"It's almost as if history is trying to erase the whole affair."
- Anthony Croix

The triple murder and failed suicide that took place at 37 Fantoccini Street in 2001, raised little media interest at the time. In a week heavy with global news, a 'domestic tragedy' warranted few column inches. The case was open and shut, the inquest was brief and the 'Doll Murders' - little more than a footnote in the ledgers of Britain's true crime enthusiasts - were largely forgotten.

Nevertheless, investigations were made, police files generated, testimonies recorded, and conclusions reached. The reports are there, a matter of public record, for those with a mind to look.

The details of what took place in Fantoccini Street in the years that followed are less accessible. The people involved in the field trips to number 37 are often unwilling, or unable, to talk about what they witnessed. The hours of audio recordings, video tapes, written accounts, photographs, drawings, and even online postings are elusive, almost furtive.

In fact, were it not for a chance encounter between the late Anthony Croix and an obsessive collector of Gothic dolls, the Fantoccini Street Reports might well have been lost forever.

This edition first published 2022 by Fahrenheit Press.

ISBN: 978-1-914475-48-1

10 9 8 7 6 5 4 3 2 1

www.Fahrenheit-Press.com

F 4 E

Typesetting & Cover Design by www.SkullStarStudio.com

THE PERCEPTION OF DOLLS:

The Fantoccini Street Reports

by

Anthony Croix *(deceased)*

Edited by Russell Day

Fahrenheit Press

*Dedicated to the work of
Guy Lyon Playfair*

*Dedicated to the work of James
Randi*

Foreword

Toward the end of 2018 I received a parcel containing 500 sheets of printed paper, 57 photographs, scores of pen and ink sketches and a collection of exercise books. The documents had been neatly packed into a pair of box files, but not before being wrapped in multiple layers of tinfoil.

I decided I had some phone calls to make.

A few weeks earlier, I'd been contacted by a friend who worked in a small law firm. She'd asked me if I'd be willing to look over a manuscript with a view to formatting it. The manuscript wasn't hers, she explained, it was the work of a client: Anthony Croix. When pressed for details she invoked client confidentiality but did allow that Mr Croix was 'having a bad time of it'. On the understanding that I couldn't promise anything I agreed to look at the manuscript.

What I'd been expecting was an email with an attachment. My experience of formatting and proofreading extended no further than beta reading work presented as Word documents or e-reader files, where changes could be made with a few keystrokes. What I'd been given was a much larger undertaking.

The package had no return address for its author and, it transpired, neither did my friend. She assured me she'd contact Mr Croix, pass on my apologies, and find a way to return the manuscript to him. Weeks passed. Finally, I reapplied the layers of foil and put the manuscript in my attic.

More than a year later, my friend contacted me again, this time acting as executor of Mr Croix's will.

The 'bad time' Anthony Croix had been having had stayed with him. When he died, in a shelter for the homeless, his worldly possessions consisted of the clothes he lay in and the manuscript in my attic. The latter he had bequeathed to me, with no instructions or requests as to what I should do with it. If I wished, I was within my rights to throw my inheritance into a bin.

I found I couldn't. Homeless, penniless, and alone, Anthony Croix had entrusted to me the only mark he would leave on the world. I retrieved the manuscript from the attic and got to work.

What follows differs in many ways from the manuscript I was given; however, these differences are, mostly, in presentation not content. Much of the text takes the form of interviews with people affected by or connected to 37 Fantoccini Street and the events that took place there. In the unedited version, these interviews appeared in full and in isolation. As the content of these interviews often covered shared experiences, I have edited them to reduce repetition. Where appropriate, I have overlapped witness accounts, so events are presented in a logical order, rather than being revisited throughout the course of the book. This has been done with clarity in mind. Likewise, book sections and chapter headings have been added with the intention of making the content more accessible.

Most of the 50 plus photographs that accompanied the manuscript were views, internal and external, of 37 Fantoccini Street and the doll's house that replicated it. Many of them were overwritten with notations and calculations. All these images, except the one appearing on the flyer for the band *Doll's House Autopsy*, were copyrighted to London North University, and permission to reproduce them was expressly denied.

Throughout the text the word *doll*, when it refers to a figurine, toy or model, will be encased. When not so presented it is a reference to the family name Doll. Any profanity used has been censored. These peculiarities of formatting were evident in Mr Croix's original manuscript, and I have chosen to carry them through to this version out of respect for his sensibilities.

The dedication at the start of this book is Mr Croix's. All foot notes are attributable to Mr Croix unless expressly stated otherwise. All descriptions of photographic, video or audio material are assumed to be Mr Croix's unless credited otherwise.

The title *The Perception of Dolls*, the section and chapter titles, and the addition of a bibliography are attributable to me.

Russell Day
2021

'Reality is that which, when you stop believing in it, doesn't go away.'
                                                                    - Philip K. Dick

'The sceptics always talk about evidence, always want something tangible.
When you give it to them, they get scared and talk themselves out of
believing it. Play the early recordings from the attic room and they'll tell
you it's ambient sound, or interference. They insist those noises are always
there and can't be eliminated. Then they hear the later recordings, those
hours of utter, utter silence, then it's, 'what did you expect? You were
recording an empty room'.
                                                                    - Steven Ward

'Whatever it was in there, it didn't want to be recorded or photographed.'
                                                                    - Carol Crossland

'That house could make me disappear. All I had to do was speak.'
                                                                    - John Pelton

Part one

Dolls, dolls and do!!s

Introduction

During the early hours of Monday 11th September 2001, in an unremarkable street in Cradlefield, north London, Kenneth Doll murdered his wife and two stepdaughters. After calling the emergency services he attempted to take his own life. The attempt failed and left him in a vegetative state from which he would never recover.

That much is a matter of public record. Much of what happen in 37 Fantoccini Street subsequently has been observed by credible and intelligent witnesses with nothing to gain by lying. Many of their testimonies are supported by recordings, visual and audio, made by accredited professionals using high quality equipment. Yet, it is unlikely the whole story of the Doll family, their deaths and what occurred in their house, will ever be known. There are too many gaps in the history and far too few facts to fill them with.

Those with first-hand experience of what happened are not always willing to speak about it. The relevant recordings and documents tend to be elusive and prone to vanishing. For every person claiming things happened that defied rational explanation another claims the opposite.

37 Fantoccini Street, Cradlefield does not exist anymore. In fact, the entirety of Fantoccini Street has been swept away, its destruction necessitated by the regeneration of NW12. Even the route of the original roadway has been largely eradicated. Anyone wishing to visit the home of the Murder Dolls will find themselves standing in the lanes of a dual carriageway. Even then they could, at best, only estimate the point where the house had stood. Less than a month after the demolition order was executed there was a fire at Cradlefield's Civic Offices. The blaze was quickly contained, with damage limited

to a corner of the building's archiving department. Some original documents were lost but few were of great importance, and most were backed up.

Among the items irrevocably lost were the plans and maps of the predevelopment Fantoccini Street and its surroundings. It is possible that copies are lurking quietly in a hard drive somewhere, but as yet, I've been unable to find them.

It is almost as if history is trying to erase the whole affair.

Chapter One: Sno Glo Elsa

My interest in the events that took place in 37 Fantoccini Street, in fact my first awareness off them at all, stem from an ill-judged promise made in 2014. December that year found me huddled over a PC, desperately searching the internet. As the calendar counted down relentlessly to Christmas and my desperation increased, I could take some solace in the knowledge that up and down the country others were also trying to make good on the same promise. Although physically alone, spiritually, I was legion.

By the end of 2014, Disney's merchandising arm would have tallied up an impressive 14 billion dollars' worth of sales. Much of their profit that year was made on the back of the hugely successful movie *Frozen*, released the previous November. Cuddly snow men and Frozen Castle Playsets sold in implausible numbers; however, they were little more than also-rans compared to that years must have Christmas toy, Sno Glo Elsa.

According to Oliver Wainwright, writing in the Guardian that year, sales of the miniature Elsa would prove high enough to bring Jakks Pacific, the doll's manufacturer, back from the brink of failure. More than just a pretty face, Sno Glo Elsa wasn't only the saviour of failing businesses, she was also a singing talent who could blast out *Let it Go* when her arms were raised in, what Wainwright described as, 'a kind of Heil Disney salute'.

In a moment of guilt induced rashness, I had assured my nine-year-old niece that Sno Glo Elsa would be under the tree that Christmas. I quickly discovered demand had outstripped supply. A friend, with more online shopping savvy than I possessed, suggested a site that listed misspelled eBay postings.

It's not unheard of for sellers on eBay to mistype the name or descriptions of what they hope to sell. The effect of this is their adverts being missed in most searches. If they don't spot and rectify their mistake the auction will go unnoticed, and bidding will be low. Bargains can be found in this hunting ground of the misspelled. If I was lucky, and quick, I might be able to procure a misnamed Elsa.

The layout of the misspelled listings site consisted of page after page of thumbnail photos with an accompanying title and link. Because the listings, by their nature would be largely invisible to specific searches, browsing this truncated web market consisted of scrolling the pages hoping one of the thumbnails would be what I wanted.

Mostly I saw cast aside plastic toys or Victorian collectables, the latter almost invariably with a typo of Victorian. At the start of my quest, I'd lost time opening pages that had piqued my interest in some way but, a few hours in, I'd become hardened to their allure until I found a listing for,

Faithful Reproduction of the Fantoccini Street
Mother Do!! / Kitchen Do!!

Mainly it was curiosity as to what *mother do / kitchen do* meant that led me to pull it up.

The mistake, in a way, was mine. What I was reading as *do* followed by a pair of exclamation marks was in fact a particular, but deliberate, reordering of the word doll. This strange quirk was consistent throughout the listing, with any reference to doll, or dolls being spelled with a pair of exclamation marks.

When expanded the thumbnail showed a head to shoulders shot of a carved wooden face. The details of the face were basic but clear, if slightly hermaphroditic. Another five views of the *do!!* were offered, left and right profile, rear of head and full-length shots front and back.

At the time the details of the doll itself meant nothing to me.

Offered for sale here is a faithful reproduction of one of the Fantoccini Street Do!!s.

This 'mother' or 'kitchen' do!! is a wooden do!! of Swiss manufacture. These semi-poseable figurines were common in Europe until the mid-eighties. The example here is an earlier model dating from the late sixties. The exact age of the Fantoccini Street do!!s is not known, but given the style and condition of the examples found at the scene it is reasonable to assume this do!! is an extremely close match.

Using the original crime scene photograph and the later pictures, published in The Cradlefield Chronicle, as reference, this do!! has been dressed, wigged and distressed to replicate the one found in the Doll family's attic.

See my other listings for reproductions of the daughter / dining room do!!s.

Do!! will be shipped with a protective plastic sheath fitted over head.

Intrigued by the mention of a crime scene and the matter-of-fact way the writer name-checked events I had no knowledge of, I saved the description to my computer before continuing my futile search for Sno Glo Elsa.

When I returned to the seller's description a few days later and read it through again, I realised I had misinterpreted a line in the third paragraph. Tired and wrongfooted by the oddity of the listing, on first reading, what I'd thought I'd seen was, *the doll's family attic*. Only now did I see that the line read, *the Doll family's attic*. In this instance Doll, used as a family name, was spelled normally.

Curiosity led me to google The Fantoccini Dolls and this in turn led me to film maker Maindo Ningyo, the knowledge lode that is Ella Caine and, ultimately, to the remaining members of the London North University research team.

Chapter Two: The Murder Dolls

Tapping Fantoccini Dolls into google produced a huge number of hits. I had to delve through twenty pages of largely unrelated material before I found *The Murder Dolls - short film*. I came close to passing it by, assuming it was yet another music video[1], but the words Fantoccini Street, included in the description caught my eye. What I found when I clicked the link was a documentary made by a student film maker in Japan.

The Murder Dolls was made in 2007. Although it is now almost impossible to find, it was, briefly, an internet sensation.

The film is a little over twenty minutes long and narrated in English with Japanese translations appearing on screen. Composed mainly of stock footage from BBC News archives and shots of still photographs, it relates the known details of the deaths of the Doll Family in 2001.

Despite predating the subsequent incidents at Fantoccini Street by three years, the film employs a tone of other worldliness.

---

[1] The Murderdolls (written as one word) were an American punk and heavy metal band known for the disturbing imagery in their music videos. Given their name and horror film aesthetic I did wonder if they had been influenced by the story of the Fantoccini dolls. The band was formed early in 2002, less than a year after the bodies of the Doll family were found.

As I no longer have access to the film, I am forced to rely on my memory to recount its content. I will ask the reader to take me at my word when I say, on this subject at least, my memory is trustworthy. Over the course of approximately six months, I would estimate, I watched *The Murder Dolls* over a hundred times. To this day I regret not making greater efforts to secure a hard copy.

The film opens with a short segment in black and white, shot using a handheld camera. The filming quality at this point is quite poor and the subject matter suggests the viewer is watching a home movie. The scene is of a long back garden in which two young girls are playing. The speed of the film is fractionally too fast, giving the scene a slightly surreal feeling. The girls wear long dresses, suggestive of the Victorian era, the lack of colour adds to this impression.

It is hard to judge their ages or height from the film, they are in the middle distance and light quality isn't good. The girls seem to be playing catch, however it becomes apparent they don't have a ball. They are engrossed in their odd game and appear unaware that they are being filmed. This carries on for approximately thirty seconds. The camera shakes slightly but is otherwise fixed.

When one of the girls 'misses' a catch, the route to retrieve the make-believe ball causes her to notice the camera. She gestures urgently to the other girl and, abandoning the game, they both run towards the house. At this point the camera moves, tracking the progress of the girls until they run up a short flight of stairs and through the open backdoor of the house. The door closes behind them. The camera lingers on the door for a few seconds before panning up. We see the house is a three-story townhouse in natural brick with the window frames and heavy lintels painted white (as far as it is possible to ascertain colour when watching monochrome film).

At the top of the house, set within the apex of the roof, is a circular window. The panning sweep of the camera halts at this point. In frame are the window, the roof and a small

8

section of sky. The sky is heavy with dark clouds. A light comes on in the attic window. The shot cuts away and shows, in quick succession, a street sign: FANTOCCINI STREET N.W.12, and then a door number: 37. In contrast to the footage of the girls, these still images are in colour.

It is now that the limited narration starts, until this point the film has been silent. The narrator's voice cannot be clearly identified as male or female.

"On the morning of September 11th, 2001 the Metropolitan Police received a call from Kenneth Doll, owner of 37 Fantoccini Street."

The use of English is correct and largely accentless. The only indication that the speaker may be using a second language is the overly precise way the narration is delivered.

Just before a second voice is heard, the image on the screen is replaced by a block of Japanese characters. White against a black background, they read:

Recording of call to police dispatcher. Received on Tuesday, September 11th, 2001 at 03:07.[2]

The second voice in the film has a British accent. The speaker is clearly male and, just as clearly, in a state of distress. What we hear is one side of an emergency call,

"You have to send someone. I think they're dead."

---

[2] At the time I had access to Maindo Ningyo's film, I happened to work alongside a Japanese speaker. She agreed to watch the film with me and provide translations of the Japanese text. On her request I have not credited her by name, but I extend my thanks for her anonymous assistance.

9

The sound stops at this point and there is a pause where, presumably, the police dispatcher attempts to obtain more detail. The tape resumes after approximately twenty seconds.

"I don't know, I don't know. I think they're dead."

Pause.

"All of them, my wife the girls. All of them. I couldn't ... I was — "

Pause.

"Yes. The address is ... "

The recording stops. Until this point the white Japanese characters have remained on screen, now we see a shot of a residential street at night. It has been raining and the camera lens is spotted with moisture. Two police cars and an ambulance are parked in front of a three-story house. Although shot in colour the scene is rendered largely monochromatic by the lack of natural light. Only the flashing blue lights of the police cars provide any relief.

The house is accessed via a narrow flight of steps that services both it and its neighbour. The shot zooms into this detail to show two ambulance crew carrying a stretcher down the steps. The figure on the stretcher is enclosed in an oblong of pale material. The camera, in a parody of the earlier scene with the girls, tracks the attendants as they take the body to the doors of the ambulance.

The rest of the film details, mainly in silence, the positions of the bodies of the Doll family and the way they were mirrored by the figures found in the doll's house.

To a westerner's eye, the film seems incomplete, posing many questions but ultimately answering none of them.

The long stretches of silence, use of black and white film and screen shots of Japanese text appearing white on black, have led some people to regard *The Murder* Dolls as a tribute to Hollywood's early pioneers.

Maindo Ningyo, the film's maker, is adamant that this was never her intent. The sparse commentary and reliance on text was due to a technical fault wiping out the film's original audio track. The first version featured a detailed account and discussion of the Fantoccini Street incident, and an especially commissioned musical score. Two drama students were employed to voice this more comprehensive soundtrack. Ms Ningyo was unwilling to provide their names.

Despite *The Murder* Dolls going viral in 2014, today, like much of the story of 37 Fantoccini Street, it is almost impossible to track down. The internet's oft repeated claim of permanence seems, in this case, to be overstated. The YouTube account, where I found the film posted, has long been dormant. On rare occasions, forum sites, catering to the curious, feature offers of the film on DVD or CD-ROM. The prices are normally extortionate, and the same sites are peppered with complaints of customers who have received low quality fakes[3].

Ms Ningyo long ago destroyed her own hard copies. She holds no affection for the film, which was failed by her tutors, costing her the degree she had been striving for. Reticent about sharing details of their criticism she simply states that they didn't like it. She no longer makes films and claims that she seldom goes to the cinema anymore.

Now in her early thirties Maindo Ningyo manages one of Tokyo's largest pod hotels, but as a child she dreamt of being

---

[3] I contacted one disgruntled customer and agreed to buy the disc from him. What I was sent was indeed low quality and fake. It was clear however that the disc's manufacturer was at least familiar with the original film and had attempted to recreate it.

a film director. It was a dream that eventually led her to the doors of the Tsukuba University and enrolment to their Film and Media degree course. *The Murder Dolls* was her final year project piece. The remit was to produce a self-funded documentary between twenty and forty minutes in length.

We spoke briefly via a video link and when I complimented her on her command of English she winced. It transpires she had honed her language skills as a child, watching Western cinema obsessively. It was largely that which set her on the path to being a film maker. Her near mother tongue standard is a left over from her determination to be part of the industry. Like most reminders of that ambition, it's a sore point.

The interview we had was less structured than I had intended and was to be my only contact with Ms Ningyo. She made it clear that she considered her infatuation with film making over and she had no desire to rekindle it or discuss *The Murder Dolls* any further. What follows is a recounting of the discussion we had. It was agreed I could record it on the strict understanding that I would not upload it to the internet.

I have included my questions and comments only where I feel they add clarity. Often Ms Ningyo's responses set the context without need of explanation.

"I was trying to make something for as little money as possible. I was hoping to show I was capable of making something engaging and entertaining and serious on an ultra-low budget. The first edit of it was pretty good, even if I do say so myself. I put the bulk of the budget into the soundtrack, not the one you'd have seen on YouTube, this one was much better.

"My tutor, who was going to be marking the film and awarding the grade, had this thing about motifs. Motifs and themes. When I heard about this strange case in England, with a family dying and their positions matching the staging of a doll's house, I thought I'd found a sure-fire theme and motif to please my tutor. I wanted to compare the dolls in Fantoccini Street, seeming to mock the living, with the traditional geisha culture of Japan. Where living woman act

12

like dolls for their male clients. Living dolls, making a mockery of their own humanity.

"I commissioned a local reporter to write a script for me and paid a pair of drama students to voice it. One of them had a very distinctive voice, she sounded like a sexy doll. The other was male, he always sounded very severe. He read translations of the news clippings and bits of the reports I had. I put another chunk of money into hiring a traditional samisen player to compose and play an original score.

"The night before I was due to submit my film, my computer picked up a virus and nearly all the files in it, including the soundtrack, were corrupted. All the audio was effectively gone. I had to put something together at the last minute. That's the one you'd have heard."

"How did you manage to get a copy of the 999 call?"

"I didn't. I read the account from one of the local papers."

"They printed a transcript?"

"No. it was just the outline of what was said. I can't remember it exactly, but the report said Mr Doll made the call and there was something about him saying he thought they were dead. I based it on that. I had a neighbour at the time who was seeing an English guy. It was about one in the morning when I realised the original soundtrack was gone and I called her in a panic and asked to borrow her boyfriend. He didn't want to help at first, but she talked him around. He wasn't an actor and found it very embarrassing to read out loud. He couldn't do it if we were watching him, so he hid in the bathroom with an old cassette player that I happened to have. It worked better that way in the end. Because he was so stressed on the tape, he sounded upset and scared, and the bathroom had an echo that gave the recording an authentic feel."

"I always assumed it was a real recording of the call."

"No. none of it was real. Most of it was pieced together using stock footage. The homegrown shots I treated so they looked like scenes from Great Britain, but really most of it was ripped off. All the scenes of the police outside the house and the views of the garden, they were just clips I culled from old movies or bits of old news casts. I don't even know what the real house looks like, all I had to go on was the description from a newspaper clipping I was sent by Ella.

"No, I don't have it anymore. I think it was from a paper called The Cradle Chronicle, something like that anyway[4].

"I wasn't really concerned about the details of the family if I'm honest. That sounds horrible I know, but it happened years before, on the other side of the world, to people I had no connection to. My film, the one I was trying to make, wasn't really about the Doll family, it was about the concept of public faces and the masks and images that society transposes onto those faces, particularly women's faces. I only contacted Ella because of the link I'd made between dolls and geisha girls. It was all incredibly pretentious, but I was very young.

"No, I didn't stay in touch with Ella. If I'm completely honest dealing with her was a little awkward. She's very … enthusiastic about her collection and the Doll case. I couldn't keep up with her level of excitement. To be polite, I exchanged emails with her for a while, but when the film went viral, I had to stop. She started to … never mind. We lost touch."

"How did the film come to end up on the internet?"

"After I'd pieced the second sound track together and changed the film from a piece about the perception of women into a cut and dried documentary about a bizarre crime scene,

---

4 It is probable that Ms Ningyo is misremembering the name of The Cradlefield Chronicle. A local free sheet, it gave the death of the Doll family more coverage than any other paper and also printed photographs of the figurines found in the doll's house. It ceased trading in May, 2006.

14

I was in a bad way. You need to understand how much the degree I was chasing meant to me. Being a film maker was all I'd dreamt of since I was a child. I'd asked for an extension to the submission date and was given two weeks. I'd done what I could to edit the film into something that made sense, but it didn't go well. I remember crying a lot, and I was in contact with Ella a lot at that time, fielding endless emails about tiny details of the dolls. She was deep into making replicas of them, she thought she could market them and make a fortune, a killing, as she put it. For some reason she'd got it into her head that my film was going to publicise her replicas and make them big sellers. The best films the university get tend to get quite a lot of exposure in Japan but that's it. There's no Hollywood connection, even for the best, I don't think I got that across to Ella very well.

"I knew when I submitted my film that I'd failed. My tutor was receptive to oddities, but they had to be good and, frankly, what I'd made wasn't. When I told Ella the film had sunk without trace, she was very disappointed. She began asking if I could make another. In the end I told her I'd post it online, to get the story and the fame of the dolls out to the people.

"I uploaded it to YouTube, a lot of film makers do. I expected it to vanish."

"But it didn't?"

"No, at least not straight away. It was that Warhol thing, fifteen minutes of fame. For a while the film was all over the internet. For a time, I thought I'd pulled it off and I was about to become the next Spielberg. Of course, that was just a fantasy. After a couple of months, interest dropped off and it was just another oddball film with a lot of strange comments attached to it. When the threats started, I took it down."

"Have you made any films since?"

"No. The whole experience made me fall out of love with the industry. Not just the failure but the contact with the people who actually liked the film. It was too strange. I sell bedspace now. People are less passionate about being asleep."

"You didn't even want to make a film about what happened

in the house later?"

"No, I didn't. I'm going now, good evening."

Chapter Three: Number 37

Kenneth Doll, habitually known as Kandy, had inherited 37 Fantoccini Street from his mother at the beginning of 1996. However, it wouldn't be until the closing days of the new millennium that he would legally be allowed to live there. Even then it would take another six months of legal wrangling before he was able to move in.

The reason for the delay was primarily the complex conditions of the late Mrs Doll's will. She had left instructions that on her death ownership of the house would be transferred to the younger of her two sons, Kenneth, on the condition that he would not reside there until the standing tenant had either found new accommodation or passed away. To further complicate matters another condition of the will was that, for as long as the tenant remained at number 37, Mrs Doll's elder son, Guy, would be in receipt of the rent and have residency of the property's ground and first floors. The second/attic floor was to be the exclusive domain of the tenant. In exchange for the rent money and the right to live in the lower part of the house, Guy was expected to maintain the property.

This bizarre codicil was stranger still considering the tenant, Mrs Phoebe Reese, far from being an elderly lady was in fact five years junior to Mrs Doll.

Aunt Phoebe, as she was known, had moved into the upper part of number 37 at some point in the late seventies. Mrs Doll's husband, Sydney Guy Doll, had left the family unit some months earlier. The event was never spoken of by Mrs Doll and, too young to be privy to the details at the time, Guy could only guess at the reasons for his father's departure and seeming abandonment. The assumption he has reached may be completely wrong, but perhaps it gives an indication of the atmosphere in the household.

During my interview with him, Sydney showed me his meagre collection of family photos and pointed out that he and Kenneth bore little resemblance to each other. I asked him which of them took after their father and he laughed,

"I think we both did, that was the problem."

Whether Sydney Doll left because of a real, or perceived, infidelity or for other reasons entirely, the resulting hole in the family finances needed to be filled. Guy recalls theirs wasn't the only property on the street to have multiple occupancy. Many of the once single-family homes had been divided into flats or bedsits.

Where Mrs Reese came from, or the exact connection she had to the family is unclear. Guy has only a vague memory of a time when she wasn't in the house.

"I remember playing in the attic room. Because it was in the roof, the ceiling was angled and came to a point, I think I was pretending it was a tent or something, make-believing I was camping. I do remember I was a little bit scared of the attic, so I was sort of daring myself to be there, pushing myself, you know the way you do when you're a kid. Mum come in and told me I'd have to go back downstairs because we had someone coming to stay. I guess that must have been Phoebe. I don't remember being introduced to her or saying hello to her, not in a welcome-to-the-house way. Suddenly she was just there. Mum always called her Aunt Phoebe, but I don't think there was a family connection.

"As best I remember, she never left the house. I know Mum did all her shopping for her and she'd join us for meals quite often. It wasn't a regular thing, but it happened enough that it wasn't something we'd comment on when she sat down to eat with us. I suppose she must have been a pretty good find as tenant's go, low maintenance, very quiet. I know after Mum died, and I inherited the rent, she never made a late payment. I'd go to the house every month or so and there would be an envelope with a cheque, dated the first of the month, on the table in the hallway. If I missed a month, there'd be two envelopes waiting on the table. I'd never see her, I never saw her at all, not until the last time of course."

The last time was the occasion of finding Mrs Reese at the bottom of the staircase. It appeared she'd fallen, the angle of her neck indicating she'd died instantly. The last cheque she'd written for the rent was laying on the floor.

Despite the woman's strong connection with the house and the Doll brother's childhood, there was no great emotional bond. When I ask if he was upset by her demise Guy shakes his head.

"It's not fun finding a dead body but, other than the shock factor, I'd be lying to say it affected me. I suppose it's strange now that I think about it, considering she was a fixture of the house I lived in for eighteen years, but she didn't really figure in my world at all. She was just this old woman who lived upstairs. Once she was in, I don't think I ever went up to the attic again, I don't think Kandy ever went up there as a kid. It was just Aunty Phoebe's part of the house and we never thought to go there.

"Mum might have decided to make her an honorary aunt to take the edge off the idea that it was just about money, but we, me and Kandy, never thought of her as a part of the family. Like I said, she was just this old Woman."

It was only at the inquest into her death that it was revealed 'the old woman' had, in fact, been younger than Mrs Doll. At the time of her entering the household she'd have been barely into her thirties.

"Don't forget how young I was," Guy says. "At that age all adults look much the same, the world is divided between kids and old people. Anyway, she was one of those people who seem to wish old age on themselves. I'd bet her first words were *I'm not getting any younger.* She always wore drab, miserable colours, and this was the seventies, when everyone dressed like a migraine. She also smoked like a chimney. That I do remember because Mum would fret about her smoking in bed and setting the house on fire. I don't remember Mum going up to Phoebe's floor, but it was a safe bet she smoked in bed.

When she'd eat with us, she'd smoke through the meal, between mouthfuls. As soon as she finished one cigarette, she'd use the end of it to light the next. I swear, if she struck a match to light up the first fag of the day, she'd not need the box again until the next morning. Her face was actually stained yellow, you know the way some smokers get yellowed fingers, her whole face was like that. She looked like she'd been carved from wood."

I ask if it was Mrs Reese that brought the doll's house to the attic room.

"I wouldn't swear to it but can't think how else it would have got there. I don't remember it being there when I used to play in that room."

Like so much of the history of number 37 and the doll's house within, the presence of Mrs Reese isn't fully understood. If, as Guy claims, she never left the house it begs the question where was she getting money for the rent? At the time she moved in she was years from pensionable age, and the attic floor of a small townhouse in a poor area would seem a strange choice for one of the idle rich. And, if she maintained her hermit-like existence after the death of Mrs Doll, then who took over the shopping detail? It certainly wasn't Guy, who, in his own words, *Collected the rent cheques and left the house to rot*. This callous attitude had nothing to do with Mrs Reese and everything to do with the toxic relationship with his brother and mother.

Guy and Kenneth Doll were born two years apart, almost to the day. Guy on July 5th '64 and Kenneth on July 3rd '66. Questions of paternity aside, it is undeniable that the siblings, at least physically, were always poles apart. Guy's slim volume of family photos is almost exclusively composed of pictures of the two boys. The earliest shows them side by side on a brilliantly patterned bedsheet. No more than a few days old in the picture, Kenneth is a chubby and robust baby. Guy smiles ruefully as he regards the picture,

"He always was the looker. Right from day one, or ground

zero." He tilts the album almost as if seeing the picture for the first time, an idea that the dog-eared pages refute. "I was the runt of the litter."

By the age of two the older of the Doll brothers had lost any hints of infant chubbiness. In the photo he sits at the side of his younger sibling and, despite the size advantage gifted by his seniority, somehow looks smaller. It doesn't help that the composition of the photo is slanted to frame Kenneth. Anything else in the photo is stage dressing.

It is a theme that continues throughout the album. Nevertheless, in the picture, Guy is beaming at his new brother.

In the collection of two dozen photos Mrs Doll appears only twice. Generally, she is behind the camera. The two pictures that include her are on the same page along with a third, the only picture including Mrs Reese, the lodger.

Unusually, Guy remembers the occasion of these photos. The rest of the album, he maintains, has little connection to him and he only knows they are of his childhood because he recognizes them as such. The occasion of these three photographs is Kenneth Doll's tenth birthday.

The first picture shows Kenneth, Guy and their mother. They are in the back garden of number 37. The photographer – in this case Mrs Reese – has captured a view of most of the rear elevation of the building. Kenneth is shown in the bottom left corner of the picture, unaware that he is playing in front of the building where he will one day murder his family. His brother is in the righthand bottom corner and only just in shot. Centred perfectly is Mrs Doll, who appears to be levitating. All three of them are looking up at a point that is not obvious to the viewer.

"We were playing piggy in the middle. Mum was piggy and I had just thrown the ball to Kandy when Mrs Reese took the picture. I threw it high, trying to get it over Mum's head, that's why she's jumping. I put too much muscle into it and the ball went into the garden next door. They had some kind of thorny bush so we couldn't get the ball back. I got told off twice, once on the day and again when the roll of film came back from the chemist. This was back in the day; years before anyone had heard of digital photography, or the idea of taking photos with your phone. Mum did the thing a lot of people did and brought two rolls of film a year, one for Christmas and one to go on holiday with. Only we didn't go on holidays, so the second roll of film was for the birthdays. When we got the pictures back that year mum got to this one and gave me a big lecture about showing off and being selfish and ruining the game.

"I know this sounds petty, and I guess it is, but I was just a kid remember, but it always riled me that Mum wouldn't buy a separate roll of film for each birthday. Kandy's was first and she'd always use up more than half the roll on his day. Once I was old enough to count it pissed me off. Now I'm going to sound melodramatic as well as petty, but that year, Kandy's tenth, was the year we really started to drift apart. The resentment began to turn sour. I expect a part of that was just my age, I was heading into being a teenager and sulking became easy."

Guy looks at the photo again and is lost in thought. It is an intensely private moment and I feel uncomfortable witnessing it. To give myself something else to think about I idly try to locate the ball in the picture. The direction of everyone's gaze suggests it should have been caught somewhere to the left of the frame. I'm unable to find it; the three figures appear to be playing with a ball that has already been lost.[5]

---

[5]At the time of the interview with Guy Doll, when I noticed the lack of a visible ball in the picture, I didn't make the connection to the opening scene in Maindo Ningyo's short film. Some days later, I contacted Guy again and asked if Ms Ninygo had sought him out at some point, he told me she hadn't. When I asked him for permission to reproduce the photo for use

The second picture in which Mrs Doll appears was captured inside number 37. It was taken in the front room, that served as a dining room[6]. Kenneth and Guy are sitting at a Formica topped dinner table. A flash has been used and the colours of the tabletop and the party food on it are painfully bright, particularly in contrast to the brown walls in the background. Kenneth is blowing out the candles of his birthday cake. His mother is caught with her hands in the air, clapping. Guy, in the foreground, looks on. Mrs Doll has applied makeup with a heavy hand and her hair has been coloured. From what I've heard of the family's situation it would be reasonable to assume she spent much of her time worried, but other than a faint tracing of lines on her forehead, this is not reflected in her face. Her skin is incredibly smooth.

The third picture on the page is of the two boys and Mrs Reese. Again, at the party table, the two boys are each seated with a slice of cake in front of them. Kenneth smiles happily for the camera, Guy's face is neutral and, as the picture has been taken, he has looked away. Mrs Reese is in the rear of the picture, two or three steps back from the table. Like Guy her face is blank, her gaze however is fixed on the camera lens. She is holding a plate with a slice of cake on it, a half-smoked cigarette is clamped in one side of her mouth.

Guy's description of her is apt; she does appear to have been carved from wood. It is hard to believe she is younger than Mrs Doll.

"She didn't look any different the day I found her dead in the hallway," Guy says as I look at the image. "Poor old Aunt

---

in this book, he claimed that since our interview he had destroyed the album.

[6] This room is variously referred to as the front room or dining room. In regard to 37 Fantoccini Street both terms describe the room where the bodies of the Doll twins were found.

Phoebe."

His use of the honorific title surprises me slightly as it's the first time he's used it to describe the woman. I ask again if he thinks it possible she was actually a relative.

"I don't think so, but then I'm basing that on how different her and Mum were, hard to believe they could be sisters but then ... look at me and Kandy."

The name Kandy was awarded to Kenneth Doll by his older brother during their time at St. Julian's co-educational secondary school. The name Doll, at least for boys, was always going to draw a certain amount of teasing but finding a Ken Doll in their ranks was a gift to playground bullies and clowns alike. Guy, at the school two years ahead of his brother and, by his own admission, already unpopular was quietly hopeful that the presence of his brother would, if not lend him support, then at least drew some of the heat away. Sadly, for him, it was not to be.

Maybe bolstered by natural charm, or just lent a greater degree of confidence by their shared but uneven upbringing, Kenneth became popular and well liked. Also, physically bigger and stronger than his older brother he was not a natural target for bullies. When the jibes about Ken and Barbie dolls began, he simply abandoned his name and resolved to answer only to K.D. His brother, who now claims not to remember if the gesture was a rare show of solidarity or an attempt at an insult, corrupted the sound into *Kandy*.

If it was an attempt to increase his brother's torment, it backfired. The invention of the name coincided with the rise of American comic actor John Kandy, and the Hollywood-tinged nickname was considered cool.

Matthew Pew, headmaster at the time the boys attended St Julian's, remembers the Doll brothers and their mother. He wasn't surprised that Ken's nickname was well received.

"Ken was popular, he was ... well charming. It's the only word for it, and that's not a word you have call to use often working with that age group. Everybody liked Ken, even some of the staff called him Kandy. He was the school star. Every school I've ever worked at as a star, a child you expect to do well, well in exams, work, life. We were all surprised when the stories about him began to filter back to the school after he'd left. I was less surprised than most perhaps. I'd had a lot of time dealing with his brother and because of that had a lot of contact with the mother. An attitude like hers has a negative bearing on a family, even the favoured ones. It just takes longer to come out for them. Really the only thing that surprised me about the scandal with the shares was that Ken was caught. Escaping a prison term, that was just to be expected, I mean ... it was a jury trial."

It was the school as much as the home life that put the final wedge between the Doll brothers. Guy was far from being a model student. A situation not helped by his undiagnosed dyslexia. Socially and academically challenged, lacking a sympathetic school and home life, his descent to the bottom of all subjects was almost inevitable.

"My behaviour was never that bad. I wasn't causing trouble; I just wasn't getting ahead. It might have been better if I had been in trouble all the time. St Julian's had a lot of real bad lads in it, it was geared up to delinquents. They had dedicated courses and a special unit to get them before they appeared on the police radar. I really don't think the school knew what to do with kids like me who just couldn't keep up. If I'd been sent to the Fraggle unit - that's what we called it - I'd have been eaten alive. So, they just kept me back a year. When I should have been in the third year, I was pulled back to the second. The few friends I had were all in the class above me. It still might have worked out but then Kandy was moved up a year."

An academic student, as well as a popular one, Kenneth completed only one term of his first year before being moved up. It was an exceptional step, that of course only served to highlight the failings of his older sibling. Why it was decided to put both brothers into the same class is not known. A charitable interpretation might be that it was thought the siblings would support each other, although by the ex-headmaster's admission the favouritism of Mrs Doll was well known to the school staff.

Weather misjudged or negligent, the move was to drive the brothers further apart.

"By the Christmas holidays of '78 we'd stopped speaking to each other. Even with Aunt Phoebe taking up the top half of the house there was enough space that we could avoid each other. We had to eat together, but mealtimes were the only time we'd see each other outside of school. Even then we'd sit at either end of the table, as far apart as we could get."

From the records of Edward Bartlett

PHOTO ID: FSI/Archive-001
SOURCE: Cradlefield Chronicle, 13 – 03 – 2002. Credited to Michael Huddart.
SUBJECT: Interior of Doll's House. Dining Room.
DESCRIPTION: The room has been modelled in the Victorian style, although not accurately. The dining furniture comprises a table with seating for eight. It is clear that the doll's house is in a bad state of repair. Patches of mould are visible on the walls.

Although there is nothing in the photograph to give a sense of size, the house and the furniture within is known to be 1/12th scale (the common scale for hobbyist doll's houses). From this it can be estimated that the table is approximately seven inches in length. At the head and foot of the table lay two wooden dolls. Both are dressed in faux Victorian style and at first glance appear identical, the only difference is that the doll to the right of shot has its hair in a ponytail, the one on the left has a bun. Both dolls lay on the floor, facing up and orientated with their heads towards the front of the doll's house.

Part Two

37 Fantoccini Street

The 2010 Fieldtrip

Monday 5th July to Sunday 11th July

Members of investigative team

Viola Mezco	*Sensitive*
John Pelton	*Audio Capture Technician*
Edward Bartlett	*Archivist/Investigator*
Mabel Noakes	*Sensitive*
Steven Ward	*Audio Visual Capture Technician*

Chapter Four: The Records

Viola Mezco talks easily about her experiences during the initial fieldtrip to Fantoccini Street. Her manner is casual, almost off-hand, but I get the impression her sanguine air has been hard won.

She agrees to see me in the holistic therapy clinic she operates, under a professional pseudonym, from a home office in her neatly kept garden. The nature of her business requires privacy and so the bi-fold doors are glazed with translucent glass, as are the space's two windows. Any feelings of claustrophobia this might suggest are countered by the ceiling that consists of three immense skylights that flood the room with natural daylight. The room itself is panelled with blond wood and furnished with two comfortable armchairs and a therapy couch. The hard practicality of the vinyl upholstery is muted by taupe-coloured throws. The space balances between warmly comforting and clinically professional.

This is a very different space from the one she was in for the first week of July 2010. The contrast between her present working environment and the dark shuttered confines of 37 Fantoccini Street couldn't be greater.

Mezco herself is equally changed. Before we start recording, she shows me a 6" by 8" photo. It was taken by Steven Ward as the group were about to enter number 37. Left to right, the picture shows Edward Bartlett, Viola Mezco, John Pelton and Mabel Noakes. With the exception of Edward Bartlett, no one in the group is smiling. John Pelton appears to have been caught glancing towards the camera, as if taken unawares. He looks uncomfortable. It may be a trick of the light or just the ungainly position in which his image has been captured, but his expression radiates hostility.

Mezco is standing slightly forward of the group. The contrast to her open and natural appearance today is marked. If I didn't know the woman I was sitting with was the one in the picture, I wouldn't think to connect them.

I press record as I hand the photo back. Her first comments are in relation to the photo.

"That was taken in the front garden. Steve took it for me, I asked him to take a snap of us all before we went in. I remember he made a fuss about my camera. I'd bought one of those disposable things you could get back then, they were about seven pounds to buy and that included developing the film. The camera was made of cardboard. Steve took it between finger and thumb, like I'd handed him a dead rat. I guess he was joking but it annoyed me at the time, that's probably why I'm scowling in the photo. I was excited about the trip, and wanted a few photos of my own, I was studying occupational therapy and was hoping to get something I could use in my thesis. When he interviewed me, Steve had said he had no objections to me doing that but warned me it wasn't the point of the visit. He suggested taking my own camera and recording gear if I needed something different[7]. Steven and

---

[7] At the end of the interview, I ask Viola Mezco if she had any more photos of her visit to number 37. She forces a smile and shakes her head. The disposable camera that worked perfectly to take a solitary expose of the group in the garden returned nothing but blank squares when used inside the house. Of the 24 exposures only two produced images, the group shot before entering the house and one more partial image taken on leaving. Viola discarded all the photos including the partial, although she does remember it. A shot of the empty house she took just before she got back

John were both a bit protective of their roles and could be rude about other people's efforts.

"John could be really nasty if anyone questioned his expertise. He had a lot of anger in him. He was also more receptive to what was going on in that house than he would like to admit.

"There was a bad atmosphere in that house, you could feel it, well I could, the moment we stepped inside. I could tell John was doing his best to ignore it, but you could tell by the way he was banging around and making so much fuss that he was on edge."

In contrast to Mezco, John Pelton doesn't seem to have left the shadow of Fantoccini Street. We meet at his home, a basement flat, crowded with sound gear of various vintages. It is uncomfortably hot. I mention this at one point and am told the walls are sound proofed, this lends a degree of heat insulation. The lack of natural light and, once I'm aware of it, the lack of ambient sound gives the impression of a small, hot cell.

Physically, Pelton has aged well, changing little since being photographed by Steven Ward. Also unchanged is his look of barely supressed hostility, although in person it is more likely to be a look of hard-set boredom. When I ask if I can record our conversation, he laughs and tells me he's been recording

---

into the minibus. She remembers taking it because she noticed there was one last exposure on the roll. The picture, when developed, showed a slither of weed choked garden and the bottom edge of the house, the rest of the picture was obscured by a black cloud, as if the house was engulfed in its own night. When I ask if she finds this strange, she shrugs and says, *a lot of odd things happened in that house.*

since I walked through the door.

"Could you tell me about the first trip to number 37?"

There follows a silence that is to be the corner stone of the interview. In contrast to Mezco's openness and ease of discourse, Pelton is guarded and requires frequent questioning and prompts. When I play it back, the tape I record, is peppered with long silences.

"What do you want to know?"

"How did you end up on the team, were you interested in the Murder Dolls case?"

Pelton shakes his head. Shakes or nods are common currency in his conversation. It is hard to tell if he is acting out of habit or out of a deliberate attempt to be awkward. It's hard to imagine that he's not awake visual responses are worthless on an audio record.

"You weren't interested in the case, or you hadn't heard of it?"

"I don't remember hearing about the murders at the time, but it was nine eleven, that's all anyone was seeing on the news that day. I heard mention of them much later, but I didn't know anything about the dolls' house photos until Eddie Bartlett got in touch. He was working with Steve."

Pelton puts finger quotes around the word *working*. I ask him why.

"All the time he devoted to sniffing around hauntings and events, he did off his own bat. He was a retired bus driver, but he'd always say he was working (finger quotes) with someone. He made it sound like he was some sort of expert, constantly being sought out."

"You didn't believe that to be the case?"

"He called himself a spiritologist or something. He knew people would laugh if he called himself a spiritualist, so he came up with that. It's the same way all the s__theads who collect pictures of alien sightings call themselves Ufologists. It sounds better than w__ker."

"Edward Bartlett believed there was a presence of some kind at work in number 37."

"Eddie was desperate to see a ghost. Again, it was like the flying saucer nuts; he wanted to believe so bad it was sort of pitiful."

Pelton stops talking and I'm about to prompt him again, but on this occasion, he beats me to it.

"Eddie saw phenomena (finger quotes) everywhere. I was talking to him once in one of the recording studios at the uni, there was a drum kit set up and someone had left a pair of sticks on one of the high toms. One of them rolled off and bounced off a snare. We both jumped but Eddie was up and across to the kit before the reverb had stopped. He was down on his hand and knees, peering around like a cat looking for mice"

"He thought it was significant?"

"I don't know about that. My point is, his first reaction was always to look for something significant. I saw a drumstick roll off a tilted surface, people's movements cause vibration, air currents, things move. Ed saw an inanimate object mysteriously move when no one was near it."

"You didn't share his beliefs?"

"No. I think that's why he wanted me along to do the sound work on Steve's dopey fieldtrip."

I don't see the logic of this and say so. Pelton looks slightly abashed.

"I've probably given you the idea I thought Eddie was an a__hole, but I didn't think that. He was a smart bloke who happened to have a very odd believe system, and he was desperate to be proved right. Thing is, he had a degree of self-awareness and that put him in a f__king minority on that trip, I'll tell you. He knew he'd read things into events because he wanted to. I think he thought having me along was going to give him cast iron proof. If I could find a hole in something, then I would. Trouble was he was so committed to finding proof of some presence he assumed I wouldn't find holes."

"Did it work out that way?"

"Not as far as I was concerned."

32

Some of the few documents relating to number 37 still in existence and open to scrutiny, are the records kept by Edward Bartlett.

Bartlett had spent almost fifty years investigating the paranormal. His fascination with the subject can be traced back to his early childhood and a family tragedy.

Shortly after his tenth birthday, Bartlett's two younger sisters and father took a coach trip to visit the children's grandmother. Bartlett and his mother were meant to be traveling with them but had had to cancel at the last minute when he came down with a stomach complaint. It was a chance event that may have saved their lives. The coach collided with a HGV, left the road and rolled down an embankment, killing eighteen of the passengers. Bartlett's father and two siblings were among the dead.

His mother, Rita, had no extended family of her own and, largely alone with her grief and surviving child, sought the council of a local spiritualist. It was move that alienated her husband's family, who were devout Catholics and took a dim view of the practice. Inadvertently her search for solace increased her, and her son's, isolation. Possibly to fill the gap, she began to regularly attend séances at three or four different spiritualists, often taking her young son along.

Young as he was, Bartlett, was an intelligent and observant presence at the gatherings and was quick to spot fakes. Rather than expose them to his mother, who took great comfort from making contact – real or manufactured – with her late husband and daughters, he confided in writing; keeping detailed accounts of what he saw in a school exercise book.

Over the next five decades the exercise book grew into a vast collection of journals, folders, photographs, video and audio tapes. Along with one of the most comprehensive libraries on the paranormal ever compiled.

The account he wrote of his visit to 37 Fantoccini Street was to be the last addition.

The collection survives today but for how long is debatable. As per his wishes, Patricia Bartlett, his widow, offered it in its entirety to the British museum[8]. She is tight lipped about the museum's reaction, but it appears the offer was rejected, and the collection may soon be leaving the country. Whether the collection will remain available for study or will become part of a private collection is something else Mrs Bartlett was not willing to discuss[9].

Patricia Bartlett was keen to speak on most matters concerned with her late husband's work and delighted in showing me his collection of journals. It is a large body of work completely occupying the master bedroom of the house. Every inch of wall space is filled with shelves containing A4 notebooks and box files. There is also a sizable library of VHS video tapes and DVDs, holding over 500 hours of audio-visual records. It represents Edward Bartlett's life work. Indexed and cross-referenced, everything is there from his first jottings in a school exercise book – the first three pages

---

[8] I contacted the British Museum regarding this matter. They declined to comment.

[9] Some weeks after I visited Mrs Bartlett a source at the ASSAP*, who asked not to be named, contacted me and told me the collection was rumoured to have been purchased by John Zaffis, founder of the Paranormal Research Society of New England and owner of the John Zaffis Museum of the Paranormal**.

*ASSAP: Association for the Scientific Study of Anomalous Phenomena. (R.D)

**I did, while editing Mr Croix's manuscript, try to contact the John Zaffis Museum of the Paranormal in order to confirm or deny this comment. To date I have received no reply. (R.D)

of which contain schoolwork – right through to his account of the initial investigation of the Doll's house.

In contrast to the early scribblings in a school jotter, the report on Fantoccini Street is a master class in record keeping. Neatly printed and encased in a file, it is also stored digitally on one of many USB memory sticks. The digital record at least will stay in the country but, like the journals, their availability to the public is in doubt. Nearly all her late husband's digital records were entrusted to IronKey memory sticks, and a record of the passwords has yet to surface. It is possible none exists. This is one of the great tragedies of the collection. Keen to adopt new technologies for his investigations, Edward Bartlett was an early convert to digital cameras and much of his vast collection of photographs has never been printed out. For the time being they remain hidden in the depths of digital encryption.

I wasn't allowed to take away the file pertaining to Fantoccini Street nor, as the electronic file is locked from me, could I print off a copy, but I was permitted to photograph it[10].

What I have reproduced here is only a fraction of the complete document. Edward Bartlett prided himself on his thoroughness, and his accounts are incredibly detailed. Much of that detail would be incomprehensible to layman and the idly curious. All editing has been by way of omission; nothing has been added.

---

[10] These photographs were not included in the package of documents I was sent by Mr Croix. I have no idea if still exist. (R.D)

CASE#:128.01/HH.XVI/P.III – IP.IV (?)[11]
Fantoccini Street / Doll Murders
Monday 5th July 2010 – Sunday 11th July 2010

LOCATION:
37 Fantoccini Street, Cradlefield, London, NW12

BACKGROUND:
The events that took place in 37 Fantoccini Street on the morning of Tuesday 11th September 2001 were investigated by the usual authorities. Their conclusion was that Barbara Doll (32) and her twin daughters, Patsy and Ann (both 12) had been murdered by Kenneth Doll (45) while the balance of his mind was disturbed. Kenneth Doll was found in the attic room of the property, having attempted to take his own life. The failed suicide bid left him beyond the reach of the judicial system, and the case was officially closed.

By chance, a police photographer making a record of the attic room captured a partial image of the Victorian doll's house that stood (and at the time of writing still stands) against the north wall of the room (see image #128.Bg.P.003/IK06). The doll's house is clearly modelled on the real house it

---

[11] Edward Bartlett's method of cataloguing his investigations gives an indication of the scale and thoroughness of his work. Mrs Bartlett was not privy to the exact method behind the complex series of abbreviations, but she could tell me HH stood for *House Haunting*, P for *Poltergeist* and IP for *Intelligent Prescence*. She suspected that the bracketed question mark meant her late husband was still debating the exact nature of what he had witnessed.

resides in (see image #128.Bg.CC.007/IK06)[12]. In the photograph a portion of the lower righthand room of the doll's house (the kitchen) is visible and a small doll can clearly be seen laying on the floor. The same photographer also took photographs of the real kitchen where the body of Mrs Doll was discovered (see images #128.Bg.P.017/IK06 to #128.Bg.P.020/IK06). The doll closely approximates the position and posture of the late Mrs Doll. These similarities were not directly commented upon at the inquest.

Subsequent photographs of the doll's house, taken by Michael Huddart, staff photographer for the Cradlefield Chronicle, the taking of which were witnessed by Max Whitgift, court reporter, revealed that the location and position of the two Doll children had also been mirrored by dolls. A fourth doll, this one representing a male, was found in the attic of the doll's house. There is no visual record of Kenneth Doll's position when he was found, he was taken for medical treatment before the police photographer arrived at the scene. However, from position of articles left on the floor[13] (see image #128.Bg.P.008/IK06) it is reasonable to

---

[12] To the best of my knowledge this is the first time anyone noted the doll's house was a representation of the real 37 Fantoccini Street. Sadly, as with most of the photographs referenced by Edward Bartlett, it is not possible to actually see image #128.Bg.CC.007/IK06. While I had no way of checking my assumptions, I did hazard a guess that IK06 might mean IronKey #06, and that CC might equate to Cradlefield Chronicle, and the series of photographs taken by Michael Huddart.

assume he, like the male ⬚doll⬚, was discovered lying before the ⬚doll's⬚ house[14].

It is not known if these facts went unobserved by the investigating officers or if it was noted but not considered significant. It is hard to believe that trained police personnel, including a SOCO team, would be so unobservant as to 'not see' the arrangement of figurines within the miniature counterpart to the house they were in. It seems more likely the attending officers were, consciously or unconsciously, dismissing anything that could not be explained by conventional science as merely coincidence. Sadly, this practice is regarded as logical by many people.

Although the placement of the ⬚dolls⬚ could have been the work of Kenneth Doll, this would not explain the strange atmosphere reported by Max Whitgift and Michael Huddart, nor could it account for the barrage of clicks and knocks both men heard while they took photographs in an empty house.

Monday July 5th, 2020

As chance would have it, I happen to live between London

---

[13] Edward Bartlett makes no other reference to the 'articles' on the attic floor and image #128.Bg.P.008/IK06 is not accessible. No one I spoke to was able to shed any light on what these articles may have been.

---

[14] Without the photographs for reference, it is not immediately what this refers to; the ⬚doll's⬚ house in the attic of number 37, itself contained a ⬚doll's⬚ house, or at least a model of one. This miniature within a miniature was also situated in the attic room and stood on a three-legged, halfmoon table.

North University and Fantoccini Street, and so it was agreed the rest of the team would assemble at the campus and pick me up on route. The arrangement was for them to collect me from my house at 11 a.m. I received a phone call from Steven Ward at approximately quarter to. He told me the team was running late and not to expect them before noon. The revised deadline came and went. A second phone call informed me they were underway at last and would be at my house by one.

I finally boarded the minibus at quarter to two. Disgruntled at the delay, I demanded to know why the team was so late. The delay had been caused, at least in part, by an argument between John Pelton and Miss Mezco. Steven rolled his eyes and told me the pair had fallen out over the amount of equipment John had insisted on bringing. Miss Mezco had complained about the lack of space this left on the bus, and John had apparently made a comment about not meaning to tread on her aura.

The drive to Fantoccini Street was quiet with even Mabel Noakes seemingly subdued.

This may have not been the best start to a fieldtrip, but it does serve to show the team was selected for their individual worth to the investigation, rather than for their ability to sing the same song.

Steven Ward still works at London North University. His role has changed since the summer of 2010. Now, as Departmental Undermanager of Visual Technologies, his work involves far more paperwork and admin duties. Teaching time and exposure to students is reduced and field studies are a thing of the past. While he doesn't say so directly, I suspect this situation suits him.

It has taken a long time to reach the stage where he is willing to talk to me. As with many of the interviews I undertook while gathering information for this book, I'm told it'll have to be brief, and it will be the only one. We meet in his office. I have been told there's no possibility of it taking place in his home. I regard the stipulation as a warning to proceed carefully rather than a genuine rebuff. Anyone not wanting to talk would have simply ignored my letters.

The office is very different to the complex order of Edward Bartlett's archive. Both in content and atmosphere. Where Bartlett's passion for his subject was almost palpable, Ward's office reflects indifference. The few books on the shelfs are professional titles and the files are strictly admin related. I ask if he still pursues an interest in the occult. He shakes his head without elaborating and offers me tea. He uses making it as an excuse to ignore me. When the props of tea making are exhausted, he sits behind his desk, and I assume the interview has started. Before I've had a chance to ask any questions, he holds his hand up to silence me.

"It's going to be hard for me to talk about this. Once I talked about it a lot, and what needs to be understood before we start is this: I know what I saw, I know what I felt and I'm not about to justify it or attempt to explain it away. I'll answer your questions, but I'm not going to be interrogated. I'm going to give you the facts, whether you believe them or not is your concern. On this subject, the only person whose opinion matters to me ... is me. Is that understood?"

During this short speech he holds his left his hand in the air. It gives the impression he's making a vow or swearing an oath. Or asking me to. I nod that I understand, and the hand is lowered.

"Okay, so, there were several trips, where do you want me to start?"

"Well, at the beginning. When did you first decide to investigate the Doll family murders? Was it a subject that had always interested you?"

"I've always had an interest in the paranormal, but I'd never heard about the Doll family or seen the doll's house photographs. Sometime around 2007, 2008 the faculty did some work for a journalist who was doing a piece on poltergeists. She wanted help setting up cameras that could be triggered by drops in temperature. It was mostly down to the tech department, but they hauled me into it. It was a slow week for news because it ended up in one of the nationals with some snide headline about getting a degree in ghost hunting. People started contacting the uni. A lot of them where cranks or just people playing silly buggers; *help me, my bicycle's possessed.* That kind of thing. My name was the one that appeared in the paper so most of them were directed to my desk. It became a standing joke. I started off trying to be polite and returning calls, putting people off gently if I could, after a couple of weeks the letters petered out. But a few months after all the fuss had died down one arrived that was more professional than the others. Most of them were just scrawled notes with a list of weird events they wanted the uni to come and investigate, often with a bible quote to round them off. This one was a very polite letter telling me about a case that might be of interest."

"The Doll murders?"

"Yeah. I nearly put it in the bin, but she'd included copies of the photographs taken by Michael Huddart[15] and a very factual description of their significance.

"I thought the writer was more together than the rest, but I've had other letters off her since that make me wonder. She was only really interested by the whole affair because she has an obsession with dolls"."

---

[15] When I asked if it was possible to see the Huddart Photographs, Mr Ward told me he'd returned them to the sender at their request.

Chapter Five: Ella Caine

I contacted Ella Caine, via her eBay account, during my infatuation with Maindo Ningyo's film. If I am honest, I'm not entirely sure why. Perhaps I was hoping for contact with somebody, anybody, who was familiar with the case and who might be a fan of the film. In the latter respect I was to be disappointed. Ella was less than impressed with Ms Ningyo's documentary. To understand why, you have to appreciate Ella's passion for the subject of dolls.

As with many niche communities, whose fascination with a particular subject seems all encompassing, the world of doll collecting is a far from unified mass. Instead, it is woven from many different threads, each strand believing they are the true holders of the faith. However, where collectors of antiques might look askance at a shelf full of Bratz dolls, and lovers of folk dolls hold lovers of Victoriana in low esteem, the clans share a partisan distain for devotees of the Gothic.

Gothic dolls, creepy dolls, horror dolls or weird dolls are commonly regarded as 'toys' rather than collectables. The word 'toy' holding a particular weighting among adult collectors. The high regard Ella Caine is held in among serious plangonologists – doll collectors – is a tribute to her expertise. Not only is she given credit for amassing one of the world's finest collections of creepy dolls, she is also frequently contacted for opinions and valuations of rare and hard to find dolls. Her opinion is also sought on occasion by folklorists and social historians who find their areas of interest invaded by tales of dolls.

Ella's collection is not open to the public. In part this is because of its location. Personal circumstances make it impossible for her to have the dolls with her and they are currently housed in the converted loft of her sister's home. While not practical to admit the public, private viewings are arranged on occasion. These are not regular and are for the most part by invitation only. I'd been in semi-regular contact with Ella for three months when, out of the blue, she asked me if I'd like to see the collection. My interest in dolls didn't extend much beyond my curiosity about the 'Murder Dolls' but, having some inkling of the fascination they held for Ella, I realised that offering a viewing was not something she did lightly. I told her I would very much like to see her collection. Arrangements were duly made.

Nothing about the home of Lydia Lalka, née Caine, hints that it contains one of the world's most respected doll collections. Ella is resistant to having her collection put online, so I'm one of a small group of people to actually see it. Concerns for security make her reluctant to reveal her sister's address. Her sister and her husband share her concerns, they tell me they never speak of the collection.

The loft conversion is accessed by a narrow staircase. If the collection was to ever be the subject of a Hollywood film the staircase would probably be dark and oppressive. In reality, it is brightly lit with a large window to one side and strip lighting overhead. In accordance with her sister's request, Lydia keeps the door to the loft space locked. Lydia has a young daughter, who answered the door to me. I ask if the door is locked to stop her playing with the exhibits. Lydia shakes her head, momentarily displacing the careful arrangement of hair that curls over her right ear and cheek – she's quick to reposition it.

"Jessie's seen the collection. She's got no interest in it."

She opens the door and we have a slightly embarrassing moment when she steps to one side to let me in first. It's a slight squeeze and, thinking she would simply go in ahead of me, I wait. Misinterpreting my hesitation, Lydia offers me a concerned smile,

"They don't bite. They're only dolls."

43

Once inside the room I have to wonder if the comment was meant as a joke; the first thing I see on entering are a trio of free-standing dolls, blank eyed and equipped with serrated metal teeth. They're replicas of the 'piranha dolls' from the 1960 sci-fi film, Barbarella. In the film a horde of the dolls attempt to kill the titular character[16]. The menace the trio emit is no way reduced by the clear plastic bags that they, in common with all the dolls in the room, wear over their heads.

Hollywood, even with the aid of badly lit stairs, wouldn't be able to do the room justice. I try counting the dolls and quickly give up, when I ask Lydia, she answers without hesitating; 897. With two more 'waiting'. The two newcomers have been donated by what Lydia describes as fans. They are currently with Ella, being prepared for their admission to the collection. Lydia shows me the space that's been made for them.

Other than the plastic bags all the dolls wear and the general air of … well … creepiness, there is little unity in the collection, and the ordering of the display appears random - though I doubt it is. The exhibits range from carved wooden figures that might be a hundred years old to soft plastic items that could have been moulded the day before. Chubby toddlers recline in miniature bassinets and miniature glamour models pose in evening gowns, babies, toddlers, children, women – there are no males in this world – sit, stand, lie and crowd the shelves and cabinets. Not immediately apparent, and perhaps the realisation is more disconcerting for not being obvious, is that all the dolls, with the exception of the piranha triplets guarding the doorway, have been arranged to give the impression of staring at the same point. Even the dolls lacking

---

[16] The roll of dolls as murder weapons is considered by Christopher Noessel on the Sci-Fi Interfaces website: https://scifiinterfaces.com/2013/03/04/pira nha-dolls/

eyes or wearing blindfolds appear to be giving their full attention to the glass case at the far end of the room. Facing the doorway, it contains a single doll, standing and posed with its arms lifted in the air, as if acknowledging the cheers of an adoring crowd.

"That is Lydia Doll," Lydia tells me. "Doesn't she look pretty?"

As she regards her namesake, the curl of hair she uses to disguise the scarring slips again. She doesn't notice and this time doesn't hurry to reset it.

She and Lydia Doll are dressed identically.

My correspondence with Ella took place over three years. The early contacts between us were guarded, but my enquiries about the details of the Murder Dolls dovetailed with her own interests in the Doll's incident and our exchanges gradually became easier.

The issues around personal visits made conducting interviews in the usual way impractical. Only after much wrangling with the necessary case workers and doctors was it agreed that I could submit a written list of questions. The questions, subject to approval, would be passed on to Ella. She in turn would be permitted to write her replies to me without censure[17].

Occasionally Ella would repeat facts/incidents that had affected her. For the sake of clarity, I have removed these repetitions along with Ella's references to previous correspondence that are not directly related to the questions and would be confusing if taken out of context. As with the transcription of Edward Bartlett's journal I have edited only

---

[17] One of the submitted questions that was not approved was an enquiry regarding Ella's strange spelling of dolls. I was given no explanation as to why the subject was taboo.

by deletion. I have not included the questions I put to Ella as they add nothing to the clarity of her replies.

I found out about the Doll's case through my sister. She saw the article in the Cradlefield Chronicle, the one Max Whitgift wrote after he'd gone back to the house and photographed the dolls house[18]. She knew I'd be interested in the dolls. It was her idea that I make some replicas, she thought they'd go well in the collection. The ones I'd put up for sale were my first attempts. The ones I kept for the collection were far better.

My interest in what people now call creepy dolls started in the seventies. If you feel it's something that needs to have blame attached to it, then you can blame NationWide. It was a TV magazine programme. All the old ITV regions did a segment each. It's what they used to call light entertainment. The sort of thing nobody wants to see anymore, jokes about things that were funny, not like today when every punchline has to be about making someone feel bad about themselves.

Anyway, they also did consumer reviews and price comparison articles. One year they did a review of the must-have-toys that were due to be big that Christmas. One of them was Baby Alive. It was the original one, so I suppose the TV show must have been transmitted in 1973, because that was the year Kenner first manufactured Baby Alive. I'd have been seven or eight then, about the right age for that type of toy I suppose. Not that dolls interested me then.

The segment about Baby Alive was handled by a really drole presenter called Richard Stilgoe. He reviewed various toys and got onto Baby Alive, completely deadpan he held the doll up and explained that Baby Alive came in a cardboard box with a plastic bag over its head. I remember my Dad laughing

---

[18] The photographs in questions were taken by the Chronicle's staff photographer, Michael Huddart, who accompanied Max Whitgift to 37 Fantoccini Street.

himself into one of his turns and needing his oxygen to be turned on.

Mum was really surprised when I asked if I could have a Baby Alive for Christmas, but part of her was pleased too. I could see she was relieved that I'd asked for something normal. She said, 'we'll see', which was the house code for 'we can't afford it'.

She found me something cheaper instead. A no-brand doll from Taiwan that wet itself. There were hundreds of manufacturers making cheap dolls back then. I could see Mum was worried when she gave me the package on Christmas morning, she was afraid that I'd be upset. I wasn't really, the only let down was that the doll, I called her Lydia after my sister, didn't have a plastic bag over its head. It was okay though, I found a carrier bag in the kitchen and cut one of the corners off. That did just as well. I told everyone that the bag was to keep Lydia doll pretty.

I've put plastic bags over the heads of all my dolls since. The other alterations I make are just window dressing and detail work really. It's the bags that are the important thing. Doctor Kenner (isn't' that funny?)[19] thinks that might be significant, but I don't know really. I've still got Lydia doll, and I was right; she's stayed pretty. My sister hasn't.

When I saw that article, the photographs of the dolls fascinated me. I spent a lot of time researching them, trying to pinpoint exactly the age and make, but the story behind them couldn't be ignored. The way they were placed in exactly the position of the bodies, as if they'd known what was going to happen. Do you know the collective noun for dolls is a perception? A Perception of dolls, you see?

I had a dream about those pictures in the paper. The ones

---

[19] I missed the significance of the this 'joke' at first; Kenner happens to be the name of the company that manufactured the first Baby Alive dolls.

47

of the do!!s house, the different rooms, all open at the front so you can see in. It wasn't a nightmare precisely, I was never scared, but I had this dream repeatedly, sometimes three and four times a week. It was always the same, more or less. I'd be in a house, it was a real house, but the front wall was gone, so it was totally open, like the do!!'s house. I wouldn't always be in the same room, sometimes I'd be upstairs in the bedrooms or the attic room, but most of the time I'd be downstairs in the hallway or halfway down the stairs. I'd be looking out into the garden and one of the do!!s, most often the mother do!! Would be on the floor in front of me. She would always be pointing behind me. You know how it is in dreams, you sometimes know things. I'd know the do!!, whichever one it was, was trying to get me to look behind me. That was the nearest the dream got to being frightening. I wasn't frightened of the do!!, but I was scared of looking behind me. I didn't know what was there, but I knew I didn't want to turn and see it.

Back then, back when I was having the dreams, well dream really, my medication was under review. I don't know if the drugs were making me have the dream or if they were just making me paranoid about it, but when I came across an article about the London North Uni getting involved in ghost hunting, I decided to write to them.

I didn't contact them about the house really, or even the Doll family, I thought the do!!s were the important thing. I suppose you think that sounds horrible, but I'm not saying my interest in the Doll case is only about the do!!s, it's just I think they're the most interesting thing about it. I don't think I'm alone in that. I'm aware that collecting do!!s makes a lot of people uncomfortable, especially the style of do!!s I gather, but the people who've been caught up in looking into the incident have all gravitated to the do!!s, haven't they? I think subconsciously people know something is going on.

By that time I'd already been in touch with the Cradlefield Chronicle and bought copies of the photos off them. I sent them with my letter, the uni. I wish I hadn't because I didn't get them back. They cost a lot and we only get pin money in here. By the time I'd saved enough money to get another set the paper had gone out of business. I never did find another set and I'd thrown out the newspaper my sister gave me.

Chapter Six: Playback

Transcript of audio recording from attic room/doll's house room. Recorded Friday 9th July 2010, on 1" tape using a Grundig TK146 reel to reel tape deck connected to a Shure SM63 omnidirectional microphone. The microphone was suspended centrally on a boom style stand at a height of 2m. The tape deck was situated in the ground floor stairwell. Connection to the microphone was via 12-gauge oxygen-free copper bi-wire with PVC insulation. Approximate length of wire was 25m.

At the beginning of the tape a voice, identified as John Pelton, states:

"Attic. Tape four. July 9th. fresh tape inserted, continuous recording starting at zero-zero hours and 45 seconds."

Foot falls are heard and the sound of a door closing. Other than a low whine, which has been identified as normal tape hiss, these are the only things the tape registers for the first 37 minutes of recording.

At 37 minutes and eight seconds, a series of unidentified noises can be heard. They have a duration of one minute 32 seconds. At one point a brief burst of music is discernible. Silence resumes for 47 seconds then a sibilant voice, possibly male, is heard:

"I'm free for it ... what's (unintelligible)... left where (unintelligible)... they (unintelligible) sick (unintelligible)."

There is a high-pitched noise, possibly a whistle, and the voice is gone. The remainder of the tape is silent.

From Edward Bartlett's written report on the Fantoccini Street Fieldtrip, submitted to the faculty of London North University.

Conclusion

The amount and quality of evidence gathered at 37 Fantoccini Street proves, beyond reasonable doubt, that activity is taking place there that cannot be explained within the framework of conventional science.

Currently, the exact nature of the activity is not clear. There were signs indicative of the survival of consciousness, possibly of more than one individual, but there were also incidents of a stone tape nature[20]. While events inside the property were atypical of poltergeist activity it is worth noting the high level of reception/connection evident between the youngest female member of the team and the presence.

The connection was evident even after we had left the house. When Attic Tape Four was played in the minibus, some miles distant from Fantoccini Street, the individual in question became increasingly upset and showed clear signs of agitation. While the tape invited lively discussion among the other members of the team, only the individual in question was so deeply affected.

The ability of psychic phenomena to act at such a distance from the house might be an indication of latent poltergeist activity. Ideally, the person concerned would return to the house, but she has stated she will

---

[20]Stone Tape theory speculates that sightings of ghosts can be attributed to a traumatic event leaving an impression, or recording, in the surrounding environment. Under certain circumstances this 'recording' will 'play' and can be witnessed. This is offered as a reason for multiple sightings of the same activity being seen at different times. Stone Tape hauntings are not thought to represent a form of survival after death.

not be willing to do so. If she cannot be coaxed back to number 37 I believe there is a strong argument in favour of finding a replacement psychic of similar demographic.

Sadly, the biggest find by far, the presence of a previously uncatalogued doll *in the attic room* doll's *house, will in all likelihood be dismissed.*

The new doll *(D#5), discovered on Sunday 11th July 2010, was not present in the* doll's *house at any time during the previous six days of the fieldtrip. This fact can be collaborated, by all five members of the team.*

D#5 was found, by me, quite by chance, when I happened to return to the house to retrieve a personal item. This happened after the team had made ready to depart and most of the record keeping gear had been stowed away.

Unfortunately, by that point most of the team where physically and emotionally drained and, when I returned to the minibus with news of my find, there was little enthusiasm for further investigation. Only one member of the team was willing to re-enter the house and make a record of D#5. It was agreed that the find was quite extraordinary.

D#5 is possibly one of the most significant paranormal artefacts to come to light this century. However, I have no doubt that it will be dismissed as a hoax because I was unaccompanied when I found it, leaving me open to accusations of planting evidence – which is the standard response of so called 'rationalists' to items that fall outside of their somewhat narrow field.

I ask John Pelton what he remembers of Viola Mezco's agitation in the minibus. He rolls his eyes.

"This'll sound stupid, but I think if something real had happened, she'd have been okay. When we left on Sunday evening, she was alright, a bit spooked maybe but that was all. It wasn't until we were in the minibus that she went into hysterics.

"Ed and May[21] were hyped up, getting themselves hyped

---

[21] Mabel Noakes, the older and more experienced of the team's two psychics/sensitives.

up. Don't know if you've ever seen people dragging their kid around a park, when the kid would sooner be at home on the computer. You know that way they start talking, getting all enthusiastic about seeing a couple of ducks, trying to make out everything's amazing when it isn't. Ever seen it work? No, course not. The kid'll usually throw a tantrum. That's pretty much what happened with Viola.

"Ed, when he finally stopped going on about that f__king doll, insisted on playing the tape from the attic. We'd all heard it. The voice on it was really indistinct, but Ed kept playing it back over and over. All the time he's frowning and shaking his head, like he's trying to unlock the Ark of the f__king Covenant. Then he decided he's deciphered some of it. I'd tried to tell them it was radio interference, but I was shouted down. May came out with some s__t along the lines of *it couldn't be from a radio, none of us have a radio*. When Ed started reciting the dialogue he'd thought he'd heard, May joined in. Once they'd worked out as much as they could they started trying to figure out what it meant."

"Did you agree with what they thought it was saying?"

"Yeah. It's not that hard to hear really, not if you're listening to it somewhere quiet, or on a set of headphones. We were in the f__king minibus though, driving through traffic, that's the main reason it was hard to make out. That and Ed getting worked up. Like I said, it was radio interference. Have you heard it?"

I have. In fact I have a recording of it with me, stored on my PC. At Pelton's insistence I boot up the device so I can play it. I ask if Mable Noakes was correct in saying nobody in in the house had a radio when the recording was made. John Pelton looks at me the way you might look at a dull child.

"It doesn't matter if she was right or wrong. Radio interference wouldn't come from a radio, it'd come from radio waves. We're surrounded by them all the time, it doesn't matter if you're holding a f__king radio or not. By that logic if you close your eyes the sun goes out".

53

To cover my embarrassment, I find the recording on my computer and play it. John Pelton is right, the voice is broken in places, but, when heard in relative silence, much of the recording is relatively clear.

"I'm free for it ... what's (unintelligible)... left where (unintelligible)... they (unintelligible) sick (unintelligible)."

"Yeah. Spooky," Pelton's voice is flat, clearly he does not find the recording 'spooky'. He asks for the PC and sets the recording back to the start. "So, how about we try this? Pick up from the station. Anybody free to take it?"

He presses play, the 'voice' supplies an answer:

"I'm free for it ..."

He carries on, supplying answers or questions to a possible dialogue.

"What's"

"...the drop off? Grandma's house, Riding Hood Lane. I know it ..."

"left where ..."

"... the chip shop used to be."

He shrugs and hands my PC back.
    "You think it was a minicab company?"
    He shrugs again.
    "It might have been. You could probably fill the blanks in a dozen different ways. It's just a random bit of radio chatter."
    "And you said this at the time?"
    "Of course I did."
    "What did the others think?"
    "May looked at me like I'd just said the moon was made of

54

cheese and says, *'well, it's not very likely, is it?'* Personally, I think it's more likely than a restless spirit coming out of the ether."

From the records of Edward Bartlett.

The Ouija board was set up in the dining room[22]. This was at the behest of Miss Mezco, who found this room to be the strongest focal point of the presence. This contrasted with Mrs Noakes, who registered a stronger presence in the attic. There was much debate as to why this should be. The conclusion reached was that number 37 probably contains multiple entities and their dissimilar natures emitted differing types of psychic energy, a state comparable with different people having differing personally types on the physical plane.

As this was the conclusion drawn by the team's two most sensitive members it is safe to assume it is correct.

Steven Ward and I were both aware of a presence within the house, but we experienced it only in vague feelings of being watched or a general sense of unease. John Pelton denied any feelings other than those attributable to the physical environment.

Miss Mezco's rationale for setting up the board in the dining room was further influenced by her belief that the presence there was not only stronger but benign. Mrs Noakes agreed with this statement, saying she felt the signal, as she described it, from the attic room, and particularly the doll's house, was angry and very possibly hostile. There was some speculation that the presence in the dining room may have been one of the Doll children.

I had expressed some reservations about the use of a Ouija board but was reassured by the participation Mrs Noakes, who has had considerable experience in their use.

---

[22] The ground floor room at the front of the house, where the bodies of the Doll twins were found. See foot note #6

Miss Mezco's Ouija board was a practicable, no-nonsense item consisting of a wooden base board in the traditional style[23]. The lettering was white (set against a black background) and in a clear typeset, leaving no room for ambiguity in the messages coming through. The planchette was an ovoid shaped piece of flat wood, highly polished and employing a 'view hole' in instead of the more common pointer. This meant that to be read the planchette had to be precisely positioned over an individual letter or numeral. Again, this precluded any ambiguity regarding messages.

The dining room, fortunately, contained one of the house's few pieces of remaining furniture: a round hard wood table. As they are of significance in recounting events, I will record its dimensions: Height 30" Diameter: 47".

Proceedings were recorded on VHS video tape with a secondary audio recording being made on 1" magnetic tape. The session began at 7:30 p.m. All members of the team took part in the session.

We sat around the table, spacing ourselves evenly. Mrs Noakes was seated facing the rooms only door, Miss Mezo sat at her left, then myself, then John Pelton and then (at the right of Mrs Noakes) Steven Ward.

As instructed, we all placed our fingertips, lightly, on the planchette.

Although the table had been left in the room there was no sign of the chairs. As the conditions inside the house were expected to be uncomfortable the team had been equipped with fold-away camping chairs. These were serviceable, but

---

[23] This consists of the letters of the alphabet set out in two arching lines, the numbers 0 to 10 beneath them in a straight line and the words 'yes' and 'no' in either the top or bottom corners. Some boards also have the word 'goodbye' along the bottom edge of the board.

noticeably lower that convention straight back chairs. When seated at the table our view of the board was not ideal and the positioning of our arms wasn't comfortable. I mention these facts to emphasize how difficult it would have been for any member of the team to have deliberately spelt out the messages that came through. Miss Mezco in particular, being rather short, had to stretch to keep in touch with the planchette. I also noted that she kept her eyes shut for much of the session, allowing others to read out the letters.

Under the conditions we were working with, fakery would have been impossible.

Video: #128.01/VHS008/IC039/10.07.10
Title: Fantoccini St. First Attempted Contact

The picture quality of the tape is good, but the angle of the fixed-point camera and the level of light makes it hard to define details of people's faces.

When the tape begins, Steven Ward, who has just activated the camera, enters the shot and takes his seat at the table. The view we have of him is of the back of his head. The rest of the team are already seated.

There is a digital counter in the lower righthand corner of the shot. At 00:01:27 Viola Mezco instructs everyone to place a hand on the planchette. There is a degree of shuffling as people adjust their positions. The Ouija board is not centred on the table and both Steven ward and John Pelton, sitting to his right, must lean forward to reach the planchette. John Pelton raises slightly from his seat and supports some of his weight on the table. Because of their changes in posture, the heads of Ward and Pelton obscure around a third of the Ouija board.

At 00:02:17 Viola Mezco, who sits almost opposite the camera, and is stretching uncomfortably to keep her hand on the planchette, asks if anyone in the rooms wants to speak. There is no response and at 00:02:49 she repeats the question. The planchette jerks to the top left-hand corner of the board, stopping at the word *'yes'*.

Someone gasps, on the sound recording captured by the video camera it is not clear who. On the audio recording made using 1" tape, it is clear the person who gasps is Mabel Noakes.

"Oh, that f__king Ouija board."

John Pelton appears to be less reticent about my questions regarding the first incident with the Ouija board.

"Viola brought it along, now…" he holds up an index finger, making a point "I'll give her her due here, she wasn't pushy about bringing it. When she got on the minibus she was holding it under one arm and asked Steve if he thought it might be worth trying in the house. May was really into the idea. I didn't give a s__t either way and I don't think Steve did either, but he said to bring it along and we'd see what Ed thought about it when we picked him up.

"I can't remember what Ed's problem with the board was, but when Steve asked about it there was a lot of huffing and puffing, like it was a big deal. He might have had his nose out of joint because we were running late. Then again Steve and Ed tended to make a meal out of everything. I remember them having a big discussion about taking temperature readings in the house; should they do it every three hours or every four? In the end I was the only one who hadn't weighed in on the big Ouija board question, so they sort of handed me the casting vote. If I'd known all the s__t it was going to bring down I would have set the f__king thing alight."

He falls silent and is clearly debating with himself how much he wants to say. Finally, he sighs and resumes.

"Viola, was trying to look all cool and 'not bothered' about it so she didn't blow her vampire aesthetic, but I could tell she was desperate to bring it along. And who was I to throw cold water on her trip?"

There's another silence that I have to nudge him through.

"You didn't want to upset her?"

He sighs again and, again, weighs up how much he wants to say.

"Thing is, I was about to spend a week in a cold damp pit with Steve, Ed and May. Steve was, and still is, so far up himself his voice is muffled, and Ed and May were both fanatics. Viola might just have been the only one there with any sense of having fun, you know? And yes, she was a pretty young woman. You could ask Ed about that is he was still alive."

There's another long silence. I get the impression that whatever he wants, or doesn't want, to tell me is a decision he's going to make alone. I keep quiet for fear of bringing the interview to a premature end.

Another sigh and he runs a hand through his hair. I notice that since the group photo, taken on the first visit, his hair has thinned.

"I said this at the time, told everyone the next morning when we'd calmed down a bit. It was me that pushed the pointer thing on to 'yes', when Viola asked if there was anybody there."

After Mabel Noake's outburst the table is still and silent. The only movement is from Steve Ward who looks from Viola Mezco to Mabel Noakes and then back again. Due to the camera angle, it is not possible to clearly see Viola Mezco's expression.

At 00:03:07 Mabel Noakes says,

"Ask her a question."

Viola doesn't want to watch the tape. I have it downloaded to my PC and offer to play it, believing it will help her recall the events.

"No, I'm willing to talk about it but I don't want to see it again."

Has she ever watched the tape?

"Yes, Eddie was very thorough. He did several follow up visits to me when he was writing up his accounts. He asked me loads and loads of questions. I don't want to see it again."

I have re-watched the tape while playing back Viola's description of the event that night. Where there is a discrepancy between her account and the recording, I have noted it. This is done in the spirit of transparency rather than to give the impression that Ms Mezco is an unreliable witness. The few discrepancies between what she recalls and what the tape shows are minor or can be attributed to the view she may have had at the time.

"It took a long time to set it up, the table was a big sized dining table, very high. We were using these canvass chairs, so we had to reach over the edge of the table. That's the thing you see, it was really difficult to see the board. We could only read where the planchette came to rest by getting out of our seats. Eddie was doing that. The planchette would move then, once it had stopped again, he'd get out of his chair so he could read out what it said. At least at the start that's what was happening."

This is a minor discrepancy. The first message read out – 'yes' - is read out by Steven Ward. Who at that point was half standing and, judging from the tape, would have had a perfectly clear view of the Ouija board and planchette.

"Once everybody had got themselves comfortable May asked me if I was ready. I told everyone to breathe deeply and try to empty their minds."

Again, the tape shows a slight difference. Ms Mezco is asked if she is ready. She nods and says,

"Okay. Everybody take a deep breath, relax and open your minds."

"We sat in silence for a while, tuning in, if that makes sense. I was aware of something being in that room. Something unhappy and scared. I asked if it wanted to speak, I think I had to ask twice, and the planchette drifted toward the top left corner of the board. We'd set the board out so it was facing me, I mean it was the right way up. I could tell the planchette was moving toward the 'yes' just by the direction of the pull. May caught her breath. She sounded exited and I think that broke the connection because I felt the presence back off. It's very hard to describe the feelings because if you don't have that sort of connection, there's no way to give a reference point. It's like asking someone what the colour green smells like. Anyway, I was trying to tune in again, but I couldn't feel it. Then May said, 'ask her a question'. She must have been tuned in more than she realised because she said ask *her*. She picked up on the presence being female before I did. Once I knew that, I was able to tune in again.

"I asked if she had lived in the house. And this time the planchette jumped into the top left corner. I actually felt it lift

61

off the board. Eddie leaned over the table and told us the planchette was resting on the 'yes'. But to be honest I knew that.

"I can remember hearing Steve's breathing. I think he was really shaken up by it. He told me later that he'd never seen a planchette move like that before.[24] May told Eddie to sit down because his interruption would break the connection."

On the tape Mable Noakes says,

"we can all see what it says, Eddie, lets carry on."

"I asked for a name and the planchette began to waver back and forth, as if it couldn't decide where to go. And the table started to tremble. I remember that distinctly, although it didn't show up on the video. It was very slight, more a vibration. Then Pelton suggested the presence might not be able to spell, and the planchette jumped again, straight over to the 'yes'."[25]

"I should have used what we call closed questions, yes or

---

[24] In the course of researching this book I interviewed Steven Ward once in person and questioned him further by phone and via email. I contacted him to ask about this statement. He told me that he was indeed shaken but didn't specifically remember Viola speaking to him about Ouija boards. He said the 11th July incident with the Ouija board was the first time he had used one.

[25] John Pelton remembers this incident. He claims the remark was meant as a joke. Although indistinct on the video his words are clearly audible on the reel-to-reel recording, as is his chiding tone of voice.

no answers, but I was flustered and asked 'are you Patsy or Ann'[26], which of courses isn't a yes or no response. The planchette moved to 'yes' but it was less sure of itself, then it shifted quickly to 'no'. So I asked, 'are you Patsy?' Again the 'yes', quicker this time. Then I asked, 'is Ann with you?'. 'Yes' again, and again, it happened really fast. That was when the table started to tilt. It jumped right up. We were all dumbstruck for a moment. Then Pelton said something like, 'f__k this', and walked out."

It's on this point that Ms Mezco's recall and the tape mismatch most strongly. On the tape Ms Mezco asks:

"are you Patsy?"

And the planchette moves without hesitation to the 'yes' corner. John Pelton says,

"I've had enough of this," and moves away from the table.

It is as he turns, the planchette jerks rapidly onto the 'yes' marker and the table tilts alarmingly. Mabel Noakes yelps as if in pain and everyone lets go of the Planchette.

Steven Ward watches the tape of the Ouija board session. At point where the table drops back onto the floor and the planchette and Ouija board both appear to jump slightly, he pauses the picture and takes the recording back. We watch again: the table tilts, everyone jumps away, the table falls and the Ouija board jumps.

"None of us could agree what happened," he says. "And this recording is next to worthless".

The video was made using a Panasonic M50 VHS camera

---

[26] Patsy and Ann, the Doll children.

63

loaded with Fuji Film Pro VHS-C TC-30 tape. The camera had been positioned on a tripod at a height of 170cm. These details have been recorded by Edward Bartlett.

Unfortunately, his obsessive note taking was carried out with the aim of forestalling later accusations of sloppiness rather than with any real understanding of the techniques of filming. No information has been recorded regarding the distance between the camera and the table, the angle of the camera mount or the type of lens used. Because of this it is impossible to ascertain the exact angle of tilt the table reaches or the height any of the jumping articles on the table reach. These factors are compounded by the arrangement of the group at the table.

"I set up the camera to give a clear view of the board. I used a wide angle 35mm lens, that's pretty standard, and manually increased the gain, to allow for the poor light. I didn't worry about the sound quality because John had his gear set up and I knew he'd get far better results than I would. I set the tape running and we all sat down. Of course, in retrospect that was all a__e about face. What I should have done is get everyone sitting then set up the camera."

On the screen, John Pelton is moving away from the table. He starts and moves quickly, turning to his right. As he leaves shot it is possible to see the table is tilted. The elevated position of the camera makes it hard to judge the degree of tilt.

"We all saw the table tilt, everyone except John who had turned around by that point, but even he allowed he might have felt something brush his arm as he moved away. Trouble is, nobody tells the same story."

Steven Ward replays the video again and shakes his head. What he regards as his mistakes in setting up the camera still trouble him.

"From where I was the tilt looked quite slight, I'd have said somewhere around 15 degrees. Bear in mind I was partially over the table, reaching for the planchette. May insisted it was much more, she said it was at least 45 degrees. She was at the end of the table that stayed on the floor, at the hinge point if you like, but the surface of the table hit her on the chin. It didn't hit her hard, but it made her bite her lip and she was bleeding. Eddie, immediately afterwards, estimated it at 30 degrees. Viola said something I found very odd. She said 37 degrees, which seems a strange figure to come up with as an estimate.[27] It occurred to me later that 37 was the house number and she might have been attempting some black humour.

"The point remains; the table tilted. That much we did agree on. We all jumped away, and it dropped back onto the floor again. Then the board and the planchette levitated."

It's another point where the group couldn't agree the details. Steven Ward maintains that the board and planchette bounced into the air, going much higher than could be accounted for by the jolting of the table returning to earth. Mabel Noakes, in the written statement she provided for Edward Bartlett, denied seeing the items leave the table (a fact contradicted by the video evidence). She insisted both planchette and board held their position, despite being on a severely tilted plain. There was some agreement between Edward Bartlett and Viola Mezco who both stated the items lifted from the surface of the table and held their position for an unusually long time

---

[27] In his writings Edward Bartlett settles on a figure of 31.75 degree. I was puzzled by this strangely precise measurement and wondered where it had come from. Steven Ward pointed out it is the average of the different estimates.

before falling. However, Mezco disagrees with Bartlett's assertion that the planchette rotated in the air and pointed in the direction of the door before falling.

Edward Bartlett's written account of the contact session acknowledges the lack of cohesion among the accounts of those who saw it – although he doesn't mention the differing angle of tilt accredited to the table[28]. He suggests that the lack of a clear and uniform recounting of the event is indicative of paranormal activity.

"The fact that four witness, each specialist in their field, could sit at the same table, with a clear view of the same event and not be able to give a consistent account of it, is surely proof that forces beyond natural experience were acting on our senses."

It is not clear from the notes why Bartlett refers to four witnesses not five. It seems likely that in this instance he was discounting John Pelton, who had his back to the room during the tilting and levitating incident.

Steven Ward has read and agrees with Edward Bartlett's recording of events. His signature along with those of Mabel Noakes and Viola Mezco, appears on at the end of Bartlett's report on the subject.[29]

---

[28] ibid

[29] John Pelton's signature is absent. According to Pelton it was Edward Bartlett's practice to ask witnesses to sign a document stating they agreed with his reports. If the witness felt the facts were inaccurate or misrepresented and didn't want to sign then they simply didn't sign, rewrites or codicils were not on offer.

Although Ward is satisfied with the accuracy of Bartlett's reporting, he has concerns about the syntax used.

"I thought the language Eddie used gave the wrong impression. Not long after I'd signed it, I re-read his report and realised it would be easy to get the impression that what happened took place very slowly. The word levitated came up several times[30]. Now, that's not inaccurate, as such. Things lifted into the air, lifted with no clear reason. But levitated implies things were floating around, and it just wasn't like that. It's clear when you see the video, but if someone was just reading that account, they'd get the wrong idea.

"What happened with that table wasn't something gentle or graceful, it was fast and violent. The table didn't hover gently at one end, it jumped, so did the board and the planchette. That board was solid wood, and it went up in the air like a rocket."

When I ask how he would account for the discrepancies in the accounts given by the people at the table he cites the speed of the actions.

"It was over and done in the blink of an eye. If you look at the time signature on the video it takes less than two seconds. On the audio John captured you hear May cry out and then, almost instantly, you hear the bang as the table hits the floor again. A lot of things happened in a very short space of time; the table jumped, May yelped, and was actually hit by the table top, then the table lands again and the items on it jump far higher into the air than they should have. That's a lot to take in, and don't forget, everybody was already shaken up. Adrenaline makes us hyperaware, and that can affect our perception of time. Ask anyone who's been involved in a bad car crash. It's quite common for people to remember events

---

[30] I counted; in the ten-page document the word levitate appears 27 times.

as if they were slow motion."

I ask if it's possible his own senses were playing tricks that night.

"I make my living by teaching people to record what they see. I know what I saw."

Was signing the witness agreement a mistake?

"Not at all. I just think Eddie's account fails to get across how frightening it was. If anything, I'd say he's bordered on underplaying events. I can why the heads of departments didn't want to give approval for the next fieldtrip. In a bizarre way it's a compliment to Eddie that everyone was so underwhelmed by the report they received. It goes to show the lengths he went to not to sensationalise what was happening. It's sad that he didn't live to see them change their minds."

Chapter Seven: D#5, The Walking Doll

D#5, the doll discovered by Edward Bartlett on the final day
of the 2010 fieldtrip, goes by many names[31]. Mostly though, it
is referred to as the *Lost* or *Walking* Doll – as in *it walked away*.
Aside from being melodramatic, this term isn't particularly
helpful; none of the Fantoccini Street dolls can be found.
Among the communities of doll collectors, gothic/macabre
collectors and true crime aficionados there is much discussion
about their possible whereabouts, and much in the way of
stories, rumour and hearsay. Like so much online content,
speculation is often delivered as fact. The dolls reside in the
Met's black museum, they were bought by the British
museum, they were bought by Stanford Research Institute for
part of an ongoing study into the paranormal, they were
bought by the New Orleans Historic Voodoo Museum, they
mysteriously vanished from a police evidence store/Sotheby's
Auction House/the private collection of … the list goes on.
There are also those who claim to have the dolls in their
possession and are willing, invariably, to part with them … for
a price.

   Ella Caine, believed by most to be the leading authority on
creepy dolls, puts little store in any of the rumours and refutes

---

[31] I have found D#5 referred to as the
Bartlett Doll, the Bedroom Doll, the Final
Doll, the Lying Doll, the False Doll, the
Prophet Doll (also the *Profit Doll* and
BS#5).

69

all the claims of ownership.

"I've often been sent photographs of Murder Do!!s, for my opinion on their validity. None of them are genuine, only one of them ever came close. Even if I wasn't a do!! Enthusiast, the quality of the fakes would be annoying. It you're going to pass off a forgery as a genuine item, at least make an effort to produce something plausible. False modesty aside, the best reproductions of the do!!s I've seen are the ones I made, but I was honest about it and sold them as replicas."

The most likely explanation for the disappearance of the original Fantoccini Street dolls, and the one Ella espouses, is that they went to land fill. Aside from the highly atmospheric photo spread of the dolls in their 'death set' positions in the doll's house of number 37, Michael Huddart and Max Whitgift also produced several pictures of the dolls against a plain white background. It is these photographs Ella referred to when authenticating do!!s being passed as genuine and when making her own replicas.

These shots, given the quality of the lighting and the cleanness of the background were most likely taken away from number 37. The most probable explanation is, having taken the shots of the dolls in the rooms of the doll's house, Huddart and Whitgift took them back to one of their homes or back to the newspaper offices, where, after being photographed again, they were likely thrown away.

When I raise the subject of the Walking Doll, Steven Ward looks pained.

"If I'm completely honest, at the time I half suspected Eddie had planted it. He didn't find it until we'd packed way all the gear and everyone was sitting in the minibus. John literally had the engine running, he'd agreed to do the driving on the way back to the uni. We were running late, and everyone had had enough, everyone aside from Eddie.

"It wasn't what you'd call a lark, camping out in that house for a week. Aside from the fact it was like living in a squat, Eddie and May had kept everyone up all night. Every time there was a crack or a creek one of them would get up and investigate it. It had worn a bit thin with all of us. Not least of all because it made the job of deciphering the tapes nigh on impossible. John was a pain in the neck sometimes, but he took the job seriously, recording was that man's reason d'état. He'd sweat blood setting up the gear properly, so we could tell natural disturbances from what he called the Twilight Zone stuff. Then Eddie or May would blunder into a room at the first hint of noise and all we could hear was them stamping around and chattering. It made it hard to get excited about anything we found. Most of the recordings from that trip are pretty much worthless.

"The problem with May and Eddie, especially Eddie, was they couldn't understand the difference between evidence and proof. They both thought if we played the tape back and one of them could say 'that was me dropping my notebook' or 'that wasn't me, that was a presence' then the tape was valid. I gave myself ulcers trying to explain we weren't in a court of law, it didn't matter what people believed, all that counted was being able to produce something that couldn't be explained away as two people in a room stomping around.

"The only audio we had that was worth a damn was the voice in the attic. John only managed to record that by setting up the mic and then sleeping at the top of the stairs so Eddie or May couldn't get into the room.

"Any way, we were ready to go, and Eddie said he'd lost his lighter, he had a cigarette in his mouth and was patting all his pockets down. He smoked like a chimney. He went back into the house to look for it. John groaned and put the radio on. I remember it was playing *Feelgood* by the Gorillaz, I can remember thinking it was the least appropriate song we could be hearing.

"It felt like we waited for a long time, but later when I thought about it, it can't have been more than a few minutes

71

because *Feelgood* had only just finished when Eddie burst out of the house again and wrenched the door of the bus open. He was excited, really excited. He told us, all of us, there was something we had to see, and he wanted me to bring my camera because his had died on him. He'd taken a basic digital camera along with him. I'd taken a pair of Hasselblad 500 medium format cameras for the serious work, and my old 35mm Sigma, for the day-to-day stuff. The 500s and the video gear were all packed up, and I'd burned up the last of the VHS tape just as we left. I grabbed the Sigma and went back to the house with Eddie. Everyone else stayed in the bus.

"He'd left the front door open and went straight up stairs to the attic. I feel bad for thinking it now, in light of what happened, but later it struck me as odd. He'd only been back in the house a few minutes, but he'd had time to go to the top of the house. I remember thinking, if you're looking for your lighter, surely you'd check the bottom floors before hauling yourself up two flights of stairs?

"When we got to the attic room, he rushes over to the doll's house but draws short of it by about five feet and just points. I went closer and there was, the new doll."

He shrugs as if acknowledging that the end of the story is an anti-climax. I press him about the lack of photographs and his discomfort becomes more pronounced.

"Eddie was very excited about his camera dying at that moment, but that wasn't any kind of surprise really, he clicked off hundreds of photos, snapping away constantly, and that drained the battery pretty quick. Don't forget that place had no electrics, all our kit was running on rechargeable batteries that we had to recharge either in the minibus or with this tiny camping generator. As I said, we'd been roughing it. We'd managed to get Thames Water to put the water on, but that was it.

"Once I was looking at Eddie's doll I realised I didn't have any film in the camera I'd brought with me. I didn't want to

72

traipse all the way downstairs again to load up, and as I've said, I wasn't entirely sure he hadn't put it there himself. I was wary of spending anymore of the budget on something that could easily be dismissed as a hoax. I pretended to take a dozen shots of the thing, letting the flash off and making the motor whir. I suggested Eddie took a couple of pictures on his phone so they could see them downstairs. Then he started on whether we should move the doll or not, maybe take the whole house away, the doll's house obviously. In the end I told him it would be best to leave it and come back later when we'd examined what we had already. It was lucky the estate agency had put those heavy security panels over the doors of the house, because being able to lock the artefacts away safely was the only thing that persuaded Eddie to leave.

"When we got back to the van, he was all for bringing everyone back in and breaking out the Ouija board again. Viola got really upset at that idea and ended up saying it was her Ouija board and she wasn't going to let anyone have it. Making contact the previous night had affected her more than we'd realised. Once she started getting upset, May said we should leave. I could see she was really disappointed, May I mean; she wanted to go back inside and see the doll for herself, but she let it go because she didn't want Viola getting any more upset. That was the thing with May, she could drive you insane at times, but she had a heart of gold."

I ask if he still suspects Edward Bartlett planted the doll. His response is emphatic.

"No. There is simply no way. I'm ashamed that I ever entertained the idea. The thing that made Eddie such a poor researcher was the same thing them made him such a committed one. He believed absolutely that the world we inhabit is just one aspect of existence. Call it life after death, or alternative dimensions, but in Eddie's mind there was no doubt. Proving it to the world at large was his all-consuming passion. Whatever his faults as an investigator and researcher, his sincerity is beyond doubt."

It has been suggested that the Walking Doll may have been planted by a member of the team – Edward Bartlett was only one of five people in the house that week – with the intent of sexing up the findings. If this had been the case, then it might have been a wasted effort. Eight weeks after the team had returned and began the long job of sifting through their findings, the Principle of London North University called Steven Ward to her office and expressed her displeasure at the quality of both his field work and pastural care. Viola Mezco had been witnessed leaving the minibus in what was described as a state of near hysteria, and the head of the Acoustics Technologies Dept had agreed with John Pelton's assessment of the Attic Tape. It looked as if the investigation into 37 Fantoccini Street was over.

Part Three

Back to the Doll's House

Back to the Doll's *House*

The 2011 Fieldtrip

Monday 8th August to Monday 15th August

Members of Investigative Team

Carol Crossland	*Sensitive*
John Pelton	*Audio Capture Technician*
Gerald Cardino	*Surveyor*
Mabel Noakes	*Sensitive*
Steven Ward	*Audio Visual Capture technician*
~~*Viola Mezco*~~	~~*Sensitive*~~
~~*Edward Bartlett*~~	~~*Archivist/Investigator*~~

Chapter Eight: DoLS Home

Before moving on from the first fieldtrip, I feel it is only right to mention my only attempt to interview Mabel Noakes.

Although little known to the wider public, Mabel Noakes, born in 1941, was a widely respected figure within the psychic community. Unlike many of her contemporaries who sought, or at least accepted, fame or social advancement from their 'gift' Noakes tended to shy away from public scrutiny. She also steadfastly refused any payment for her services.

She came to public attention only briefly, in the early eighties when she was interviewed on Channel 4. The interest of someone on an editorial team had been roused by Noakes petitioning the House of Lords to pass a bill giving mediums, psychics and clairvoyants professional accreditation.

The interview took place live on Channel 4. *Focus 82*, described as *an edgy mix of current affairs and up to the minute pop-culture*, was one of the channel's early attempts at 'yoof' programming. The series was derided by critics for being amateurish and self-consciously crass. It was axed halfway through its first series.

It seems unlikely that Mabel Noakes knew the nature of the program when she agreed to appear on it. The aim of her campaign had been to introduce legally binding codes of practice to protect the public from charlatans and con artists. The subtleties of this were lost on the show's producers and host. At one point near the end of the interview she was asked to read the presenter's mind. Clearly upset and frustrated by the chiding and mocking tone, she ended the interview in tears. Possibly the segment would have been cut from a pre-recorded show, as it was, the camera quickly cut away from the image of a middle-aged woman crying. The clip survives on YouTube, among a collection of random snippets from the show. It is a sad legacy.

At the time of writing Mabel is resident in a council run care home. She has lived there since 2014 when worsening Alzheimer's made independent living impossible. When I enquired with her carers about the possibility of an interview, I was warned it would be unlikely to yield results. This proved to be the case and in the twenty minutes I spent with Mabel, she neither spoke to me nor acknowledged my presence. She was however in near constant motion, moving from one part of her room to another, opening and closings drawers and doors without reason. When I decided the interview was indeed hopeless and made to leave, she followed me from her room and to the reception desk where I was required to sign out.

The scene that followed was heart-breaking. As I was signing the visitors' log, to register my departure, another visitor happened to arrive. To gain entry to the care home visitors are required to pass through a glass walled antechamber, resembling an airlock. When they ring the bell a staff member buzzes them in, and the outer door opens. Only when this door has shut again will the inner door be opened.

I'd wondered at this arrangement when I entered the home, now its necessity became clear. When the visitor came through the first door and waited at the second, Mabel went to the antechamber and began tapping on the glass, clearly wanting to get out. A member of staff had to gently, but firmly, lead her away from the entrance before the visitor could come in. As soon as the door closed again, Mabel returned to it, continuing her tapping.

I realised Mabel would need to be held back again when I left, and asked if I should wait for her to move away before leaving. The member of staff at the reception desk, a surprisingly young man I thought, shook his head.

"She might be there for an hour. Mrs Noakes is one of our wanderers, she's always trying to get out. We have to stop her physically. A lot of the residents here are the same. That's why we have the dolls in place."

This last comment made me jump and I asked him to repeat it, thinking I'd misheard.

A 'dolls', he explained was the term for a Deprivation of Liberty Safeguarding order (DoLS). It meant Mabel could be restrained if her actions were deemed to go against her own self-interest or safety. The young man on the reception desk was at pains to explain the DoLS was there for her own good.

Mabel was duly held back as the inner door was opened and I passed through. My last sight of her was as she stood knocking on the door, waiting for it to open. Held in place by her DoLS

Chapter Nine: A Psychic and A Surveyor

It's debateable whether the subsequent fieldtrips would have come about had Edward Bartlett lived. Again, the facts are far from clear, and theories and rumours abound.

One fact is beyond doubt, on the morning of September 9th, 2010, a few days after being told the material gathered at number 37 didn't warrant further investigation by, or support from, London North University, Edward Bartlett was found dead.

His wife found him, fully clothed, on their bed. Beside him were his PC and a printed A4 photograph of D#5, the doll that would become known as the Walking Doll.

The computer was turned off and closed when Patricia Bartlett found her husband's body. It's a detail she is very clear on. The PC was closed, lying on the bed to the left of the body. The picture of D#5 was to his right.

Edward Bartlett had taken to working in the bedroom. It was the smaller of his home's two upstairs rooms, the master bedroom having long since been given over to his library of the paranormal. For a time the bigger room had also served as an office, but the vast archiving project had taken over all available workspaces.

It appeared he'd just settled down to do some work when it happened. *It* being a massive cardiac infarction that, according to the coroner's report, would have been mercifully quick. A point Patricia Bartlett isn't convinced on. Her husband's face, when she found him, was a mask of terror.

There was no suggestion of foul play, the investigation of the coroner's office was a rubber-stamped formality. Nothing about the death points to anything other than a domestic tragedy.

However, two factors beyond the remit, and possibly understanding, of the authorities were to come to light.

Four weeks after the funeral, Steven Ward contacted Patricia to ask if he could have copies of her husband's notes on Fantoccini Street. Although the university's faculty were unimpressed with what they'd seen of the trip and had no intention of funding or supporting another, Ward was preparing an article for publication. He thought he owed it to Bartlett's memory to make it as thorough and complete as possible. While Patricia Bartlett was happy to loan him a copy of the relevant paper file, she didn't know the password for her late husband's PC, nor for any of the IronKeys.

"I knew the IronKeys were beyond all but professional hackers and codebreakers, but I thought some of the techies on campus could probably open the PC. Pat was happy to let me have the computer."

Ward's confidence was well founded, and the PC was duly opened. What he found was, in part, what he'd been expecting. The last document Edward Bartlett had been working on had been his write up of the Fantoccini Street trip. In accordance with his widow's theory that he'd had a heart attack before starting his day's work, the computer recorded that the document had last been opened two days before his death. However, the computer history listed the last items viewed as being accessed on September 9th, the day Edward Bartlett died. It would seem likely that he'd been using the PC in his bedroom shortly before his death. The significance of this is lost on me. Surely, it was possible that Bartlett had finished what he needed to do with the PC, closed it and then had a heart attack. It is even possible that he felt unwell and closed the PC intending to rest.

Steven Ward nods in agreement.

"That's what I assumed but then something struck me about the files he'd been looking at. They were all picture files, photos. The file manager on the computer listed their location as removeable drive E, so they'd been accessed on an external drive. In all likelihood one of Eddie's USB sticks. I tried clicking on one of the links, but of course I just got a message saying the file couldn't be reached. I didn't think anything of that until I'd given Patricia the computer back and said goodbye. I was almost through the gate when I remembered she'd been at pains to tell me that she'd only found the PC on the bed, waiting to be booted up."

He watches me in silence as I try and make the new facts fit the scenario I've constructed for Edward Bartlett's last actions. It isn't a good fit: Having viewed the files on an external drive he removes the drive, shuts down the pc, closes its lid and then gets up, leaves the room to return the drive to its place and returns to lay on the bed. It begs the question, why did he close his PC if he intended to use it again? And if you he didn't intend using it again, why didn't he put it away when he was putting away the external drive?

In themselves, these questions hardly constitute a smoking gun. People are not machines, they don't always do what they should or act in logical ways. It's clear to Steven Ward that this is what I'm thinking.

"The files he'd been viewing didn't have titles. I could tell they'd been photographs because the PC told me so, but they hadn't been given a file name, they were logged as a string of numbers pulled from the SIM card of the phone or camera that had taken them.

"I asked Patricia if I could try the last IronKey in Eddie's collection. He had them all numbered. I thought there might be a chance he hadn't got round to setting a password on the key he'd been using. For a second I thought I was right. Patricia gave me an Ironkey with 012 scratched on it. She said she thought that must be the last one because it was the highest number. It opened up okay, the password hadn't been set, but it was blank. I didn't know what to make of that, but when I gave it back, Patricia put it on this tiny rack of the things. They were numbered one to twelve, and there was a gap where number seven should have been. I tried number six, and it was password protected. Number eight opened but

81

it was another blank."

He leaves the question of what became of the missing IronKey unspoken.

Playing the interview back to transcribe it, I'm reminded of the stillness in Steven Ward's office at this point. On the tape there is merely a gap; the silence of two people not saying anything. At the time though, I had the distinct feeling that this point of the story held great significance for Steven Ward. The silence had the tension of a man at the edge of a deep drop, debating whether to leap. On the tape the silence is broken by the sound of a door opening.

Someone had looked into the office and, seeing us, withdrew muttering an apology. The stillness was over.

"What do you think happened?"

The question is in relation to the IronKey. A fact I am sure Steven Ward is aware of. There is the tiniest of pauses before he answers.

"What do I think happened to Eddie? I can't *know*, but what I *believe* is something in the photos he was looking at scared him badly enough to cause a heart attack."

"And IronKey number six?"

Once again, a pause.

"I suppose it fell on the floor. Patricia's very houseproud. It probably wound up in a hoover bag."

This is the only time I have the impression Steven Ward isn't being entirely candid with me.

If the matter of the mislaid IronKey were the only anomaly connected with Edward Bartlett's death, then it would be easy to disregard Steven Ward's idea as overblown. However, during her husband's memorial service, Patricia Bartlett mentioned, more than once, that the position of her husband's body matched that of the doll in the photograph she'd found next to him. Mabel Noakes later recounted hearing this claim,

"According to Pat, it was almost as if Eddie had been trying to reproduce the photograph he'd taken."

"I asked John to come with us on the second trip because he was good at his job. We all respected that and of course he knew the lay out of the house. It would be quicker for him to wire up the equipment a second time then it would be for somebody new to do it from scratch."

Steven Ward stops talking and we are both faintly embarrassed. He has given me an answer to a question I haven't asked.

At the time of interviewing Ward, I had yet to meet John Pelton and had not heard his claim that he had moved, and admitted to moving, the planchette[32] during the July 10th Ouija board session. Ward's unasked for justification for taking Pelton on the second fieldtrip was the first indication I had of the tensions at play between the two men.

"I'm not sure if the uni authorities thought Eddie's death made the investigation more valid, or if they thought it would be disrespectful to his memory to allow his last investigation

---

[32] John Pelton's claim to have cheated with the Ouija board came to me many weeks after my interview with Steven Ward. I sent Ward an email asking for his comments. Initially he responded with a single line email saying he had no recollection of Pelton making such a claim. However, in a later email he made reference to the claim, dismissing it as 'more of John's s__t stirring'.

to go neglected. I'd like to think the latter."

Another possible explanation for the heads of faculty's newfound enthusiasm for the project is the brief flurry of interest from the press. In a slow week for news the death of *'the counties most dedicated ghost hunter'*, and the faint glamour of the supernatural, was picked up by several national news sheets. It even rekindled an interest in the Doll family tragedy.

"We wanted has much continuity between the trips as possible," Ward continues, still justifying his decisions. "May was willing to come along but she was obviously scared. Pelton agreed, for a fee of course, but Viola said she wasn't going to set foot in that house again. She took a leave of absence from her course and wouldn't return calls or emails. I could understand that. May and I agreed with Eddie's comment that the next trip should include someone similar to Viola, because the house had seemed to respond to her."

"Physically similar, a young woman?"

"A young sensitive. Obviously, that was the most important factor, but we hoped to find someone of as close a demographic as possible."

"Was it hard to find a replacement?"

"Not really, Eddie had had Carol in mind already, and she was ideal. But we wanted a second person too. It was hard to know what to look for there. Eddie's role hadn't been entirely clear. In the end we chose a student from the engineering department. We thought an engineer would take the same no-nonsense approach Eddie had. There were a lot of volunteers. The hard part was finding someone suitable.

"The publicity and the renewed interest around the Doll family gave the second fieldtrip a new appeal. We had applications from almost every department. Most people didn't really have anything to offer other than enthusiasm. Though we did toy with the idea of taking a member of the nursing cohort along."

The teams' new sensitive was Carol Crossland. A third-year degree student studying criminal psychology. At twenty-two she was the same age as Viola, and according to Ward, bore more than a passing resemblance to her.

There was no group shot taken outside the house on the second trip. There are however a great number of the team at work.

"For the documentation shots I stuck with my analogue kit," Ward tells me. "But Carol had suggested, during her interview, that it would be a good idea to keep a record of the trip itself. Meaning a record of the normal day-to-day events, rather than a catalogue of details or attempts to capture anomalies. I suppose that came from the mindset of a psychology student. Anyway, we liked the fact she'd obviously given the trip some thought and wasn't just morbidly curious."

The upshot of this was a digital album of over 400 'snapshot' pictures. Ward and Crossland both took digital cameras and, mindful of the problem with power supply, a pocket full of fully charged batteries.

"I spent about a week scrounging batteries off people," he recalls.

Unlike the image captured by Edward Bartlett, Ward's images are accessible.[33]

The digital pictures contained on the USB stick -open access- Steven Ward gives me are for the most part unremarkable. None of them are titled. This is a task I assume would have fallen to Carol, had she continued her studies. Luckily the file numbers make it possible to view the pictures in chronological order and the images all have a date stamp on them.

The first image on the disc is a view of the frontage of 37 Fantoccini Street. There are no people in this photo. The house is shuttered on the lower floors with a heavy padlock and hasp securing the front door. What strikes me, seeing the

[33] Permission to reproduce these photographs was expressly denied. (R.D)

photo for the first time, is the complete lack of resemblance to the house used by Maindo Ningyo when she culled stock footage for her film. The house, even viewed with the knowledge of its history, is remarkably bland. A two-story terrace of no particular style, it is shabby and in a moderately bad state of repair. And that is as much as can be said about it.

The next dozen or so pictures on the disc were various shots of the minibus being unloaded. Another dozen detail John Pelton tacking cables to skirting boards and door frames. More still show him positioning mics. This series contain the first shot of Carol Crossland. What, at first, I take to be a physical resemblance to Viola Mezco I later decide is little more than a similarity of style. Both women favoured DM boots and black clothing. In the photo Cross is position in the hallway. She appears to be singing. In fact she is speaking aloud to provide a 'level' for the taping equipment Pelton is setting up. When I see this picture for the first time, I'm in the company of Ward.

"That took up most of the afternoon, wiring the place for audio recording." He sighs heavily. "It was decided to record continuously in the kitchen, the attic room and the dining room. Those were where a presence was most strongly felt by the two sensitives. That amounted to about 360 hours of tape, that was a big part of the budget. The infuriating thing about it was the uni insisted the silent tape be donated to the music department and reused. They were considered blank. All the silent tapes, bar one, are lost."

The surviving 'silent' tape, taken from the cadge of recordings from the attic, has become something of a legend in certain circles. Pelton's sophisticated equipment and finely honed skill at recording failed to register anything. Anything at all. Those who study the practice of taping empty rooms to capture phantom sounds, find this total absence of sound as chilling as any message from the dead.

A smaller number of Ward's photos show a painfully thin young man. This is Gerald Cardino, invariably the photographs show him taking measurements.

Gerald Cardino was the youngest member of the team. In the first year of a civil engineering degree, he admits now to having joined the fieldtrip, in part, as a joke.

"London North Uni was a bit of a joke in itself, really. It was an old fashion polytechnic that had been up graded to a university. It offered about a thousand different courses and did most of them badly. At the time I was there they had a prospectus the size of a phonebook. In my first term a big row kicked off between the Department of Alternate and Complimentary Medicine and the Engineering Department. They were both housed in the same building.

"It was like that all through the campus, classes and courses being lashed up ad hoc. There were signs everywhere, every room belonged to a dozen departments. I've got a photo somewhere of a plaque on one of the admin offices, there were eight different names on it. Of course, the uni wanted to pretend it was the greatest seat of learning in the country, and we were all one big happy family. But really, the place was an embarrassment[34].

"I remember the place was divided broadly into techies, people doing what were considered 'real' degrees and the

---

[34] This assessment may seem harsh, but it is a fact that between 2009 and 2012 a total of eighteen courses were added to the London North prospectus. In November of 2010 the Daily Mail described it as *'possibly the worst university in Europe'*, citing its willingness to validate subjects and courses from largely unvetted establishments.

hippies, guys doing the wishy-washy stuff. Being on a civil engineering course I was very much in the 'real degree' camp. There was a certain amount of resentment directed toward the hippy crowd. The heavy tech side of the uni was pretty lame, the course I was doing was another add-on that had been squeezed into the syllabus. I don't suppose there was any truth in it, but the feeling was the money that should have been spent on funding real courses was getting frittered away on nonsense like osteopathy and new-age therapies.

"When word filtered down that the faculty was paying expenses for another trip to a haunted house, a lot of people were pretty p__sed off. Someone, I don't know who, but there was a rumour that it was one of the lecturers, suggested that everyone studying a real subject should apply to go along, because *'why should the free ride be hippies only?'* Stupid really when you think about it, Steve, Steven Ward, was department head of the Visual Technologies. That was considered a 'real' subject."

Cardino's application to join the second fieldtrip was only half in jest. Despite pursuing a career in something as grounded and 'real' as civil engineering, the possibility of survival after death and the field of the paranormal has held a fascination for him since childhood.

The combination of engineer and psychic investigator is by no means unique. Maurice Grosse, one of the main investigators of the Enfield Poltergeist, had his own engineering and display consultancy and was a member of both the Royal Institution and the Institute of Patentees and Inventors.

"My interest in what people call the paranormal or the supernatural began with Uri Gellar. By the time I was old enough to really appreciate what he was doing the spotlight had moved off him. Mention his name now and most people will draw a blank, but in the seventies, at his height, he was a household name. He's been studied under scientific conditions time and time again and no one's been able to show how he does what does."[35]

Geller came to public attention with displays of telekinesis. In brightly lit TV studios in front of live audiences, often with the show's host and other guests seated next to him, Geller would bend solid metal objects into pronounced angles with gentle strokes of his fingertips. Despite performing a range of tasks that defied the known laws of physics, Geller is most widely remembered for bending spoons. Perhaps because their distortion was most clearly visible to a TV audience.

Also, in what became known as the Geller Effect, people in the audience, and on occasion watching on TV, would find their house keys had bent. In the wake of Geller's arrival on the world's consciousness people, often young children, came forward having discovered they too had the ability to manipulate metal by nonphysical means.

"That was the fascinating thing for me. Until Geller came along these people hadn't experienced anything out of the ordinary then suddenly ... boom ... they're bending spoons just by thinking about it. What happened? Had they been hiding in cupboards too scared to talk about what they could do? Or did the Geller Effect trigger something that allowed them to tap into a kind of power we hadn't seen until that point?"

Geller and many of the so-called *Geller Children*, were tested under laboratory conditions. In the US the Stanford Research Institute put Geller through a gruelling series of experiments and concluded his powers were real. In the UK Professor

---

[35] This fact is contested by James Randi in his 1975 book, *The Magic of Uri Geller**

* Later, updated, editions of this book were issued under the title, *The Truth About Uri Geller*. (R.D)

John Taylor of King's College, London University, tested the abilities of children, some as young as ten, who claimed to be able to bend metal objects by non-physical means. He was unable to detect trickery. It is difficult to believe a scientist of Professor Taylor's standing wouldn't be able to see through the tricks of a ten-year-old.

"In my opinion the problem was all the research and testing was carried out with the view of proving Geller, and the others like him, were genuine. Or rather trying to prove they were fakes. So much time was spent on that, that no one was trying to find out the nature of the forces at play. Think of the potential of being able to harness that sort of power. And all anyone was doing was checking the envelopes were stuck down tight.[36]"

It's a natural question to ask if Cardino had experienced paranormal events previous to his trips to Fantoccini Street. His denial is adamant.

"Nothing. Ever. Most people have a few stories about the phone ringing, and they'd know who it was before they picked up, or having a feeling of foreboding before a car crash. Stuff like that. They're common currency, but nothing like that ever happened to me. When we all took the Zener test before going on the 2nd fieldtrip, I had the lowest score out of all of us. I scored lower than random chance. I think we can rule out any idea of me having a psychic gift. But in a way that's why I'm interested in the study of it. I don't think everyone can have

---

[36] Aside from telekinesis, Geller also gave displays of precognition and telepathy. These would often involve 'seeing' images, drawn by a third party, sealed in an envelope.

the sort of ability people like Geller and Zé Arigó[37] have, but not everyone can be Mozart, that shouldn't stop people studying music. If we can expand our understanding of events that currently defy logic, then maybe one day telekinesis, telepathy and astral projection will be taught in school alongside Maths and MFL."

Zener cards are a standardised method of testing and measuring extrasensory perception (ESP). Karl Zener, a perceptual psychologist, first designed and used the cards in the early 1930s. He obtained positive results when working with colleague J. Rhine, a parapsychologist, although these have proved impossible to replicate.

A pack of Zener cards consists of 25 cards each printed with one of five distinct symbols. Usual practice is for the cards to be used by two people. One acts as the transmitter and the other as the receiver. The transmitter randomises the test simply by shuffling the pack, and then focuses on each card for a few moments. The receiver says which symbol they feel the transmitter is focused on. Obviously the two participants must be separated for the test to have any value.

The idea to test all the team members before the second fieldtrip was Carol Crossland's. According to her the test results were shared between the team members but no record of them was kept. Steven Ward didn't respond to my emails on the subject and John Pelton was dismissive of the episode.

Viola's replacement, Carol Crossland, had taken the Zener Card test on many occasions. She had her own set of the cards and would test herself periodically with different subjects. She

---

[37] Zé Arigó (1921 – 1971), also known as the Surgeon of the Rusty Knife, was a faith healer who performed psychic surgery. While in a trance state he would carry out surgery with basic kitchen utensils.

noticed a definite increase in her score over the course of three years. A fact backed up by a personal record she kept of her own scores for the period (see appendix)[38].

Her reasoning for asking the team to take the test was twofold.

"I thought if we took the test between ourselves then any degree of tuning in to each other's minds would become evident. And I thought it was a wise precaution, given the events of the first trip and the strength of the forces we could encounter. If any of us was too sensitive, I believe it would have been too dangerous.

"Each member of the team sat the test with every other member, twice, once as receiver and then again as transmitter. that meant twenty sittings in all. It took most of one morning. Jed[39] did the maths on it and produced two sets of results: an average for each individual and a detailed breakdown of which people were most in tune with each other. I won't pretend to remember specific details, but a few things really stood out. Firstly, May's score was fractionally lower than mine, that surprised me, I'd followed her work and had expected her to put me in the shade. She told me it was probably her age, her powers where in the decline while I was just starting to grow into mine, which made sense. The other was Jed's score. It was stunning and I mean absolutely amazing."

I express surprise and repeat Cardino's claim that his score was the lowest in the group, below what would be expected for pure chance. Crossland nods earnestly,

---

[38] This is the first of several references Mr Croix make to an appendix, unfortunately none was included in the package of documents he left me. (R.D)

[39] Gerald Cardino.

"That is exactly my point. The base line for the test is chance. The score you'd get by randomly selecting cards, the score you'd get from guess work. Jed's score was, I remember this clearly, 99% wrong. Don't you see how far that is away from the median? It's frankly ... well, unnatural."

Unlike Cardino, who'd actively sought inclusion on the second fieldtrip, Crossland had been effectively recruited. Something she has mixed feelings about.

"Going away to uni was a big deal to me, and with hindsight I can see I was more than a little naïve. It was my first time living away from home and I was trying to define myself, and yes, I know how pretentious that sounds. It's not that I was running away from a bad home life or anything like that, but it was my first real taste of independence and I was very consciously doing my best *not* to come out of my shell. Mainly because people, my parents included, kept telling me that's what I needed to do. Without meaning to I ended up being a people pleaser.

"Maybe doing psychology gave me a better idea of how things work, so at least I avoided the more obvious pitfalls. A lot of the women there fell into this trap of writing themselves as super confident, super cool, super sophisticated. Of course, in a grotty little north London uni, sophistication meant either being deadly serious or drinking yourself into a stupor. It's easier for men, they can decide they're party animals and get a pat on the back for it. For women it's different. Party animal equates to slut and once that label had landed it can become a self-fulfilling prophecy.

"My roommate got drunk at a fresher's week party and had a one-night stand. After that, if she didn't put out, she was prick teasing, if she did, she was a slag. She didn't want to be called prissy or unsophisticated, any more than she wanted to be called a slut. She went the route of shouting about sexuality as a means of empowerment and slept with six or seven different partners in the first term. The gossip around campus added a zero to the figure.

"I could see she was unhappy with what she was doing but didn't know how to exit it. Once the course had been going long enough for people to start matching up, people's girlfriends would see her as a threat and give her a hard time – she'd been nicknamed The Maneater.

"Having her as a roommate went some way to putting me on the track I went down. There were always arguments to defuse, and I ended up being the peacemaker. I can see now, I was too quick to accept the role. I guess that's how I ended up in that house.

"Edward approached me directly about going to Fantoccini Street. There was a lot of chatter about the first trip, and it was being said they wanted a psychology student on the second one. The head of the psych department had said outright that nothing connected with the trip would be taken seriously if it was handed in as coursework, but very few people were interested any way. There was a rumour that the team really wanted to take along Slidesmith, he was a PhD student who even taught a few classes. He was someone people gravitated to, but he could be a bit well, weird, is the only way to describe him. People said he was into the occult and a lot of people had told me he did tarot readings. That intrigued me a bit, I was interested in things like that back then.

"I'd had one of Slidesmith's lectures and I'd missed laid my notes, so I wanted to ask him if had print outs of the presentation he'd given. I happened to see him in a corridor and went over to him just as Edward was doing the same. We both spoke to him at the same time. Edward smiled and made a deep bow, then he said, 'Please, lady's first, I'm sure Mr Slidesmith would rather talk to you.' Very old school and chivalrous. Slidesmith glanced at me and sort of rolled his eyes then said to Edward, 'If you want to ask me about the doll's house trip, the answer's still no.' He wasn't exactly hostile, but he wasn't trying to be polite. Edward said something about how he thought it would interest him, Slidesmith, because he'd heard he was an urban witch doctor. It must have been the wrong thing to say, because Slidesmith turned away from him and started talking to me, totally excluding Edward.

"I've always been good at reading people's body language and Slidesmith was very angry. Edward didn't seem to notice though and hung around long enough to realise I was a psych student. He asked me to come along on the trip later that day. After the scene with Slidesmith, I felt bad for him, so I said yes.

"Two days later Slidesmith was waiting for me after one of my tutor meetings. He asked if it was true I'd agreed to go on the fieldtrip. I said it was, and he told me I needed to be careful. I asked him if he meant about upsetting the head of department, but he said no, and he'd have a word with her if needed. He told me I should just watch out for myself on the trip, and to remember I could leave at any point.

"I could see he didn't like Edward for some reason, and I thought he was just talking about that. After spending a week in that house though ... I'm not so sure.

"Another funny thing, well not funny really, I spoke to Slidesmith again, the weekend before we left for the trip. I asked him if it was right, he did tarot readings. He said, 'I dabble'. I asked if he'd read the cards for me, he said he would, but he was busy right then. He wasn't nasty about it, but he put me off again the next time I saw him. By the time I saw him again I'd been to that house and playing around with the occult didn't seem funny anymore."

Chapter Nine: The Doctor and the False Cut

Carol Crossland isn't the first person to raise the name Slidesmith. He's been mentioned by others and not always kindly.

When the idea of a second fieldtrip was first being debated somebody suggested it would be interesting to have the team under the observation of a psychologist. The head of the psychology course had little enthusiasm for the idea and, after she'd made her feelings clear on the notion of 'ghost hunting', very few of her students wanted to take part.

John Pelton, in an apparently rare show of interest in the project, suggested they ask PhD student James Slidesmith, to go on the trip. In Pelton's words,

"He wouldn't give a f__k what the department thought."

James Slidesmith was considered something of a maverick in the uni. At the time of the first fieldtrip, he was in the second year of his doctorate; a study into sociopaths – a group he claimed to have a soft spot for.

It was Steven Ward who first approached him to enquire about being part of the second trip. He maintains Slidesmith showed some interest until he realised the purpose of the fieldtrip was to investigate paranormal events. Ward believes Slidesmith, who was known for a fascination with tarot reading and was widely believed to be infatuated with the practices of Voodoo, was in fact scared by the forces that might be occupying 37 Fantoccini Street.

John Pelton has a very different take.

"When it was clear the psych department wanted nothing to

do with Steve's jolly up and none of the students wanted to risk upsetting their tutors, I suggested asking Slidesmith. He didn't give two s__ts about staying on side with his tutors, didn't give two s__ts getting a doctorate either, as far as I could see."

"But he didn't accompany you? Why not?"

"He asked if they'd be paying him for his time and they said no."

"Simple as that?"

"Ah huh, simple as. But if you want something other than the usual mumbo jumbo, you should go have a chat with him. If the f__ker's still alive."

I ask if he knows where I might find Slidesmith. He gives one of his characteristic shrugs.

"Probably in a cell somewhere."

Slidesmith, both alive and still at liberty, isn't hard to find. His unusual name doesn't take up much space on the internet and a single search leads me quickly to the website of *Slidesmith Tattooing*. I ring to check if the Slidesmith who now plys his trade as a tattooist is the same Slidesmith who once studied the psychology of sociopaths.

The phone is picked up quickly and a voice with a guttural north London accent tells me I've reached Slidesmith's, then adds,

"Doc speaking."

I make the necessary enquires and once I'm sure I have the right person, I explain why I'm calling. He surprises me by laughing.

"They still banging on about those poxy dolls?"

Suspecting there might not be a right way to answer the question without closing the door on the conversation, I quietly ignore it and go straight to a request for an interview.

"Interview? I didn't ever set foot in the house."

I explain that I'd like his opinion, as an outsider, on the people that did.

"If you want to drop by the shop one evening, I generally

97

call it a day around five and shamelessly exploit the energy and youth of my work force." From the other end of the line someone laughs.

Slidesmith Tattooing is a small shop in a street that, typically for north London, is a not completely comfortable mix of residential and commercial. Parking is a problem and I have to walk quite a way; the stretch of road immediately outside the shop is filled with a row of motorcycles.

The waiting room is clean and brightly lit but the black and red paint work give a suggestion of gloom. The space is decorated with a variety of artifacts and photographs, a mix of heavily tattooed women and hulking Harley Davidsons. Given the nature of the shop and the customers it caters to, I'm not surprised by the pin-up girls or motorcycles. The voodoo images and framed tarot packs are less routine.

From a room at the rear of the shop, behind a counter that runs the full width of the room, I can hear the buzzing whine of a tattoo machine. At first glance the space behind the counter looks unmanned, and the movement of the figure there makes me jump.

Doctor Slidesmith is a striking figure. Tall and rockstar thin, everything about him is pale, his faded tee shirt - with his shop's logo printed on it - his skin. Even his eyes. This stark palette of tones makes the tattoo on his face all the more obvious. Along his right cheek, edging toward his ear, are the black outlines of a jawbone and teeth. They're reminiscent of the ghoulish face painting associated with Mexico's Day of the Dead festival. But the artist behind this piece has gone for a more realistic style, it's only the slightly exaggerated sizing that stops Slidesmith's face resembling an illustration from an anatomy text.

Possibly seeing my scrutiny of him, Slidesmith smiles at me – I use the phrase *at me* quite deliberately. His own teeth are no less disturbing than the tattooed ones.

"Help you?" He asks and has to repeat the question when I don't immediately answer. As he has spoken, I've noticed there's an open book on the counter in front of him. It's a book of prints by the artist Robert Williams. It's open on a page showing a picture of four Raggedy Ann dolls staging a puppet show with a family of human beings.

"Help you?" I realise that I've still not answered him. When I finally tell him who I am, he takes the edge off his smile and extends a hand. At the same time, he closes the book, and I have another jolt when I see its cover and title: *The Perception of Dolls*. I'm aware that I've left another gap where I should be shaking the proffered hand.

"Perhaps we better do this upstairs," Slidesmith says.

Before he leads me from the shop, he puts *The Perception of Dolls* away. The shelf it goes on is weighed down with art books, ranging from studies of flora and fauna to tombs on the traditions of Japanese tattooing, I also spot motorcycle manuals and novels. The shelf is one of three, all equally loaded. At a guess I'd say there are at least a hundred books there, and more books litter the counter and low table in the waiting area.

The odds of Slidesmith randomly picking the book at random are more than a hundred to one. I don't like to wonder about the odds of him opening it to the exact painting I'd been discussing with Ella Caine just days earlier.

My correspondence with Ella covered more than just the events in Fantoccini Street. Many of the letters we exchanged had little or no bearing on the subject of this book. It could be expected though, that no matter what the subject was, at some point Ella would find a connection to dolls.

One of our more casual exchanges was about painting. Ella, as witnessed by the work on the dolls in her collection and, more rarely, from the pieces resulting from her brief infatuation with firing pots, is quite an adept artist. I once asked her if she'd ever tried her hand at oil painting. She hadn't but expressed an interest in certain artists, or rather specific examples of their work. Not surprisingly, her favoured pieces concerned dolls.

As chance would have it, she mentioned a painter I happened to be aware of (unlike Ella, I have no artistic notions). The artist Robert Williams is a Californian abstract painter. He paints landscapes, characters, and vehicles with each component instantly recognisable yet almost totally alien. His compositions can be humorous, horrific, poignant, and sexual, often simultaneously. I knew his name because one of his pieces was used as an album cover and attracted much controversy, with some people claiming it glamourised sexual violence.

I quote here from Ella's letter to me dated March 2nd 2016. Three days before I visited Doctor Slidesmith.

"The idea that dolls have an existence and purpose beyond those that are intended for them isn't new. A lot of people talk about dolls being used in horror movies, but the tradition goes back far longer than the invention of the motion picture. It's something set deep in the social psyche, and not just the rubbish that comes out of Hollywood. If you want a good example look at Robert William's painting, Dance, Pinky, Dance. If you haven't seen it, it shows a group of dolls in the Raggedy Ann style playing with human puppets."

Many of Robert William's paintings have three identities. *Dance, Pinky, Dance*, is no exception. Along with its *Common* title, it boasts a *Scholastic definition* and a *Remedial* title. Often William's bizarre canvasses pop up without context or explanation online and, if named at all, will usually be given the short, *Common* title. A brief dip into auction house catalogues or one of the many books detailing Williams' work and the fuller titles appear. Like his art, his titles can be humorous or disturbing and all things in between. Ella's fleeting reference to it suggests that she was unlikely to be aware of its Scholastic Definition:

A Nuclear Family Watches In Awe As The Neutered Bread Winner Pitches A Fit, Unaware That They Act At The Behest Of Saccharine

100

*Laced Dreams Of Their Own Making, As The Overlords Of Childhood
Past Take Their Revenge.*

The painting is oil on canvas, measuring six feet by nine. It
was unveiled in 1993.

It's beyond my abilities to describe it fully. Like all Williams'
work it contains many elements and a host of details. The
main focus of the composition however is a family living
room decorated in a style reminiscent of fifties America. The
room appears to float in space, independent of the house it
belongs to. At one end of the room sits a TV set with old
fashion rabbit ear antenna, on its screen is a black and white
image of a 'Raggedy Ann' doll[40]. Along the back wall of the
room there is a sofa, the mother of the family sits here
attending to the contents of her handbag, unaware that the
father is in the centre of the room having some sort of crisis.
His limbs are bent into angular positions that appear unnatural
and painful. The movements could be interpreted in a variety
of ways, possibly he is dancing or shaking out a cramp, but the
expression on his face suggests something more sinister is
happening. At the other end of the room to the TV set, two
girls, both strongly resembling the mother figure, kneel in
front of a dolls house and push pins into the figure of a male
doll. The doll itself is a basic wooden figurine but its clothes
are a precise match for those of the father character. The girls
have their backs to the room but look over their shoulders at
the father. They both have malicious grins, and their faces
look older than their size and dress would lead you to expect.

The scene doesn't end at the confines of the domestic
setting. Outside the room, and seemingly invisible to the

---

[40] Ella, when mentioning this picture
pointed out that the dolls were not
accurate depictions of the officially
licenced Raggedy Ann dolls but merely
painted in the style of.

101

occupants, stand four gigantic Raggedy Ann dolls. Each of them is holding a puppeteers' controller, the strings of which lead to the limbs of the humans below. Three of these monstrous dolls are only seen from the chest up, their lower portions being hidden by the architecture of the disembodied room. The last Raggedy Ann, the one who controls the young girl pushing pins into the father doll, is standing at the right side of the room and she/it can be seen more fully.

The top half of the fourth doll is a detailed and carefully portrayed image of a typical Raggedy Ann doll. It has been rendered with the care and precision that Williams is well known for. But at the waist the Raggedy Ann doll transforms, and we see the stocking clad legs and bare buttocks of an adult woman.

The remedial title of the painting is: View From A House Inside A Room.[41]

Slidesmith lives above his tattoo shop. The flat is minimalist to the point of austerity. I'm led to a living room containing two threadbare armchairs and what, to my untutored eye, looks like an altar. Slidesmith tells me he's going to make a pot of tea and I embarrass myself by laughing. The banality of such a domestic task is at odds with everything about this interview. If my host thinks I'm rude, or deranged, he gives no indication of it.

While I wait for the tea, I try to calm myself. The austerity of the room helps, although I make a point of not looking at

---

[41] The same year (1993) Williams produced *Dance, Pinky, Dance*, he also produced *Island of Infantile Avarice*. It has no bearing on the events within this book but I mention it because, like, *Dance*, it features a Raggedy Ann style doll and a young girl with a face that seems older than her years.

the corner containing the altar.

Slidesmith comes back and hands me a mug. He settles himself into the room's other chair.

"You want to talk about the doll's house trips?"

"Your name came up a few times, different people on the trip mentioned you – independently. John Pelton suggested I talk with you. He thought you might have a different overview of the thing."

Slidesmith laughs.

"Pelton? That sounds about right. Did he tell you that it was him that suggested taking a psychologist along, in the first place? When the head of department made it known she'd take a dim view of anyone who mentioned ghost busting in their coursework, John told Steven Ward to try me."

"He did say you didn't care about upsetting the psychology department."

"I wasn't looking to rub anyone up the wrong way, but by that time I'd already decided academia wasn't for me. I'd only gone the PhD route because it came with a grant for living expenses. The grant wasn't dependant on obtaining a doctorate, so even if I failed, I wasn't going to end up liable to pay it back."

"So why didn't you go?"

"A couple of reasons. I knew Pelton was only being facetious when he mooted the idea of a team psychologist. It was a joke: *what should we take with us on a ghost hunt? How about someone to examine our heads?* The department head back then was a woman called Flanagan. Razor sharp. She saw the idea had started as a windup and didn't want to get pulled into it. I can see her point, there were a lot of ways it could end up looking bad for people. Not many of the students were that interested anyway, the Doll case wasn't exactly headline news when it happened, and the supernatural angle wasn't in the big league. I don't think the SPR[42] or ASSAP even raised an

---

[42] Society for Psychical Research. Found in 1882, the SPR claims to be the first

103

eyebrow at it."

"The team did approach you though?"

"A couple of times. Steve tried to get me interested then Bartlett came sniffing around. Those two were the only ones on campus who hadn't twigged Pelton was taking the p__s."

"Were you worried about being the butt of the joke?"

"There was an element of that, I guess. I was a bit younger then, I took myself a bit more seriously. But I didn't have the time anyway. I was working on my doctorate, even if I was doing a pretty half fast job of it, and working in a tattoo shop three evenings a week. I'd spent the grant money the moment the cheque cleared, so I needed cash. Steven and Bartlett were looking for volunteers and I'm more your mercenary type. And, when Steven approached me, he made it clear that they were only interest in the supernatural angle; they really were ghost hunting."

"And you don't believe in such things"

"It's a not matter of what I do or don't believe. Belief is irrelevant. If you're investigating something, you investigate what is there and try to work out what it is. You don't start off at the answer. If you go in thinking, *Oh, this house is haunted*, then every bump in the night's going to prove it. It's simple confirmation bias. Steven and Bartlett were going to find ghosts no matter what. Not that Pelton was any different, he just came at it from the other side; nothing weird was going on and he'd die before believing otherwise.

"Even if I'd had the time and the inclination to go, the idea of spending a week roughing it in an abandoned house didn't really appeal. Anyway, I thought they were missing the point of the whole thing. I was probably one of the few people in the uni who'd heard the news story about the Doll family when it first broke, not the nonsense with the doll's house and that stupid photo story, I mean the murders. If the papers had

---

society to conduct organised research into
paranormal events.

104

it half right it was a triple murder and attempted suicide. That don't happen every day. I thought that's what they were looking into when they started talking about fieldtrips to Fantoccini Street."

"So, you *don't* believe the paranormal angle?"

"Again, what I believe on the paranormal, or the supernatural, however you call it, isn't the point. The point is almost any investigation into it is going to go nowhere. People never go into a haunting with an open mind. If you're looking into this, I guess you're familiar with the book about the Enfield Haunting?[43]"

I tell Slidesmith I am.

"Over a year's worth of events, hundreds, literally hundreds, of events catalogued. The manhours involved were scary, they produced something like 200 cassettes tapes, photos left right and centre and what did it prove?"

Slidesmith makes a sucking noise and a dismissive gesture with his hand.

"You don't think the investigators were being honest?"

"Oh, I don't doubt they were honest. In everything I've read by them or about them, they come over as honest and above board. I would gladly hand either one of them the keys to my house and the numbers of my bank account and trust them to the ends of the earth, but they were so eager to see a

---

[43] The Enfield haunting is one of the most documented cases of poltergeist activity in history. Between 1977 and 1978 the Hodgson family were subjected to eighteen months of poltergeist activity. The centre of events seemed to be 13-year-old, Janet Hodgson (not her real name). The case was closely watched and recorded for a period of 14 months by Guy Lyon Playfair and Maurice Grosse. Playfair wrote about the case in his book, *This House Is Haunted*.

ghost they couldn't see anything else. It's been a while since I read the book so I can't quote it word for word, but at one point Playfair says something to the effect that the ghost is very clever, because it waits until he leaves the room before doing anything. Another time he decides that paranormal events don't happen in the presence of non-believers. He'd leave the kids alone with his tape recorder, even after he'd caught them playing silly buggers, more than once. He was sincere but his methodology made a big chunk of what he was recording suspect. By the end of it I think if someone had walked in the room with a sheet over their head and said they were the ghost of Mary Queen of Scotts, he'd have bowed."

When I point out that many of the events in Enfield were witnessed by Playfair himself, and ask if he trusts Playfair's sincerity, how he explains these, Slidesmith leaves the room and returns with a pack of cards.

"This is a Charlier cut, okay?" He takes the cards and using only one hand deftly cuts them. I nod, I've seen it done before, in fact I can do it myself, though I didn't know it had a particular name.

"Now, this is the triple cut."

Before he performs it, Slidesmith shows me the top card, it's the seven of hearts. With one hand he divides the pack of cards into three layers and repositions them. While elegant, the triple cut is a confusing sweep of motion. He lifts the top card again.

"Queen of diamonds. Just what you'd expect after cutting the deck, a different card on top."

Again, I agree. Slidesmith returns the queen to the top of the pack and performs the elaborate cut again. He asks me what I've just seen.

"I've seen you cut the cards."

Slidesmith lifts the top card. It's still the Queen of diamonds.

"A conjuring trick."

"If you like, but the point's is you saw the cards cut, I performed the triple cut and you saw it work, then I perform the triple cut and it didn't work. What you saw the second time wasn't what you thought you saw. If I hadn't shown you the cards hadn't moved, you'd still be believing you'd seen them cut. You saw what you were expecting to see, and that was after we'd been talking about fakery and false impressions. Believe me, if we'd been playing poker, you'd be broke, and convinced I'd won fair and square."

"So, I'm a mug?"

"No, you just see the world behaving the way you think it will. In fairness so do I, but I see a world full of card cheats and untrustworthy witnesses. Including my own senses."

The few photographs of the Walking Doll, taken by Edward Bartlett using a mobile phone, are presumed to be stored on one of his IronKeys and can't be accessed. Only one seems to have ever been printed out. The one found beside his body. It may be assumed that this picture represents the best of the batch, but such speculation is useless. The single print, contained in Bartlett's file on the Doll's case is all we have.[44]

The picture quality of the Walking Doll is poor. The lens has been held too close to the subject and while the phone's autofocus has produced a reasonably sharp image, there is a degree of distortion.

According to Bartlett's notes, it was found in the righthand room, of the first floor of the doll's house. This room represents the house's master bedroom and was one of the few rooms in the miniature house that had furniture. The wooden doll lays on a miniature double bed. According to Ella Caine, who I showed the photograph to, the doll is probably an unbranded figure, manufactured in the style of a traditional European folk doll. The general condition of the doll suggests it is unlikely to be a genuine example and is more

---

44 Again, despite referring to this print, it wasn't part of the package Mr Croix sent to me. (R.D)

likely a modern reproduction. These were produced in great numbers in China during the nineties. This example's clothing denotes it as a male.

The figure lays on its back, legs slightly splayed. Its head appears to be cranked back, but it must be noted that due to the camera angle and picture distortion, the exact details of the figure's articulation are not easily decerned. The doll's left arm is by its side with the right positioned so it rests somewhere on the doll's midriff. The doll appears, according to Bartlett's notes: *tensed in pain, clutching at its torso.*

The positioning of the doll, again according to Ella, is unlikely to be accidental. None of the dolls of this style, that she is familiar with, have any articulation beyond rudimentary shoulder and hip joints. To set the doll in the way seen in the photograph would have required either delicate modifications of, or damage to, the doll's limbs.

Again, the quality of the photograph makes it impossible to see exactly how the positioning of the doll has been achieved.

Slidesmith, if impressed by the photograph, doesn't show it. He looks at it in silence before handing it back to me, looking slightly bemused. I repeat Patricia Bartlett's comment that her husband appeared to have been trying to reproduce the picture in reality.

"His wife said he was in the exact same position as that doll when she found him."

Slidesmith shakes his head.

"No, he wasn't. He can't have been. To be in *exactly* the same position he'd have had to have had exactly the same anatomy. And he clearly didn't. He was in, at most, an approximation of the same position and, more likely, he happened to be in a similar position. Coincidence."

I point out the number of coincidences is quite high; both prone, both with one hand on their chest, both on a double bed in a master bedroom. And, what to my mind, and others, is the biggest coincidence; another doll approximating a human in death. I point out Edward Bartlett's comment that the doll looked, to him, as if it was clutching its torso in pain. The same could be expected of a man suffering a heart attack.

Once more, Slidesmith leaves the room, this time returning with a sketchbook. He rests it on his knee and begins to draw. A talented tattoo artist, he quickly outlines a series of figures. At first he draws purely by eye, but then adds a network of lines and circle that demonstrate the proportions and ratios needed to produce an accurate drawing of the human form.

The figures he has drawn are of the doll in the photo seen from different points of view. I have the impression of the figure rotating in space.

"In my opinion as an artist, not as a psychology quack, the doll in that picture isn't clutching its chest." The final sketch he's produced of the doll show it as if viewed from one side. That hand, that in the photo could be resting anywhere from the throat to just above the groin, is clearly stationed at the figure's crutch. Slidesmith sees I'm halfway to getting his point. He makes an obscene hand gesture to drive the point home.

"You think the doll was supposed to be abusing itself?"

"If this expert of yours is right about the doll being broken to get it in the right position, then I'd agree the pose is deliberate. And if someone's taken that level of care to make it grab its crutch, then they weren't saying 'heart attack'."

"Why would someone do that though?"

Slidesmith avoids the question for a moment, hiding behind a long sip of tea.

"Best guess," he stresses the word guess. "It was a nasty joke, probably at the expense of someone on the trip."

"Who?"

"Whose expense? One of the men. If I was a gambling man, I'd put my money on Bartlett."

Slidesmith falls silent. There's an obvious question hanging in the air. I try to wait him out but find I've underestimated his ability to endure silence and in the end I speak first.

109

"Why would someone make a joke like that about Edward?"

"One of the reasons the campus wasn't willing to get involved with another ghost hunt was that it would mean associating with Bartlett again. And there were rumours floating about that he was a bit of a letch. The campus had a building called the Student Hub, it was just a café really attached to a few of the help desks. The area around it was landscaped. When the weather got hot students gravitated to it on breaks. Some people would do a bit of sunbathing. Bartlett was big into taking shots of the campus grounds, rumours were he'd always find something interesting to snap that just happened to have a pretty young woman in the foreground."

I ask if the rumours were true.

"I wouldn't say categorically, but I always thought he was a bit smarmy around women. He had that way of talking down to them and pretending it was charm. If I'm being generous, it might have been a generational thing: *men are men and women are girls,* you know? But, true or not, stories about Bartlett collecting pictures of young women were doing the rounds. If Someone on the team believed them, they might have put the doll there as a snide joke."

I point out nobody involved in the trip ever mentioned playing a joke.

"Maybe they would have if Bartlett had lived to write an article about the mysterious doll he caught cracking one off. But he died. Dead fall guys don't get a laugh."

The current dean of London North University denied knowledge of any unsavoury rumours concerning Edward Bartlett. As a matter of record, no formal complaints were ever made regarding his conduct.

As a sidenote, in 2012, London North banned sunbathing on campus grounds. The official explanation for this was that the practice was deemed inappropriate for a multi-cultural and inclusive University. The rule was brought in shortly after a member of staff, in connection with a charge of stalking, was found to be in possession of over 600 candid images, all taken on university grounds.

After leaving Doctor Slidesmith, I had another brush with the world of art that left me feeling uneasy. I'd happened to get slightly lost and found myself in a cue of traffic crawling past Willesden County Court building, where a small crowd had gathered. Traffic conditions conspired against me, and I was forced to move away from the scene, having caught only a glimpse at the cause of the excitement.

The crowd had gathered to see a new 'Banksy'[45]. Sprayed onto the brickwork to the right of the court building's glass frontage, the work was a black and white rendering of a Raggedy Ann doll holding one of Banksy's trademark rats by its tail. The doll was approximately nine feet high, and, seen from the seat of my car, it appeared to loom over its audience.

The sight of a nine-foot-high Raggedy Ann doll, so soon after the 'coincidence' of finding Doctor Slidesmith perusing William's piece, *Dance, Pinky, Dance*, was disturbing.

The Banksy, known as *Dolly*, survived less than 24 hours. It had been spotted and posted to social media by 6a.m. and the crowd I saw, at around half seven in the evening, were remonstrating with the council workers tasked with its removal. Arguably, I was lucky to have seen it.

---

[45] Banksy has since confirmed the piece was one of his. Despite its size and prominent location, *Dolly* is not one of his better-known works and there seems to be no record of it online.

Chapter Ten: Dolls/Dolls in Residence

A neighbour, possibly the last person outside of number 37 to see the Doll children alive, described the family as quiet. And nothing more.

On the evening of September 10th, he saw the twins playing in the garden and heard one of their parents call them in for dinner. In the early hours of the 11th, he was woken by the arrival of an ambulance.

It is the closest thing that exists to a first-hand witness account. Inside the house, the scene that greeted the police and ambulance crews was not easily explained.

PHOTO ID: FSI/Archive-002
SOURCE: Cradlefield Chronicle, 13 – 03 – 2002. Credited to Michael Huddart.
SUBJECT: Interior of Doll's House. Kitchen.
DESCRIPTION: As with the dining room, the kitchen is dressed in an approximation of the Victorian era. Miniature kitchen fittings (cupboards, a sink, a range, etc) line the back and righthand walls.

To the right of the room there is a wooden doll. It is positioned as if sitting on the floor, slumped against the range, and facing the door. Like the two dolls in the dining room, it is dressed in a faux Victorian style. The clothing and size of the doll suggests it represents an adult female.

In the article accompanying the photograph, Max Whitgift refers to this item as, 'the mother doll'.

From the records of Edward Bartlett

Barbara Doll was found in the kitchen, slumped on a chair that was wedged into the corner, between the kitchen sink and the wall.

At the coroner's hearing one of the ambulance crew testified her body was cold and rigor mortis had already set in. Despite the assertion of countless TV and movie dramas, pinpointing a time of death is not a precise affair, and it was only possible to state she had been dead sometime.

There was a small amount of blood on her face, the result it would later be confirmed of as split lip, and her bladder had voided. A common feature in cases of death by strangulation. The post-mortem revealed her hyoid bone, a small U-shaped bone at the base of the jaw, had been broken. Another feature in cases of strangulation. Unusually, there was no bruising to her neck.

Patsy and Ann Doll were found in the downstairs front room. Reports that they were found huddled together under the table were disavowed at the inquest. They were, according to the testimony of the attending police officers who found them, laying supine about two metres apart, laid at each end of the table. Neither showed signs of violence although one (it was never established which) had voided her bladder. Both girls had enlargement of ocular blood vessels (blood shot eyes), a finding consistent with asphyxiation. As with their mother, they were cold and rigor mortis had set in.

Both girls were fully dressed, and both had mud on their shoes. There were no traces of muddy footprints anywhere in the house. It was surmised that Kenneth Doll had smothered the girls in their beds before dressing them and arranging their bodies under the table.

PHOTO ID: FSI/Archive-003
SOURCE: Cradlefield Chronicle, 13 – 03 – 2002. Credited to Michael Huddart.
SUBJECT: Interior of Doll's House. Attic.

DESCRIPTION: The attic of the doll's house is in the apex of the roof. It is the least detailed/dressed room shown in Michael Huddart's photographs. The only furniture is a miniature, halfmoon table, that sits against the room's back wall. On top of this table is a model of a doll's house.

There is a doll on the floor in front of the miniature table. It has been posed in something close to a position of worship. On its knees and bent at the waist, the doll's head rests on the floor with its arms before it, as if reaching for the tiny house on the halfmoon table.

In this photograph, it is hard to make out details of the doll, beyond the fact that its clothing denotes a male. In a later photograph (see FSI/Archive-005) it is possible to see the doll is of a different type to those found in the dining room and kitchen. More modern and probably made of plastic, the doll has fine facial detailing and is fully articulated.

In the article accompanying the photograph, Max Whitgift refers to this item as, 'the father doll'.

From the records of Edward Bartlett

There are no pictures of Kenneth Doll lying on the attic floor of number 37. When he was found the ambulance crew were called and first aid was started. As in all police actions, preservation of life was the priority.

At the inquest, one of the attending police officers stated that Kenneth Doll appeared to have passed out while on his knees. When asked to elaborate, he added,

"Mister Doll was on his knees, slumped forward, a little bit like he was praying."

Kenneth Doll had attempted to block his airways by forcing a pair of tights down his throat, using a length of broom handle. Investigation into the scene discovered no DNA or fingerprints, other than Dolls, on the broom handle or the tights. It was an unusual method of suicide that, given a little more time, would have worked.

Although suffocation brings to mind images of struggling and fighting for breath, if oxygen is reduced at a slow enough rate, unconsciousness can overtake the victim in a slow drift. Accidental deaths from auto asphyxiation testify to the fact that a willing victim can slip away with little trauma.

The inquest found that Kenneth Doll had murdered his family and tried to kill himself while the balance of his mind was disturbed.

No mention of the doll's house was made at the inquest.

The case was closed.

"It's easier to paint men as monsters than to understand what drives them to monstrous acts. Ken Doll's actions were horrendous but it's pointless to take them in isolation. There is always a motive, no matter how twisted or bizarre, in someone's mind there is a motive for their actions. Monsters are no different."

Slidesmith watches me, waiting for a reaction, while he takes another sip from the tequila I've just bought him.

Quite how Kenneth Doll made a living after his fall from grace in the investment sector is an unknown. As a discharged bankrupt he was unable to own a business and the usual ploy of recovering bankrupts, operating under their partner's name, doesn't seem to have been employed. Barbara Doll doesn't appear to have been declared as owner or director of any company. Even with ownership of the house it's unlikely that the Doll family's money worries would have disappeared entirely.

The house that had been neglected for many years was in need of modernisation and repair. The reports of the team from London North University indicate that no such work had been carried out. Further to the decay that standing empty for several years would have resulted in, there was no sign that the house had been touched at any point since the death of Ken's mother. Social benefits wouldn't have run to the costs of private school. And yet, that's where the girls were educated.

115

One thing many sources about the life and times of Kenneth Doll suggests is that it was unlikely any investigation into his practices would have unearthed all his funds. It is purely speculation, but it is possible that anything Kenneth Doll may have stashed away could have been running out, and the stress of his situation was beginning to close in on him. For the want of anything concrete to explain his reasoning for committing the atrocity he did, I find myself contacting Doctor Slidesmith once more. The man with, in his own words, *a soft spot for sociopaths.*

I find sociopath isn't a word he's quick to apply to the late Kenneth Doll.

"Sociopaths aren't known for remorse. They don't automatically fit the pattern of family annihilators. Particularly ones who kill themselves, or try to."

Sadly, Kenneth Doll reacting to stress and failure by murdering his family is not a unique phenomenon. According to a study by academics at Manchester University there were 39 cases between 1996 and 2005 in England and Wales. In America the crime has achieved the dubious honour of entering law enforcement nomenclature: family annihilation.

What research there has been into these awful events indicates two recurrent factors, spontaneity and debt. It's in the US, where both financial ruin and guns are easy to obtain, that figures for family annihilations are greatest. Spontaneous, or at least ill considered, events are a characteristic of sociopaths. When I put this to Slidesmith he disagrees.

"Sociopaths, and I'm talking in board brush here; are self-centred, arrogant and get bored quickly. They make fast decisions that often go wrong, sometimes fatally wrong. But as a rule, they don't regret the consequences of their mistakes. A sociopath kills his entire family; he won't think, *how can I live with myself?* He'll start coming up with a plan to get away with it."

I've furnished Slidesmith with all the information I've managed to obtain on the crime scene and the events that took place in number 37. He's read through them once in a busy

116

public house, between sips of tequila.

My initial annoyance that he didn't seem to be taking the information seriously has turned to admiration. Without referring again to the stack of documents and clippings in front of him, he recalls times, dates and details with ease. I am beginning to think Slidesmith's lack of interest in the Fantoccini Street fieldtrip was a loss to the endeavour.

"There's two things about this that strike me as out of kilter," he says. "The first one is the call to the police. Ken kills his wife, her daughters then calls the police to tell them, and he says, reportedly," – I've been unable to obtain copies or transcripts of the 999 call Kenneth Doll made and Slidesmith's remarks are made in light of the report given in the Cradlefield Chronical - "'I think they're dead'. Now that's unexpected. That doesn't tend to happen, the a__holes that kill their families are single minded, they kill everyone then themselves. If they had the capacity for soul searching, they wouldn't be in the situation. The call to the police has the feel of a classic sociopath's move: fuck up then try to get out of it. 'I think they're dead', that statement implies he's just a bystander. *I just got here, I don't know what happen.* It's the set up for an excuse and an alibi. Then it don't come, instead he goes and chokes himself before the police get there."

The other thing that doesn't gel with Slidesmith is in a similar vein to the fascination others have with the events. The ritualistic nature of the crime scene.

"Spontaneity remember. These events aren't thought out blow by blow and then carried out with surgical precision. You expect mess. Panic, people in fear of their life running and screaming and fighting." Slidesmith gestures, noticeably with a now empty glass, at the pile of documents he appears to have digested by barely glancing at. "There's no mention of that in there. Even in the second report from Whitgift and Huddart, when they recapped the case to showcase their doll pictures."

The accounts of the crime scene are sparse. And it is this sparsity that Slidesmith is referring to. There is no mention of gore, or scenes of struggle, violence. From the descriptions it would be possible to conclude that what the police and ambulance crews found in number 37 were four corpses, unwrapped and placed at various locations about the house.

The coroner's report gives the cause of death for Barbara Doll as strangulation. Her daughters as suffocation, possibly by means of smothering. The only signs of overt physical violence or struggle was that Barbara Doll had sustained a split lip. It was this in part that led the assumption that the case was a straightforward incidence of family annihilation, perpetrated by Kenneth Doll.

It is another assertion that doesn't sit well with Slidesmith.

"One of the reasons I left psychology was the underlaying premise that vast tracts of human activity could be explained away by a single narrative. Then you can't get a consensus on the narrative from the very people claiming the model's valid. One of the proposed narratives for a__holes murdering their kids is of a caring father who reacts badly to stress and acts out of shame.

"The story goes: alpha male, breadwinner loses face, either 'cos his job or business fails, or his wife has an affair or walks out on him. The event constitutes a threat to his self-identity and he lashes out. Then, having punched his wife in the face or thrown her downstairs he's consumed with shame and remorse. Then kills all the witnesses and himself to spare them living with the horror."

Slidesmith waves his hand, dismissing the idea.

"If you believe that s__t, I've got a bridge for sale. In nearly every case of family annihilation there's a history of domestic violence. This idea of a caring man driven to murder by self-remorse is nonsense. It's the usual suspects, pathetic losers knocking their wives and kids around to make them feel powerful, or habitually violent individuals who don't know any other way to react. Ken wasn't either, not from what I've seen."

Is Slidesmith suggesting the police got it wrong?

"I'm in no position to say what happened that night, no one

118

is. At least no one with a pulse. But three murder victims and a botched suicide in a locked house ... there's an obvious conclusion to draw ... or jump at. I don't doubt the police went by the numbers, did a house to house, asked the neighbours if they'd seen anything odd. And I don't doubt the neighbours told them, no. Look into the financial records and what do you find? A desperate man with money worries and a police record. Lucky not to be in the shovel[46]. Well, luck runs out. True enough there are things about the case that make me wonder, but wondering is a luxury afforded to people with nothing better to do.

"Don't forget the Doll family were largely isolated, no grieving relatives to make a fuss and the timing was guaranteed to get the story a low profile. No one outside of the immediate area heard about it really, and if they did, what's three deaths against what was happening in New York? No public outrage. Police are human, they saw a simple answer and when no one objected, they closed the case. But I keep coming back to that 999 call and the neatness of it all."

I ask what he thinks happened.

"I don't really have any theories, nor does anyone else, it's a mystery and it'll stay that way. But family annihilators, the suicidal ones, run amuck. They don't set stages.

---

[46] Rhyming slang: Shovel and Pick = Nick.

Chapter Eleven: Family Matters

I ask Guy Doll if he ever went back to Fantoccini Street after his brother and family had moved in. He shakes his head.

"The last time I saw that house was the day I found Aunty Phoebe's body in the hallway." He looks into the middle distance. It's a fanciful thought, but I wonder if he's searching for an emotional response. If he is, he doesn't appear to find one.

"The last time I'd seen Kandy in person was when Barbara walked out on him, and that was just after the trial. That would have been a year or so before Ms Reese died."

In fact, the trial of Kenneth Doll came to a close on 3rd August 1999, Phoebe Reese's body wasn't discovered until 27th February 2001. Almost 18 months later.

Having little background on Ken and Barbara's relationship, it's unsurprising that this was the first I'd heard of a separation.

"I'm not sure exactly when Barbara walked out with the girls, but from the way Kandy told it, it sounded like a matter of days after he was released. Fair dues to the woman, she stood by him all through the trial, that's more than anyone else did."

Again, Guy lapses into silence, glass eyed and searching the distance.

"I don't know if she waited on the verdict out of loyalty, or pity, but almost as soon as he was home, she packed up and went. Kandy took it real hard. I mean, he came round to my place, that's how low he was. Then again, where else could he go?"

For many years Kenneth Doll had marketed himself as a freelance financial consultant. His qualifications for the title were, to quote the prosecuting council, *a head for numbers and an unusual degree of personal charm.* For almost a decade he ran a series of, what amounted, to Ponzi schemes, using new investor's money to produce over inflated returns for existing ones. An endless cycle of robbing Peter to pay Paul. It was a scheme that relied on a constant influx of fresh investors. As with all such schemes its collapse was inevitable.

Kenneth Doll's lifestyle, which if not lavish was certainly beyond his means, vanished overnight. Frightened creditors clamoured for payment and investors demanded their money back. He lost everything and was lucky to escape a custodial sentence. Even the family home that, with a foresight unusual for him, had been put in Barbara's name, was eventually sold to pay some of the more persistent creditors. Friends and colleagues were quick to distance themselves.

By the summer of '99, when Barbara left him, Kandy had indeed few other places to go.

I ask Guy where his brother was living at the time.

"I'm not entirely sure. And I know that sounds bad, but other than a few evenings when he'd roll up at my bedsit looking for a shoulder to cry on, we still weren't close. He crashed out on my sofa once or twice but that was about it."

"Did he ask about moving into number 37?"

"The idea came up, eventually. We kind of skirted the subject a lot. I think he was waiting for me to offer, and I was waiting for him to ask. We hadn't moved on from when we were teenagers. He didn't want to ask directly for my help, but I needed him to ask. It was the only time in my life where it wasn't me who'd f__ked up and I wanted him to admit it. He didn't, of course."

"So, you were at loggerheads?"

Guy laughs. There's a sour note to the sound.

"No, Kandy won. Of course. He was a great salesman; it was what he did. Talking to Kandy was like watching a magic trick. You'd never know how it was done, you'd just know you'd been fooled. Then you watch the trick again and get fooled again. He was kipping on my sofa one night and the

121

next morning he left with the keys to the house, so he could have a set of copies made."

Guy's expression hardens for the first time since I've been talking with him. Until then he's looked vaguely sad, and it was easy to regard the relationship between him and his brother as a particularly nasty bout of sibling rivalry. However, at this point I have the feeling of gazing into a pit, possibly bottomless, of resentment and loathing. The moment passes and neither Guy nor myself speak. I am aware that I have just witnessed something very personal and find I can't meet his eye.

I may also have witnessed something of a turning point. From that point on, Guy appears to open up more. The sense that he is being guarded drops away.

"We agreed that he could use the house if he had to. I don't remember exactly how we left it, but I remember offering him a set of keys and telling him it would be helpful to me to have someone in the place. It amounted to, I'd let him have free board and lodging and then be grateful to him. When he left with the keys that morning, it was the last time I saw him. When I got in that evening there was an envelope pushed through the door with the keys in it. Oh, and a note."

Guy leaves the room and returns with a slip of paper. Written on it in very neat script:

> *On consideration, I don't think I'll have time to undertake caretaking at #37. So, I am returning your keys to you. Sorry I am unable to help you at this time.*
> *Kandy*

"So, he never used the house until after Ms Reese died?"

"I don't know in all honesty. I never saw him again, he didn't come around asking for the keys once Phoebe was out of the way, so I suppose he must have had a set of copies made up."

Guy shrugs.

"Either way he won ... You know what would have been

122

perfect? If mum had lived just long enough to see him arrested. Then died before they let him off. That would have been sweet."

There is no way of knowing if Kenneth Doll visited Fantoccini Street in the year and a half between his trial and Ms Reese's death. Even the option of asking neighbours if they remember seeing him isn't easily available, as the Street no longer exists.

It is possible to state that Kenneth Doll, with his wife and two stepdaughters, started living there fulltime at some point in March 2001 - the day-to-day business of home occupancy leaves a paper trail. It can also be stated that by the end of April, ownership of the property had been transferred solely to Barbara Doll. If this move was put in place by Kenneth to protect assets or by Barbara to afford her and the girls a degree of security is another unknown. It is likely that the legal situation, regarding the codicils of the late Mrs Doll's will, saved number 37 from being swallowed by the court settlement placed on Kenneth Doll's financial consultancy business. Speculation aside, in the spring of 2001, apparently reconciled, the new Doll family took up residence in Fantoccini Street.

Within three months, Barbara and the girls would be dead. Kenneth would survive for a further two years in a persistent vegetative state.

Although I have attempted, throughout my enquiries, to maintain an impartial viewpoint, and to gather empirical facts rather than questionable impressions, it is sometimes hard not to view the events that took place in number 37 as an entity of some kind. Time and time again I come across blanks where there should be pieces of the story. Almost as if the events themselves were trying to hide, like a criminal covering his tracks and eliminating evidence.

The internet, that we are told frequently is written in ink, appears to have swallowed, whole, Maindo Ningyo's film. The

123

paper that broke the story of the bizarre arrangement of the doll's house folded, leaving no records. Number 37, the street it occupied, even the road it stood on, were ground under the tracks of bulldozers and city development. Guy Doll, estranged from his brother is, to the best of his knowledge, the sole remaining member of his strand of the Doll family.

Barbara Doll, nee Boneca, according to Guy had no contact with any family of her own. My own searches on her have yielded nought. Even the photographs I have managed to find of her shed little light on her. From frame to frame, Barbara Doll changes her appearance. Between a second birthday party for the twins and a snap taken next to a Christmas tree, she transitions from a blond to a brunette. Hair style, length, colour all change, as does makeup and wardrobe. Her appearance is as malleable as plastic.

I was less then surprised then, when enquiries into the schooling of the Doll girls led me from one dead end to another. One of the few photos I have been able to trace of the girls, beyond the age of three or so, shows them standing outside the gates of a large dark building. Almost perfectly square, the frontage of the structure looks entirely unwelcoming. Beyond the gate is an empty quadrangle of featureless tarmac. A sign on the gate reads:

ST. JULIAN THE HOSPITALLER GIRL'S SCHOOL.

The sign is dark green with gold lettering. It is peeling. Both girls are in uniform, dark green blazers with an indistinct badge or crest on the breast pocket. The posture of the girls conveys nothing of their feelings, but their lack of animation seems to rule out excited.[47]

---

[47] I have included this as a footnote. In the early drafts of this document, I had made this observation within the body of the text. In subsequent drafts I edited it away, fearing that I was jumping at

A little investigation revealed St. Julian The Hospitaller was a private school. It closed in 2004 and lay empty until a property developer sent in the demolition teams nine years later. At the time of writing, the space it occupied is lying undisturbed as the courts debate the legality of that move.

I anticipated another series of dead ends in tracing the

---

shadows. On reflection I have included it here and charge the reader with drawing their own conclusions. The photo taken outside ST. JULIAN THE HOSPITALLER school is typical of the small collection of pictures that survive of the Doll girls. The girls are posed for the camera, few of the shots in my procession capture them at a moment of spontaneity. They appear to have stood stock still, as the images are clear and well-focused, however their faces are blurred. Something appears to have caught their attention as the photo was taken, and they have both turned to the viewer's left. This is the norm. In 12 of the 15 pictures I have featuring the girls, both of them have moved as the shutter clicks. In the remaining three only one them is in focus, and even then she (I cannot distinguish between Patsy and Ann) has her eyes closed. I showed the pictures to a local portrait photographer, asking if she thought there was anything significant about the photos. Her response was dismissive, she told me she could produce a thousand pictures of children who moved just as the picture was taken. Some people she said, adults and children, had an uncanny ability to blink as the shutter dropped.

school life of the twins, and entered the name of the defunct school into a search engine with little expectation of a result. I found the school's official website and was duly led to a webpage telling me the domain name was up for sale. Another link took me to a story of the school's closure. Most useful was the *Saint Julian Ex Pupil* forum. The home of the site used the school's less formal name, St Joolz. This gave the page header an affectionate tone that, for the most part, wasn't reflected in the discussions and comments that followed.

Under the heading *'History of St Joolz'* I learned that the school had once been a state school with a Roman Catholic curriculum. A series of disturbingly low OFSTED reports were blamed for the school's closure, at least in a state guise, in 1995. It was to reopen as a secular private school two years later. No one seems to know why it was decided to keep the original name, which must have carried little or no kudos.

The bulk of the web site is made up of postings of photographs connected with the school, followed by a list of responses from ex pupils. For the most part these responses are little more than chit chat and often bland in the extreme. Under a picture of a coach waiting on the road outside the school and labelled French trip 2000, a dozen people had comment that the rear end of the coach smelled of the chemical toilet.

On occasion though there is something that suggests something at the school wasn't right. One or two of the staff, identified by nicknames, are referred to as *creepy* or *handsy*. With remarks like that in mind it begins to strike you how few positive comments there are about the school. One in particular stood out, the writer of it, identified only as 'Guest' wrote.

"Has anyone seen the nonsense in the History of the St Joolz page? OFSTED my foot. The council shut St Fiddlers down before the scandal broke."

I'm going to deviate into a side story at this point and ask the reader's patience. The St Joolz website represented a chance to contact someone who might have something to say on the subject of the Doll girls. The website was in the form of a Facebook page. To contact anyone through the page meant opening a Facebook account, and, as I wasn't a member I had to join. After signing up I sent a message to Mrs Cindy Smythe[48] introducing myself and explaining that I was writing a book that would touch on the lives of the Doll family. Within an hour of sending my first, and as it would turn out my last, FB message, I received notification that my account had been suspended for violating Facebook's terms of use. I requested the suspension be reconsidered and was informed that it could not be lifted. I have yet to be given a specific reason for the suspension and it is still in place.

When I have mentioned this to people in relation to my difficulty in researching the events at Fantoccini Street, they are quick to blame coincidence or - the 21st century equivalent of an act of God - a software glitch.

Fortunately, my Facebook message included a list of references vouching for me, and my email address. Mrs Smythe contacted me via that.

Shortly after I was contacted by Mrs Smythe, the St Joolz website was closed.

Cindy Smythe, the administrator of the St Joolz website had no personal knowledge of Ann and Patsy Doll, but she was familiar with their names and at least part of their story.

"I joined St Joolz in 2002. That was the year after the Doll twins were murdered. The class I went into had been the one they were in. Of course, this was some months after the event and between the murders and my joining there had been the Christmas holidays to distract everyone. That sounds harsh but it the way it is at that age. By the time I got to the school there were other things to talk about and a lot of us were discovering boys. I think belonging to an all-girl's school

---

[48] Not her real name.

ramps up that obsession.

"Their names came up now and then, but no one seemed that concerned about it. It may have been a deliberate decision on the part of the school not to harp on about the deaths, the staff were very good about things like that. We were one big family, that's how I remember it, the staff were always very concerned for the girls' welfare.

"There was one girl who talked about it, about them rather. But she was a bit of an outsider, not popular. She would mention them every opportunity she got. She always claimed the twins had been her closest friends but I'm not sure if that's true."

When I ask if she remembers the name of the girl claiming to be close to the twins, Cindy apologises. This mysterious girl seems to have made little impression on her and she remembers nothing about her other than her dramatic claim on the Doll's story.

Cindy was unwilling to put a general call out on the St Joolz site for enquiries about the Doll twins. She was worried the morbid tone would 'cast a shadow over the memory of a wonderful place', but she did put me in touch with a retired teacher who had been her head of year and would have known the twins.

Francine Corn took early retirement in 2004 when St Joolz closed its doors for the last time. A year later she had a stroke from which, by her own account, she has never fully recovered. Her speech in terms of pronunciation is perfectly understandable, but she suffers from a degree of expressive dysphagia. During our interview she occasionally used the wrong word, sometimes she was aware of this, and tried to correct herself, other times she was not. In transcribing our conversation, I have written the points where she corrected herself as if no slip up had been made. Where she had clearly substituted one word for another without realising, I have used *italics* to recount what was actually said and put the most

128

likely meaning, based on context, in brackets[49].

"I remember the *kitchen* (Doll) girls very well. I'm sorry to say this because it sounds cruel, but they were a little odd. Something there was off. That's the only way I can describe it. I'd come to teaching late, it was my second career, but you quickly get a sense for the girls who are troubled, as opposed to the girls who are trouble. The problem is in terms of managing a classroom and a timetable and everything else, the one who are trouble tend to take up all your *floor* (energy). The troubled can get forgotten, if they've *beneath* (quiet). The Twins came into that category. Certainly, in St Joolz.

"When I was at St Joolz the school was in trouble. After it had been closed by OFSTED there were a lot of rumours doing the rounds about inappropriate behaviour from members of staff. I didn't waste time committing any of them to memory really. The school I was in was totally different. The whole teaching staff were new, even the caretakers were fresh hires. Most of the old St Joolz people had been church people. And the few that weren't didn't get rehired when the school went *table* (private). I think that's why the school was sold off to the private sector. It allowed a clean cut from the old employees. If the local authority had kept the running of the school than there would have been issues of employment law to consider.

"The history of the school, the rumours about it, were a taboo subject. The governors of the school had made it quietly known that mentioning anything about St Joolz time before it went private was going to be frowned upon. Being in the private *top* (sector) had advantages and disadvantages, job insecurity was the downside. Making the history of the school

---

[49] Although he made no other reference to them in the body of his manuscript, Mr Croix later listed these substituted words, repeatedly, in his sketches and diagrams (see figure, iv).

129

taboo only made it intriguing. The governors made the mistake a lot of people make, they thought the children were inherently stupid or living in a controlled environment. The new *thoughtless* (influx) of students had heard stories about the school, in was in the papers and even if none of the papers said it out right, people could read between the lines. No one sends their child to a fee-paying school on a whim, they wanted to know what was what. The parents were reassured that the staff were new, the governors were new, the school was secular. But obviously the sort of worries they would have had would have been spoken about at *mindless* (home). Children hear conversations, being young or being ignored doesn't change that. The girls who came to St Joolz knew something had happened. Because they didn't have all the details, they filled the holes with whatever they liked. The rumours outstripped the truth.

"When it reopened the decorating and refit were still on going. The last room to be done was the main hall. The governors were working hard at distancing the school from any comparison with its state school, catholic school past and the buildings were fanatically secular. Because of that the main hall underwent a huge amount of *maison* (refitting). The space was remade into a stage set; the school was big on drama. In the days before everyone got paranoid about their children being posted on the internet, the school's end of year plays would be *altar* (videoed) so parents could buy copies. The problem with the assembly hall, was it had been designed and modified over the years to look like an *imaginary* (church). The stage at the front of the room looked very much like an altar and there were crosses and reliefs of the Virgin Mary wherever you looked. I think if the *numbers* (governors) had left it in peace, it would have gone unnoticed. It would have just been another room that happened to look like a chapel. But because it was still being dismantled when the first girls came to the school it took on a special *ninety* (significance). I was on my way to a class one time and moving behind a group of the younger girls. They hadn't realised there was a teacher behind them and were *square* (talking) in a way they might not have if they'd known. Just as we passed the entrance to the main hall two workman came out carrying the massive carving of *twists* (Christ) on the cross. It was a huge thing, at least *irons* (feet) high. I don't know what it *equal* (weighed), but it must have been heavy. To make their job easier they'd cut the arms off, well hacked them off.

"A pair of the young girls in front of me exchanged a look and one of them whispered

'I bet they'll take that to the cellar.'

Another girl giggled but it was that shrill giggling you hear a lot in *pretty* (schools). Laughter trying to hide fear. Another girl made a tutting noise and said the school didn't even have a cellar – which wasn't true in fact. The first girl was adamant,

'There is a cellar, it's where they took them all.' Then she thought about it for a second and added, 'there were crosses everywhere and pictures of the crucifixion and Mary and … '

At that point her imagination wound down. I cleared my throat and said, too loudly,

"I'm sure the workmen are just going to take it to the *still* (skip)."

"That was years before the Doll girls were at the school, but the story about the cellar had taken hold somehow or other. It was never clear what was meant to have happened there, but then the best stories never are fully formed. The cellar of crosses and hidden things was passed on down the school to each new intake. The story about the hall once being decorated with crosses and Virgin's turned into a black shrine and voodoo dolls.

"One funny, or maybe not funny, thing though. Some years after seeing the carving taken away, I happened to go into the cellar, and there it was. I heard the drama teacher had intercepted the workman and saved it from the skip. I think the idea was to use it in a production, of course it was too heavy to move again so it stayed down there.

"I'm sure the majority of the old staff were totally innocent of any wrongdoing, but *sister* (clearing) them all out was possibly the best thing to do. Of course, it meant the school opened with a mix of inexperienced staff, like myself, and there was no chemistry, if you get my *ironed* (meaning).

"Even the girls attending the school were new. When the state school closed the pupils were re-placed at other schools. NW12 wasn't a wealthy area, and the locals weren't in the market for private education. Most of our girls came from outside the area. Again, that's something that's frowned on now but I'm pretty certain the school advertised out of borough to try and get girls that hadn't heard the stories. That was another reason the Dolls stuck out, being local.

"They were very *face* (quiet), I mean beyond the point of being shy or even just keeping their heads down to avoid trouble. I'd take the morning and afternoon register and they'd both say 'here Miss' when I called their names. That would be as much as I'd hear out of them for the day. If I happened to catch their eye when I called their names they'd try and get away with just nodding or lifting a hand. I've seen kids doing that before, trying not to engage, but normally there was a clear reason why, they might have a stammer or English wasn't their first language. But with them it was different, they had normal articulate voices and If I asked them something directly, a question in class say, they'd answer without needing to be coaxed, but they'd never *front* (volunteer) anything. That was the unsettling thing about them, at least I thought it was, that element of control. They were deliberately not speaking and that was that. And it didn't seem to bother them. They weren't like the Silent Twins, they weren't tormented by their self-imposed isolation."

The Silent Twins refers to June and Jennifer Gibbons, sisters born at the RAF hospital in Aden, in 1963. Physically healthy, they were inseparable from birth and as they got older began to communicate less and less with their family and the wider world. Their lack of interaction with the local community earned them the title the Silent Twins. Their story came to national prominence when a journalist, Marjorie Wallace, wrote a book about them that was adapted for TV and broadcast by the BBC in 1986.

I ask Miss Corn if she had concerns about the homelife of the Doll twins. Her expression is hard to read, in part because of a degree of paralysis caused by the stroke.

"I don't know if concerned might be putting it too strongly. And of course, in light of what happened I have to ask myself if there were *behind* (signs) I *back* (missed). But I do know they caught my *forward* (attention), though, as I said, they didn't do it in a way that required *stairway* (input). The other problem was they weren't popular, so it was natural for them to be quiet, because the other girls weren't playing with them. Even if there were concerns there was nothing *scribe* (concrete) to pin them on. I do remember being curious about their parents and being *writes* (eager) to meet them on parents' evening.

"Mrs Doll didn't attend, I do remember that because it was more usual to see the mothers. Fathers seldom came alone, if they did they were normally widowers.

"Knowing what he went on to do it's hard to distinguish memory from hindsight. Mr Doll was charming, it was hard to believe the *recordings* (girls) were his[50]. I don't remember him being particularly handsome, but he was very well *snow* (groomed), very smooth. I'd have liked to have seen him with the girls but the policy at the school was to talk to the parents without their children being present. We had a ten-minute slot in the evening and at the end of it I realised we hadn't really spoken about his children at all. All I knew was that he was a charmer and that I didn't like him. Although in the same way the girls worried me, I didn't know why I didn't *painless* (like) him. I intended to watch him leaving the school because I wanted to see him interact with girls, but as soon as he left his seat the next parent jumped in and started talking at me.

"That would have been the end of the summer *burning*

---

[50] Miss Corn was unaware that Kenneth was the twin's stepfather.

133

(term). The autumn term started late that year because the boiler broke down and the repair took longer than expected, so the summer holiday was extended a week. The school opened again on Monday, 10ᵗʰ September, and of course there was an inset day, so the pupils didn't come back until Tuesday, Nine Eleven. I won't pretend I remember anything about that day other than the Twin Towers. No one does. The twins didn't come in for morning registration. I remember that much but it wasn't something I'd have *wooden* (worried) about really. If a child was too sick to come into school it wasn't uncommon for the parents to forget to ring in and tell us, or for the office to fail to *board* (pass) the message on if they did. I would have made a note to tell the office to check. By lunchtime the news reports had started to come in and after that we were just trying to keep calm and make sure the girls weren't distressed. A few parents came to the school and took their girls home. I don't know why, they might have had relatives in NY.

"The next day we were contacted by the police, telling us about the twins and their mother. There was a meeting at first break, and it was decided to tell the girls en masse. We called them into a special assembly after lunch and the head addressed them.

"I have to say, for me that was one of the most horrible things I've ever been part of. The form heads sat at the sides of the room and the head took the stage. He called for quiet and finally got it. Or for what passes for quiet in a school. That low background hum of whispering.

"The girls' reaction was ... nothing. I don't know what I'd expected, it was a biggish school, and three quarters of the girls wouldn't have known the murdered girls at all, not even to nod to in passing, but the lack of concern was deeply upsetting. I thought so anyway.

"I suppose if the school hadn't been so evangelically secular the head would have led a *black* (prayer) and drawn it to a close. As he couldn't do that he stood there for a moment until the indifference made it awkward. Then he said if anyone felt upset by it and wanted to speak to someone, they could go to the school *white* (nurse). If I remember *glass* (rightly), only one girl did. She said the girls were her best friends. She was a girl from my form group; Ruth Haggerty[51]."

The photograph Ruth Heggerty shows me is of the twins standing in front of a tree. They're in the St Joolz uniform and their faces are blurred.
"They moved as I took the picture," Ruth explains. "That was a week before they were murdered."
We're sitting in the same garden twenty years later. Ruth points to the corner where the twins had stood. The tree is gone and the patch of garden beyond is now a brick-built extension.
The photo is creased, and the edges are slightly tattered. It's unsurprising given its history.
"I was incredibly melodramatic when I was young," Ruth tells me. "I carried that photo with me for about two years, showed it to everyone in the school." She affects a breathless, ominous tone, "this is the last picture of them alive. I don't even know if that's true."
I hand the picture back and Ruth smiles at it a little sadly before slipping it back into an envelope.
"It was currency of a sort, I suppose. My brief sojourn as one of the cool kids. I stopped doing it when I overheard

---

[51] For the most part Miss Corn's dysphagia didn't require me to ask for explanation. It seemed to be centred largely on nouns and normally it was simple enough to infer the word she had meant through context. However, I did ask her to repeat Ruth Heggerty's name and when she still couldn't manage it, I asked her to write it down. She had replaced the name Heggerty with Raggedy, as in Raggedy Ann.

another girl doing an impression of me waving my photo about. A new girl had joined the school that day and I'd sought her out so I could show her the famous photo of the two dead girls. That was how I thought of it, 'the famous photo'."

I manage to find Ruth through the St Joolz website and by an exchange of messages on Facebook, via a friend's account. Now in her thirties, Ruth, is a social worker and has twin girls of her own.

"They truth is I didn't know them that well really. We weren't part of the popular set and I think we were friends through lack of choice, not out of mutual affection. I made a lot of mileage out of my friendship with the doomed girls after their death than our friendship warranted. And I know that sounds horrible, but at that age it's hard for most children to really process the idea of death. And, in defence of myself as a teenager, the school mishandled it. There are ways to deal with a tragedy like that among a group of children and the school didn't do that. I remember they made an announcement about the deaths in assembly. Now I swear this is true, I'm sure he'd deny it now, but the head of the school called me up on the stage because I was known as the twin's best friend, and he asked me if I'd been told anything about it. As if a twelve year old girl was going to be privy to anything the press didn't already know. Fool. At the time I didn't think anything of it, in fact I was excited about being the centre of attention, but now I look back and wonder what the hell he thought he was doing."

The photo was taken when the girls had visited Ruth's house, the only time they'd done so. Like most of the school's intake, Ruth lived out of borough and getting to her house required a considerable journey. Despite the rarity of the visit and the morbid celebrity it afforded her, Ruth, has very little memory of how it came about. She does remember that Kenneth Doll dropped the twins off at the front gate and didn't get out of the car. As soon as the front door opened and Mrs Heggerty answered it, he drove away.

"I didn't see that, but I heard my mum comment on it to

Dad. She thought it was rude and I remember her saying that the girls hadn't had time to wave goodbye before he pulled away."

Memories of the visit are thin.

"I can't for the life of me remember how the visit was organised. Our houses weren't close, and I don't remember asking my parents to organize a visit, but somewhere along the line I supposed that's what must have happened. They stayed about six hours or so I'd guess, because they came after breakfast and had lunch with us, but Mum drove them back to their place before supper.

"I went in the car with them, they didn't say much. They sat in the back of the car, and I sat next to Mum. I think that says a lot about the sort of friendship were had. When my brother had friends over if Mum or Dad gave them a lift anywhere, they'd all pile into the back of the car regardless of space, three or four of them crammed into the back, inseparable. I do remember cranking around trying to chatter with them, and them not responding. I must have been embarrassed by it and rabbited on to fill the silence, because I remember Mum telling me to calm down and take a breath. When we got to their house, we walked with them to the front door. Their dad let them in, told my mum, *thank you for driving them home*, and the door closed."

Ruth shrugs and hands the envelope with the photo of Patsy and Ann in it, to me.

"You might as well have this." When I defer, she insists. "No, take it. It might be useful for the book. I've only kept it because it seemed disrespectful to throw it away. But if you're keeping the memory alive it's better for you to have it." She smiles, "I'm still a little melodramatic."

When I ask what she and the twins did on the solitary visit to her home she laughs, almost.

"Not much really, we watched a DVD in the end because they weren't that interested in playing or doing anything. We were an awkward age, too old to play with dolls and too young to talk about boys. I didn't want to suggest things for fear of

137

looking childish, but I do remember they had a thing about miming. That's what we were doing in the garden, they'd tried to get me interested in this game they played were they pretend to throw things to each other. It sounds strange now I say it, but at the time it was just boring. I wanted to take photos and pose, but all they wanted to do was pretend to throw things back and forth. Odd really. They only wanted to play with stuff that wasn't there."

Chapter Twelve: Teamwork

Guy Doll's sparse description of how his brother took occupancy of number 37, and the details of what the emergency services found there six months later, represents almost all that is known about life within its walls.

The Dolls made little impact on the local area, which was already in a state of urban decline. Neighbours were few and, because the surrounding houses had been carved into a variety of low-cost rental properties, often transient.

This situation may have been another factor in London North University giving Steven Ward the go-ahead to continue his fieldtrips. Added to the emotional load of not letting Edward Bartlett's last investigation fizzle out was the somewhat dubious addition of not letting the Doll family be forgotten.

Amenities for the second trip were slightly better than the previous year. Gerald Cardino had arranged the loan of a four-berth caravan, belonging to a family friend. Although it was agreed in advance that at least two members of the team would be sleeping in the house each night, the caravan meant the teams could eat and wash in relative comfort.

John Pelton, the only member of the team to receive a fee for his work, negotiated a percentage of the budget to buy several reels of 12-gauge oxygen-free copper bi-wire, to provide higher quality recordings. He also took along a selection of digital recording equipment to run concurrently with the analogue tapes.

The decision to use digital equipment was, according to Pelton, a bone of contention between him and Steven Ward.

Ward believed digital recordings were largely worthless as they were more open to accusations of tampering and fakery. He was wary of including them at all for fear of casting doubt on the honesty of the team's findings. However, as Pelton was providing the equipment, and the expertise behind its use, Ward's objections were largely moot.

Cardino too, brought along technical equipment. Although unpaid for his time he procured, at his own expense, a Fluke 64 MAX IR Infrared Thermometer and a tripod mounted, Leica DISTO S910 Laser Distance Meter. He was quick to point out that, at the time, these were tools he had anticipated needing in his working life.

The second trip was scheduled for seven days beginning on Monday August 8th. It was agreed Ward, Pelton and Cardino would arrive a day ahead of Mabel Noakes and Carol Crossland. Ward and Pelton had their recording and monitoring equipment to set up, and Cardino, aside from bringing the caravan, was to survey the house itself.

Cardino's activities served two purposes. Firstly, surveying the house made it easier to track and detail any incidents and, secondly, it addressed health and safety concerns. By this time the house had been standing, unoccupied and largely untouched for ten years. Cardino was happy to comply but, initially, regarded the survey, other than for safety reasons, as pointless.

"I was interested in the forces at work inside the house. *Something* was going on in there, pick your own label. Until we have a proper body of evidence and points of reference, they're all meaningless. I was happy to check the roof wasn't about to fall in on us and the stairs weren't about to collapse, but measuring the house seemed like a waste of time. To be honest though, on the first day, I was glad of the excuse to move around the house. Steve and John had started arguing almost as soon as we got there."

Both Ward and Pelton mentioned an argument during interviews with them but didn't give the impression that it had been more than a minor disagreement. Cardino's recounting is quite different. In fact, he feared the two men would come to blows.

The three men arrived at Fantoccini Street independently. Aside from the caravan, Cardino had burrowed a Land Rover to tow it with. He remembers arriving later than intended because of a problem with the lights on the caravan. Ward and Pelton were already inside number 37 when he arrived. Already arguing.

"From what I could gather John was waiting at the house when Steve got there in the uni's minibus. I got two versions of the story really, one from Steve and another from John. By the evening, when it was time to eat, they'd both calmed down, but it wasn't exactly cordial, and when there's three of you in a caravan it's hard not to pick up on an atmosphere, psychic or not. After we'd eaten, John said he was going to bunk down in the house and said good night. He made a slightly snide remark to Steve, something like 'if you trust me not to steal the valuables.' He said it as if he was making an off the cuff remark, something light-hearted. But ... well ... like I said, three of us in a caravan. Steve either didn't pick up on it or decided to let it go. I said, 'watch out for ghosts', trying to keep it light you know? I'd had a belly full of them squabbling and didn't want to have to listen to any more of it. John just rolled his eyes.

"After he'd gone, neither Steve or me spoke until we heard the front door of the house slam shut. We weren't exactly waiting for John to get out of ear shot, but I'd set the caravan up on the hard standing directly in front of the house, and that's sort of what happened. John shook his head and muttered something under his breath. I don't want you to think Steve was slating John the moment he left the room; whatever had happened between had wound him up and I think he just needed to vent. He wasn't asking me to pick sides or anything.

"By Steve's telling John was standing on the doorstep, already waiting, when he pulled up. He was impatient, that's what Steve told me. Steve's plan was to take a series of photographs inside the house before anything was touched. He wanted to make a record of exactly how the house stood when we entered it. I don't know why he thought that was so important. I mentioned it to Carol, this was weeks later, she thought he felt bad about not going back into the house on the first trip, when Edward found the walking doll. What Steve had wanted to do was start on the ground floor and move through each level, cataloguing the rooms if you like.

"Steve was in charge of the keys. I don't know the legal ins and outs, but there was some problem that meant the keys couldn't be copied and someone had to sign for them before the estate agency would let them go. That's what we were told anyway. Steve let John in and went back to the minibus to collect his cameras. The area was a bit rough back then and I don't think anyone wanted to leave valuables in the cars. When Steve got back to the house, John was walking down the stairs. He said he'd needed a pee. Steve didn't think anything of it. He took pictures of the front room, or the dining room, whichever you want to call it. Once that room was on record, the pair of them had unloaded all the gear and Steve started shooting the rest of the house. I don't know how long it took but he's very methodical, so I'd say it was at least forty minutes. I'd guess he got to the attic room not long before I finally turned up."

Photograph #026, taken by Steven Ward on 08/08/2011
Detail of doll's house bedroom

This is an analogue photograph taken using a Hasselblad 500 medium format camera and is of much higher quality to the ones taken on 11th July 2010. It is possible to clearly see the content and condition of the miniature room where the D#5 doll was found. The floor is badly warped, and splits can be seen along the rear wall. There is a significant amount of black mould visible on all surfaces.

In the centre of the room is a model of a double bed equipped with fabric covers. Like the floor and walls, the fabric is stained and discoloured with mould. Other than this the room is empty.

There are, in total, sixteen photos of the bedroom of the doll's house. Ward refuses to be drawn as to why he devoted so much film (all the pictures are analogue) to what would appear to be a non-event. It is possible that the decision was a purely emotional one.

"The walking doll was gone. John denied any knowledge of it. Of course, Steve confronted him about being upstairs while he'd been collecting the cameras from the bus. John just insisted he'd been using the toilet[52] and hadn't even been near the attic. By the time I got there they were getting really heated. It's probably just as well I turned up when I did, they looked about ready to start throwing punches. Eventually Steve had to give in and accept John's word. He still didn't believe him, but John was sticking to his story and short of physically searching him, there wasn't a lot Steve could do to disprove it.

"The problem wasn't that the doll had gone missing, but that there was a shadow over its loss. If John and Steve had stuck together and found it missing at the same time it could be catalogued as a paranormal event, but now because the loss couldn't be verified it was open to ridicule. At the time I thought he was being a bit over the top, but later I found out when they'd been arguing, John had told him, 'Maybe one of the ghosts took it'. I guess Steve was just wound up about it.

"When we settled down for the night, it occurred to me how big a deal it was if John hadn't taken it. The doll appears spontaneously, between the team leaving the house and Edward Bartlett going back into it, then disappears again

---

[52] As on the first fieldtrip, arrangements had been made to restore running water to number 37. One of few creature comforts the house provided was a working toilet situated on the first floor.

143

when the house is empty. I could see Steve's point; John going upstairs upset the chain of evidence.

"Do I think John took the doll? I really don't know. I think about that doll a lot. We never knew how it got there, and it appears to have vanished into thin air. If John didn't take it, it's one of the most significant cases of spontaneous materializations in history. Or it's just a case of petty theft. Either way, as a piece of evidence it's been rendered worthless. That, in itself, is a tragedy. On balance, I'd say I believe John. I mean, he was part of the team, part of the investigation and, in many ways, his evidence gathering was the most rigorous of everyone. I think Steve convinced himself he'd stolen it because it was less galling than believing they'd screwed up recording such a significant event."

"Steven was totally convinced John had taken the Walking Doll," Carol Crossland tells me. "He didn't say anything directly to me about it, but I did overhear him talking to May. She was trying to calm him down, because that's what she did. It wasn't fair really, May was always the one to sooth ruffled feathers. It irked me because it was always the men that needed talking down. I wanted to tell them to grow up and stop acting like children, but I didn't. It would have only fallen to May to stop them sulking. And to be honest, I think she sort of liked playing den mother.

"Sorry, I'll climb down from my soapbox. I heard Steve and May talking in the caravan. Really that was the only place they could have talked. John had spent a full day wiring the house with recording devices. On the first night we turned up he told us that every room had a mic and tape deck running. He said if we could announce ourselves going into a room it would help eliminate our natural noise from anything that couldn't be accounted for. I thought he was just being dramatic and trying to prove how vital his toy collection was, but I realised he was speaking for May's benefit really.

"Steve was ranting about John stealing artefacts. He was convinced John was trying to cash in on the project. May was doing her best to assure him no member of the team would do such a thing. She pointed out, rightly I thought, that John didn't even believe anything out of the ordinary was happening in the house. Then she said something I thought was strange, she said that was a good thing, because evidence presented by cynics held more sway in scientific circles than evidence presented by believers. I just happened to be passing and overheard. I wasn't listening at the door, you understand."

"You can stop pussy footing around, okay? I know Steve thinks I stole that f__king doll. I had that place wired for sound, top to bottom. Hours and hours and hours of tape and disc. Nearly all of it empty. I left digi recorders in the attic, the kitchen and the front room. Every room, landing and staircase was covered with an omnidirectional mic. They recorded constantly to digi and I had analogue tape machines wired to sound activated switches. At night they'd start recording at the level of a whisper. Basically, if someone cleared their throat in one of those rooms, I'd have it on record. I told everyone about them, I wanted them to announce when they went into a room, so I didn't have to waste time listening to supernatural occurrences that turned out to be someone looking for their pen. Or May rushing in because she thought something had happened.

"The first night we were all in the house[53] I saw the attic room deck had triggered at a point when it should have been empty. I pulled the tape up and it was Steve, giving Crossland a tour of the attic room and the doll's house. He went on and on about the bedroom where Ed claimed he'd found his doll. Then he went into a big rant about people selling artefacts - he actually used that word - and devaluing the work of serious researchers. I cut out the section of tape and threw it, I only used fresh, virgin tapes in that house. With analogue tapes you

---

[53] The second night of the second fieldtrip, Tuesday 12th August.

can get traces of earlier recordings contaminating your new ones. Crossland was from the same mould as May and Ed, the first sniff of anything unexpected and they'd start seeing ghosts. Jed had a more tech background, but you could see in his eyes he wanted to see or hear something. I don't know if they believed Steve, about me nicking the doll to sell it off, but I was always due to be the fall guy. The last thing you want in a haunted house is a f__king rationalist.

"Did it bother me? Well, it made the week a bit of a drag, not being on good terms with anyone, but none of us were destined to bosom buddies. I think I'd have got along okay with Jed under different circumstances, but he really got into the swing of whole psychic investigator schtick, and I wasn't in the mood.

"He'd spent most of the first day doing a survey of the house. I think he'd been allowed onto the trip mainly because it made the uni look as if they were covering the health and safety angle. I wasn't paying much attention to what he was up to at first, I had my own stuff to do. I was replacing all the wiring for the sound gear with super insulated cabling, that way it was less likely to pick up ambient radio and electrical waves. I kept bumping into him when I was running cables down the stairs. He was measuring the stairs. I mean the steps, every one of them, treads and runners. He was getting ready to shoot his bolt about it and expected me to do the same. Turned out the stairways weren't standardised."

"The thing is, the thing that struck me, was the way things wouldn't add up, wouldn't make sense, but would be connected. I mean the dimensions of 37 made no kind of sense at all. There were three floors, ground, first and attic.[54] On the first floor the ceiling height was 245.8cm and on the second it was 248.4cm. That kind of discrepancy you expect, but the stairs were something else. The flight from the ground to second floor had 14 treads, but the second flight, to attic, that flight had three less, only 11. I measured the floor depths because there was a possibility the joists were different between floors, but the floors were near enough to identical that the extra steps couldn't be accounted for. So, I measured the stair treads, all of them. They got gradually lower the higher they went. Tiny amounts, and not entirely uniform. When I measured the rooms, I found the house was tapered. It's upper dimensions back to front were almost 20cm less. When I measure the average angles of the external walls, I found they were spot on. I mean spot on. That house was built in 1903 but the external walls, even after decades of neglect were absolutely, *absolutely*, true. I find that amazing in itself. If nothing else it shows that that house was put there by masters of their trade, that house was built with an extraordinary level

---

[54] The top floor of number 37 followed the same pattern as the first floor but lacked a toilet. Despite having the same floor plan as the first floor the attic had considerably less volume because it was built into the eves of the roof.

of care. Which only makes the state of the inside more baffling; oddment staircases and sloping internal walls? The house got smaller as it rose, it was like it had been inverted. And the doll's house in the attic? That was a whole new level of weird."

Unlike the four Murder Dolls and D#5, there is a comprehensive collection of photographs of the doll's house that stood in the attic of 37 Fantoccini Street.

The earliest available photograph showing a full view of the house is one taken by Steven Ward on the first fieldtrip[55]. There were in total of 24 pictures taken of the doll's house on the first fieldtrip. Front, left, right and top elevations, and shots of each internal segments (eight in total). Most of these angles were shot twice for security's sake. Ward retained the clearest images for his records and discarded the extras, although the negatives still exist. There are two prints of the front view of the house, one showing just the house and the other showing the house and the halfmoon table it sat on.

The front view of the miniature house shows its internal structure is comprised of eight distinct parts. The first and second floors each have three separate sections; two rooms set left and right with a central section containing a flight of stairs, hallway and landing. The attic area has only two sections, one being much larger than the other. The smaller section represents the real attic's tiny kitchen.

---

[55] The ownership/copy write of the photographs is held by London North University. Permission to reproduce them for this book was denied. I viewed the pictures while interviewing Steven Ward and the descriptions are taken from the notes I made at the time. This is also true for subsequent photographs taken by Gerald Cardino.

The front panels of the doll's house, that, when closed, would represent the external frontage, are not present in this series of pictures. They appear, only by chance, in a later series taken by Ward to catalogue the rooms of the real house.

The rooms of the real number 37 were all photographed on the first trip but, Ward admits, in a slightly haphazard manner. Single pictures were taken of the hallways, landings and bedrooms. The dining room, kitchen and larger attic room/doll's house room were more carefully catalogued, with each wall as well the ceilings and floors photographed. The dates and times of these first pictures are not well indexed. Ward admits to taking them in no particular order, although he remembers starting at the top of the house and working down on the first trip. He would also take several additional shots of the dining room floor, following the bizarre episode with the table during the Ouija board trial. These photos revealed nothing that could account for the movements of the table.

The doll's house stood against the wall opposite the door of the attic room, so that it was visible immediately on entering the space. Because of the orientation of the staircases this meant the doll's house stood against the [56]north wall. The

---

[56] Note: Directions given in the interview material disagree with those given in Mr Croix's description. Although not stated within his manuscript, it seemed to be Mr Croix practice to orientate the house north, south, east and west on the principal that an individual standing in the front door looking directly through the building toward the back, would be considered to be facing North, their right would be east, left west with south to their rear. This orientation is constant in

149

frontage panels were caught in the photograph of the west wall. The west wall of the attic room was extremely low; built into the roof space, the room had angled ceilings.

The frontage panels are not immediately visible in the east wall photograph. Mounted on the lower part of the angled ceiling, unless the viewer is aware of their significance, it is easy to mistake them for a damaged or discoloured section of plaster. They are also partly covered by a strip of ceiling paper that has broken free and hangs down in front of them. In this photograph few details can be made out.

In these early photographs the depth of detail is not particularly great, but it is clear the dolls' house is in a state of decay. The side views on the model show a bloom of black spoor on its external walls. It is possible to see this is mirrored on the interior wall of the actual attic room. Ward noted this creeping infestation of mould and, after taking the initial photographs, took the trouble to pull the miniature house and the table it rested on a small distance from the wall.

The individual shots of the miniature rooms and staircases also show the doll's house to be in poor condition. Black spoor or mould is present in all the rooms. There are very few items of furniture in the miniature house, and it is not known if they have been lost or if the house was never completed/furnished. The exception is the main kitchen, which is equipped with enough pieces to give the impression of a workable, if not luxurious, cooking area. The lower floor room to the left of the kitchen contains a miniature table. The right-hand second floor room contains a bed (on which D#5 was found). The only other piece of furniture is in the attic room: the miniature halfmoon table, set against the back wall, with a model of a doll's house sitting on it.

Strangely there is little overlap between doll collectors and

---

all mention of directions within the house.
(R.D)

150

doll's house enthusiasts. When I questioned Ella Caine about the Fantoccini Street doll's house she confessed to near complete ignorance on the subject. Doll's houses, even the one where the Murder Dolls where discovered held very little interest for her. Purely by chance while Ella was reading my letter that contained a photo of the doll's house, a member of staff was on duty who happened to collect doll's houses. Seeing her interest, Ella asked her opinion of the piece.

The staff member[57] and I entered into correspondence, and I shared with her copies of all the pictures I could find of the doll's house. She was unable to identify the house or find anything similar online or in her extensive library on the subject.

This, she told me, wasn't surprizing. Few doll's houses of the size of the one found in number 37 are production line products. Commercially available houses tend to be smaller, thus keeping their price to an affordable level. Larger pieces are normally bespoke commissions or DIY projects. As the house in number 37 would appear to be a miniature representation of the house it sat in, it seems likely that it was a unique item.

This in itself raises questions. When asked about the doll's house, Guy Doll had no recollection of seeing it when he ventured into the attic rooms. This suggests that the tenant, Phoebe Reese, predated the house. Did she commission the building of the model, or build it herself? Neither seems likely. The house appears to have been made to a high standard. A bespoke piece of that size and quality would not have been

---

[57] When first approached for advice on the subject of the doll's house the staff member was enthusiastic about the project and said they were happy to be acknowledged in print. Subsequently they contact me to request their contribution be anonymous.

cheap, and there was no indication the Phoebe Reese was a woman of means. A hobbyist, with the skill required to build to the standard of the model in Fantoccini Street, would seem unlikely to be in possession of only a single piece.

Certain features of the model are unusual within the field of dolls house building. It has internal doors, a detail normally omitted from even the most obsessively manufactured miniatures. The reasoning for this is prosaic. The inclusion of doors limits the amount of light in the tiny rooms. Apparently, the builder, or builders, of 37a – as the doll's house is sometimes called – were content to build darkness into the miniature home. The other striking feature is the pitch of the roof. As with the vast majority of doll's houses 37a is one room deep; there are, in effect no front and back rooms but rather left and right. Most doll's house builders extend the exterior width wise, resulting in an overly wide front. Often this deformed architecture is accented by the practice of pitching the roof at 90 degrees to the lay out of the norm; the ridge of the roof runs side to side of the model, not front to back. This is not the case with 37a, and the pitch of the house runs front to back.

As well as the lack of any provenance for the doll's house outside of the real number 37, there are several features of the model that strongly indicate it was specifically built to mirror the actual house it stood in.

"Okay, I have to put my cards on the table at this point," Gerald Cardino is showing me a set of drawings he made during the second fieldtrip. Beautifully drawn with a draftsman's eye, they show evidence of being handled and pawed over a great deal. Some parts of the drawings, most noticeably the attic, are almost obscured by notations, lists of figures and complex calculations (see appendix). "Doll's houses creep me out. Always have done. I'm not sure why, I think it's the way they're made as 3D structures but have a 2D layout[58]. That means you pull open the front panels, go through the front of the house, but then you're in the centre of the building, as if the door has tricked you and led you somewhere else."

He laughs at his own imagery, but this is clearly an idea that troubles him.

Despite his aversion to doll's houses, the walls of his study, a light airy room on the ground floor of his family's home, is covered with photos and drawings of 37a and the attic where it stood. With the exception of a collection of framed and glass fronted prints, hanging above a draftsman's drawing board, all the pictures are liberally covered with notations, figures and calculations. Even the framed prints are graced with layered halos of post-it notes. The drafting board has a sheet of A5 paper taped to it. In contrast to the finely produced drawings spread on the desk for me to see, the drawing on the board is hastily sketched. Executed in black marker pen it is a crude likeness of number 37. Arrows in various colours lead into, out of and around rooms. Their purpose or meaning defeats me. They may have defeated the artist too; most of the arrows begin or end in a cluster of question marks. Some of the arrows and question marks have left tears in the paper.

Being in the study is slightly disconcerting, and I get a feeling for what Cardino means with his talk of being tricked by doll's house doors. To sit in one room, so thoroughly encased by images of another room - imaginary, and now lost - is disorientating. It is perhaps an indication of how disorienting that I do not immediately notice the room contains a doll's house of its own.

Cardino is quick to point out, it isn't a doll's house.

"A doll's house is a miniature house, designed to showcase miniature furnishings and figures. Or simply a toy. What that is, is an architectural model of a doll's house, in 1:1 scale."

---

[58] This is a reference to the 'one room deep' construction of most doll's houses.

At first glance the model simply appears to have the same proportions as 37a. In fact, Cardino has built it using the exacting measurements he took, and drawings he produced, on his trips to the real number 37. To use his words, 'if you were to hang it in the space 37a occupied, it would be an exact fit'. The attention to detail stops there, however. 37a was a doll's house, in as much as it attempted to make a facsimile of a building and incorporated miniature features like door and window frames, skirting boards and stair banisters. What Cardino has built is closer to a set of measurements with form. The model is a largely featureless series of cavities; windows, doors and fireplaces are simple rectangular holes. Walls that in the Fantoccini Street doll's house had been papered and finished with wainscoting and coving, here are flat plains of plywood. Even the staircases are absent, although the number of steps each flight would have had is recorded, in marker pen, on the walls. The rooms are all empty, except the attic room that, like the original 37a, contains a miniature doll's house on a halfmoon table.

The model's exterior is coated with layers of tinfoil. When I ask why, something in the way Cardino says, 'isn't it obvious?' suggests I've hit a sore spot. When she let me in the house Mrs Cardino warned me not to upset her son. I let the question go.

"That structure" He points at the foil coated model, "is two models. One built in 1:1 and the other built in 1:12."

He sees that I'm not following and pulls himself from the office chair he's sitting in. Standing to one side of the model he delivers what amounts to a lecture.

What he talks me through is very obviously something he's ruminated on for much time.

"As you see it here - orientated like the doll's house in the attic of number 37 - this open side represents the front. With this room to the left being the dining room, the one to the right being the kitchen, which of course leaves the stairways in a central position, with the risers facing the front entrance. So, if you walked into this house, you'd walk straight up the

154

stairs, you see?"

Thinking the question is rhetorical I don't immediately answer. It becomes clear I'm expected to respond. I nod.

"That's normal practice with $\boxed{\text{doll's}}$ houses, it increases what designers call play value. Now, if we turn the structure through 90 degrees, so that the right-hand room becomes the front room and the left-hand room becomes the back room, we have the model in the orientation of the full-size number 37. Now, this is where 37a is a different kettle of fish to most $\boxed{\text{doll's}}$ houses, because the depth of 37a was exactly one twelfth the width of the full-size house. And when I say exactly, I mean exactly. The biggest discrepancy I could find between 37 and 37a was less than two cm. A difference that small can be accounted for by expansion or contraction caused by temperature changes. The same is true of all the other dimensions. In this orientation the model is precisely one twelfth the width, depth and height of the full-size house.[59]"

At this point I must confess I found myself lost in Cardino's reasoning, something not helped by his growing enthusiasm for the subject. His measured and assured delivery became a little erratic. What follows is a verbatim transcript of the recording I made of the interview[60].

---

[59] This is the strongest evidence that the original $\boxed{\text{doll's}}$ house was built specifically to represent the real 37 Fantoccini Street. Although, it gives no us clue to who by and why.

[60] As with all the recordings I made during my study of the incidents at number 37, I obtained permission to do so. Having gained permission to record my interviews/discussions I would always offer

155

"The thing is, although all the external, encompassing dimensions, match up and tally, the interior ones have been altered. This had to be done to keep within the normal conventions of doll's housing. This means the stairways and landings run front to back in 37a, in doll's house orientation. But, if you maintained that orientation in the full size 37, they'd have run side to side. Now, obviously that means anyone entering the full-sized house would climb the stairway at 90 degrees to the doll's orientation. Of course, that's only true of the first stairway. On the second flight of stairs, our visitor would have compounded the effect, so now they'd be at 180 degrees to the full-size house.

"Now, there were three steps less on the second flight than the first, this is where it gets complicated. Assuming the subtraction of three from the height of the climb is significant, it seems safe to subtract three, or one of its factors, from the overall figure of 180 which leaves only 177. Obviously that number is meaningless. It's as close to a random number as you can get, given the mathematical processes needed to get there. That stumped me for a while but then it struck me; going up a flight of stairs isn't done in isolation. You go up the stairs, but at some point, you come down again. I got stuck again at that thought because if you took away three when going up the stairs, wouldn't the act of coming down require you to put three back on, leaving you were you started? That

---

the interviewee a copy of the recording. This offer was usually accepted, the exceptions being John Pelton, who made his own recordings, and Gerald Cardino. When I offered to send him a copy of my tape, he tapped his wristwatch and said, 'no need'. Like his model of 37/37a, his watch was covered with foil.

seemed completely logical for a long time, but then I had an epiphany. You enter the house, enter it on the doll's house orientation, okay? You've gone through 90 degrees just to get on the stairs, then 90, less the three steps. Agreed? But what have you done aside from turning 180 degrees, less the three steps? It's obvious really, you've made two physical turns, two turns to get to the top and you'll make another two turns to get back down the stairs. At first glance logic dictates ignoring those turns; two up, two down and you're back where you started. Except ... you're not, because you'll be facing the other way. You'll have moved physically through 180 degrees. You might be back at the location you started from, but you're not seeing where you started, you're seeing, and interacting, with something totally different.

"Okay, maths time again, 180 minus 3 is 177, but these three lost steps that reduce the height on the way up, when added back again, on coming down, reduce depth. In effect, you'd still be three steps from the bottom when you stopped descending. Now clearly, that wasn't happening, I went up and down the stairs of the full size 37 dozens of times and always, every single time, always, always, always ended up on the ground floor. Those steps, coming down, must have been absent. So, from 177 take another 3. 174, which is still a number of no significance but now, take away the physical side of this equation, take away the 180 degrees that our visitor turned through when going up and down the stairs. Minus six, right?[61]

---

[61] This wasn't a rhetorical question. Although I nodded, by that point the numbers were coming at me too fast to deal with. I remember, in fact can see in my mind's eye as I write this, Gerald nodding along with me, smiling widely. Excited and delighted. Whether at his own calculations

157

"Minus six. Now don't get side-tracked by that, of itself it's not significant. But ... but when you put it in the context of doll's house orientation and account for those .... those f__king stairs, well, well it gets very strange. So, there we are, standing back at the bottom of the stairs, stairs are behind us now and we're thinking everything's back to front but that's normal, 'cos we've turned 180 degrees. Only we've got it wrong. I got it wrong, all the times on those f__king stairs I got it wrong, standing there like a fool thinking I'd just done a 180, when in truth, in reality, when you factor in doll's orientation, I'd actually gone minus six degrees. But to get there I've done two separate journeys. One up, one down. And this was another point I was stuck on until it came to me, those missing three steps where did they go?"

I remember clearly, at this point, Cardino nodding slowly at me, as if confirming I was right, although I'd said nothing and knew nothing about where the lecture was heading.

"Minus six steps, six under, six down. I'd suspected right from the start those missing steps were there all along, right under our feet."

Listening back to the recording I made that day, is a slightly uncomfortable task. At this point the only sound on the tape is Cardino's rapid breathing. I recall him staring at me, waiting for an indication that I understood the significance of what he'd just said. I asked if he was talking about a cellar. I'll be honest, I was relieved when he smiled.

"Not one that we knew of, but, of course, we weren't looking at that point, but now ... "

He pointed to the base of the foil wrapped model. Like the doll's house in Fantoccini street, his model stood on a

_____

or at having someone to share them with, I
couldn't say.

wooden base approximately 15cm high. Featureless in both reality and in his reproduction, the base seems to represent nothing. But, looking at it then for the first time, it struck me that its proportions, if in the same scale as the model, would have been the equivalent of a low-ceilinged cellar.

"... now we know it was there. And if the full-size house had one, and it was hidden, then so did 37a. But the real point is this: three missing steps above three steps below. Six. Six steps taken by one person. One plus six, seven. To get to seven that one person goes up then down, two journeys. One plus two, three. Three before the seven, 37."

Having pulled his calculations together to reach 37, Cardino's energy deserted him, and he sat down again. Listlessly he gestured at a section of wall beside him. This was one of the few spots not covered with pictures of the doll's house. On the wall, the number 37 had been written repeatedly.

"It always came back to 37. Back to the start point. Like those f__king stairs, up and down and round and round remember? Up to the left down to the right, two twisting lines like DNA. Only not like the DNA of living things, of life. Those two strands, 37 and 37a, they were the opposite, cos' once you'd been up than down, you'd be facing the opposite way, you see? Between them, those two houses were the DNA of f__king death."

Chapter Fourteen: Pastoral Care

"They shouldn't have let him go back to the house again. Not after the first time."

John Pelton falls silent. While this isn't unusual during our interviews, on this occasion it feels different. He isn't drunk but has been drinking during this session. When the subject matter turned to the second trip, the new people who attended, and inevitably to Gerald Cardino's measurements and calculations, Pelton's demeanour changes. The silences now are introverted rather than hostile.

"I tried to speak to Steve about it, but he didn't really listen to me. When I tried to go over his head and went straight to the board of governors I just came across as spiteful. I feel guilty about Jed, if I'm honest. I mean I did try, but the fact I'd been so confrontational with everyone weaken my position, I guess. I looked like I was stirring up trouble, not trying to stop someone getting hurt."

"When did you realise something bad was going on with Jed?"

"A couple of days in. Of course, with hindsight, it was obvious from the off, but I had that stupid row going with Steve about that doll he thought I'd nicked. Me and him were both fuming. I think Jed could have turned up dressed as a clown riding a unicycle and we wouldn't have noticed. But now ... hindsight. Jed was heading toward manic from the moment he landed. He must have gone up and down those stairs twenty or thirty times. I can remember that evening, when the three of us were eating dinner in the caravan, he stank to high heaven, he'd been sweating like a pig all day. Me and Steve weren't saying much, we were both sulking like a pair of kids and Jed was rabbiting away 19 to the dozen. If I thought about it at all I guess I thought he was chattering to cover the silence. You know the how people do, they get caught up in someone else's argument and talk out of embarrassment. But I don't think it was that at all. He was hyped up about finding the flights of stairs didn't match. I remember Steve asking him if that was unusual in houses of that age. I don't remember the answer, but I know it went on for a long time and the crux of it was Jed just reiterating that he'd checked, checked and triple checked the results and there was an anomaly. He kept coming back to that word, anomaly.

"I slept in the house that night. Partly I wanted to get away from Steve, but mostly I wanted to get away from Jed's chatter, and his BO. That got worse through the week. The washing facilities were a bit better on that trip. The caravan had a water bladder that we could fill from the house and heat up with the genny, so we could freshen up a bit. And there was a fitness centre nearby that agreed to let us use their showers, so long as we didn't take the p__s about it. Jed didn't bother, said he didn't have time, he had his measurements.

"When he wasn't measuring things he was scribbling these long lists and calculations in a ring binder. The next day Steve went off in the minibus to collect May and Crossland. I was still setting the recording gear out. I'm guessing here of course, but I have a feeling Steve might have told Jed not to leave me alone with the doll's house. The second Steve took off in the minibus, Jed run up the three flights of stairs like his life depended on it. Later that morning, when I'd worked my way up to the attic, he was all over the doll's house. He had about a dozen rulers and tape measures scattered around the thing and was tying lengths of string to it, measuring the angles they formed with a protractor.

I could hear him talking to himself when I was on the landing but when I opened the door he stopped. I didn't think anything of it really, I'll think out loud when I'm alone, a lot of people do, and you stop if you know someone's listening. But by then I'd already wired up the attic room with a sensor to trigger a recording device. I figured Jed would have triggered it. It wasn't a problem; testing the systems was part of the plan for the day anyway. The recorders were set up in the next room so they'd be well away from the mics that were feeding them and whatever the source of any noise might be.

"I went into the next room, that little kitchenette thing, and saw all three recorders had triggered[62]. The reel-to-reel tape was almost at the end of its run, which I sort of expected, with Jed moving around in the room the sensors would have picked up the sounds and triggered regularly. But when I looked at the timer, I saw the recording had triggered just once. Recording was continuous.

---

[62] I later asked why there were 3 recording devices. The first one, which was to be used as the primary source of 'evidential recordings', was an omni directional mic feeding a reel-to-reel machine, loaded with 1" tape with a potential recording time of 60 minutes. The second was a backup machine used to provide an analogue copy in the event of primary equipment failure. These recording were made on a basic cassette deck. The last recording was digital. This was added because of its robustness and almost limitless recording time, it was made on a multi-track Tascam device. All three Machines would be triggered any of the four sensors placed at various points around the attic room. Once started all the devices would begin recording only stopping when the sensors registered two minutes of continuous silence. The exact time the recordings started was monitored by a mechanical timer, fitted to the reel-to-reel recorder, and a digital recorder that was part of the Tascam's software.

"When I played it back, the first thing I heard was the door of the attic room opening and Jed's footsteps. Then he started muttering numbers and measurements to himself. I skipped the tape forward a few minutes and got just the same, more numbers more measurements. I didn't listen to the whole tape, but I skipped through it in four or five minute steps. and has far as I could tell it was the same all the way through. Jed had been in the room over and hour, measuring and calculating and counting and never doing it silently."

I ask what became of the recordings. The analogue tapes were discarded and the digital one was deleted. It's a shame. I'd have liked to have heard them and compared them to the lecture Jed would later deliver to me.

"I won't lie, I didn't really get on with John."

We are in Carol Crossland's kitchen, which is a grandiose space that wouldn't look out of place in a manor house. It appears too large for the single bedroom flat it serves, but its size is a product of necessity. It doubles as on office and studio.

The sumptuous marble island unit were sitting at is home to a selection of cooking utensils, mixing bowls and a collection of exotic ingredients - all of which are completely alien to my untutored eye. It also houses an impressive desk top PC and a pair of video cameras.

We're talking between classes and Crossland has one eye on the clock. She'll be streaming live in fifteen minutes. Her live shows, available to subscribers, provide a steady income, but it's a demanding way to make a living. When not streaming live she is usually producing new videos for her YouTube channel, taking private consultations or updating her product range. The appellation 'new age' often has connotations of vapid, ethereal beings, floating gently through blessed lives. For some its stress-free image hides an iron-hard work ethic and rigorous professional practice.

"I don't have any problem with sceptical enquiry, none at all, but John wasn't a sceptic, he was a cynic. Cynics are a different thing, different mindset. The sceptic says, show me the evidence, a cynic just waves it away. Of course Jed was damaged, traumatised even. I did my best to get him some form of compensation from London North, I argued that their duty of care was breached. I spent a lot of time with his parents, going around different doctors, trying to get his PTSD[63] diagnosed. It was always the same story, instead of help and acknowledgement of what he'd been through he'd get a label: *paranoid schizophrenic*. A label and a box of pills, of course.

"John likes to think he was the only one who knew something bad was happening with Jed, but we all saw it. I'd go so far as to say we, myself, May and Steve saw what was happening with far more clarity than John could ever hope for. I could tell from the moment Jed set foot in the house that he was more connected to whatever was there than either myself or May."

"I don't think Jed necessarily had psychic gifts, as lay people like to call them, but something about him certainly drew that house to him. At the time I thought it might have been something to do with his abnormally low Zener card scores. Particularly when he started talking about the way the doll's house was laid out; at odds to the real house. The word he used first was inverted, though later he started talking about things being twisted. But the inverted thing chimed with me, I wondered if he had a psychic sensitivity that was somehow 'inverted' from the normal way. Something that made him instantly compatible with the house, well houses if you count 37 and 37a as a working couple. That's certainly what Jed's findings pointed to. But, the last time I saw him, and that was over a year ago, I was more inclined to give May's theory some credence.

"When we got back the recordings John had made with all his toys and they were all blank, I said, whatever is in that

---

63 Post Traumatic Stress Disorder.

house doesn't want to be recorded. May pointed out that Jed's measurements were a type of recording, and, unlike sound recordings, measurements are taken. they're aggressive if you like, where a sound recording is passive. I think the houses saw Jed as a threat and dealt with him accordingly."

"Me and May ended up sort of looking after Jed in the end," John Pelton tells me. "I didn't think of it that way at the time, I was trying to stop him running around the house and setting off all the sensors. I'd finally got May to understand that, without some kind of control over who was where, the tapes would be worthless. So she stopped rushing towards every click or crack she herd. I think part of it was her bad hip, she was on a waiting list for a new one, and I think she had to give a bit of thought about bolting up and down stairs. But if we didn't keep Jed busy, or at least talking, he'd start on the measuring thing again and it was impossible to know where he'd end up. He kept finding things that brought him back to the number 37, the number of the house, obviously. He'd get very excited when he found another example of the house adding up to 37. That was how he put it; *the house keeps adding up to 37*. Of course, it wasn't the number 37 coming up time and time again, it was just him playing with figures. If he ended up with a figure that wasn't 37 he switched units, convert metric to imperial or vice versa, whatever got him close enough to declare he'd found the magic number.

"What really made me see he wasn't nailed together right was the thing with the window in the kitchen. He spent all morning measuring it and jotting down figures, but he couldn't find a 37 in there. Steve, May and Crossland were doing something in the attic, don't ask me what. Anyway, Jed suddenly shouts out, 'yes', like he's just got all six numbers on the lottery. I jumped about a foot in the air. Then he started getting excited and calling me to come and see.

"He'd found a fly trapped in a spider's web. The husk, you know, the shell left behind after the spider's sucked it dry. Jed was staring at it, excited but beginning to look scared. I was a

165

bit short with him to be honest, to be blunt about it he was getting in the way. I'd thought someone with a bit of savvy on the team might make the whole thing more bearable. Turned out he was more fanatical about the house than the brown rice and sandals brigade in the attic.

"I said, 'Dead fly'. He tells me to watch, and pulls out a reel of cotton. Did I mention the cotton? He'd pin or tie cotton lines all over the place, use them as illustrations of angles, sizes and so on. He'd already started on the window and now he put the fly into the equation. He showed me that if you compared the distance from the corner to the fly, to the distance from the frame, and on and on and on. He divided and subtracted and did whatever he could and finally, managed to show the fly had died exactly 37 something or other from the angle formed between the ceiling and the back wall. Then he fixed a cotton line between the fly and the floor where they found the body of Mrs Doll. Guess what the angle was?"

"37," I say. I must sound impressed because Pelton sneers.

"Of course, 37. The area of the floor you could designate the 'death spot' was pretty big. Add in the equivalent area that the doll was supposed to have covered, and you could put a line from the window to almost anywhere you fancied. It meant nothing, but Jed acted like he'd found the holy grail. Poor bastard was totally gone.

"On the day we left he was helping me pack the tape decks into my car. I'd spoken with May about getting out of the house the previous evening, we were both worried that it might be a struggle. By the end of the week, he'd practically stopped sleeping, he be prowling around the house most of the night. I joked that he was channelling the spirit of Ed, because he'd taken on the mantel of ruining my tapes. I ended up with whole tapes of him scampering around muttering figures to himself, all of it worthless of course. In the end we decided the best thing to do was to get him to load his measuring gear first and then blockade it with all the camping stuff, so he wouldn't be able to get it easily. We had visions of him constantly grabbing pieces of kit so he could track down another 37.

"It took a long time to get him to put his stuff in the back of the minibus but when we did, he seemed to calm down a bit. Then when we were putting one of my mixers away, he froze and stared at the numberplate on my car. Perhaps there is something in all this psychic c__p; I knew what was about to happen. He shoved the box he was holding into my hands and started running around the cars. We just had to leave him to it in the end. By the time we left he'd made this great long calculation that showed all our cars, and the Landy he'd borrowed to tow the caravan, had numberplates that 'added up to' 37. Provided you played with the numbers enough. Unpicked the code was the term I think he used. It was total c__p of course, the routes he was going through to arrive at 37 were arbitrary, none of them made a scrap of sense but he convinced himself that there was some meaning to it. The stupid thing is the others believed him.

"That was when I washed my hands of it. If they wanted to play ghost hunt and waste their time, they were welcome, but I thought it was getting dangerous. Encouraging Jed's delusions was insane. Even May, who was genuinely worried about him, was agreeing with him about the c__p with the numberplates."

"It was scary, what happened to Jed. Of course, by the end of it he was damaged. I'm still in touch with his mother so I know the condition he's in. The fact his mind shattered, that doesn't mean he was wrong. Those calculations he made were always correct and his knowledge of maths was amazing. When he calculated the numberplates on the cars; connecting them all, he found at least a dozen 37s. The one that really amazed me was when he pointed out the first numbers on the plates, were one, six and three. I didn't get, it but without needing to look it up he knew 163 was a prime number. It's the 37th prime number. Call him mad if you want, but imagine being able to carry information like that around in your head.[64]

"It's the old story; cynics point out a single fact that suits their narrative and use it to disparage everything. Yes, I'll agree Jed's mental health suffered and maybe his connection to what we call reality is tenuous - the business with the tin foil - but that doesn't mean everything he's ever said or done can just be disregarded. Look at all the measurements he took, hundreds, possibly thousands, he measured and counted everything. By the end of that first trip, he had actually calculated how many floorboards were in that house. He showed me the record he'd kept and this page of equations, comparing the differing numbers of boards between each room, between each floor, the number of cut versus uncut boards, the number of nails in the boards. I don't remember the figures of course and even when I was looking at them, I didn't have the maths to follow them, but he had a series of ratios that proved even the number of floorboards in that house were designed to contain 37. The obsessive nature needed to gather that information and calculate its relevance isn't 'normal', but with that house, we weren't dealing with the 'norm'. I'm sorry, it's hard for me to talk about this sometimes. Excuse me."

Crossland uses a sheet of kitchen roll to wipe her eyes. To save embarrassment I look away. A framed photograph catches my eye. On a shelf, nesting among a miniature forest of fresh herbs, is a picture of a shuttered house. The plywood boarding covering the downstair window had been crudely sprayed with the number 37.

At the time I interviewed Steven Ward I had no idea what had happened to Jed. My assumption that it would be best to interview Steve first was based on the fact that he had attended, and overseen, all three trips and would therefore give the most comprehensive picture. Mabel Noakes also

---

[64] 163 is in fact the 38th prime number.

attended all the fieldtrips, but the relentless march of her Alzheimer's put her recollections beyond reach.

The problem of course was Ward's proviso that the interview was a one off. Initially he had been willing to field further questions in the form of email exchanges. However, as my inquiries into the events at Fantoccini Street deepened my frequent emails began to try his patience. In January 2017 I received an email politely, but firmly, requesting I stop contacting him. I exchanged two more emails with him after this point. The first was a reply thanking him for his co-operation and patience up until that point and assuring him that I would respect his wishes to be left alone. Unfortunately, I had to back track on this assurance less than three weeks later.

Following my discussions with John Pelton and Carol Crossland, regarding the mental state of Gerald Cardino, I contacted Ward again. I asked him if he wished to comment on London North University's decision, the following year, to let Jed to return to Fantoccini Street. I received the following response, and my subsequent emails were blocked.

Dear Mr Croix,

Your insinuation that London North University, or I personally, bear any responsibility for the unfortunate mental breakdown of Mr Cardino, is unfounded and frankly insulting.

Every attempt was made to support and assist Mr Cardino. The Student Welfare Dept made every effort to assist him towards the completion of his education/course.

I have already asked that you end communication with me and respect my wishes to put the incidents of Fantoccini Street behind me. As you are unwilling to comply with that polite request, I will now state flatly that I am ceasing all communication with you.

S. Ward

Chapter Fifteen: The 2nd Session Tape

The video footage of the second use of a Ouija board is far more sophisticated than the first. Steven Ward was determined not to make the same mistakes again. Four simultaneous recordings were made of the event, two using VHS tape and two using digital equipment. The decision to use digital recorders was a purely financial one. Video tape equipment of a sufficiently high resolution was prohibitively expensive, so a compromise was reached. The most important angles would be recorded to tape with records from secondary positions being made digitally.

The second attempt to make contact took place on the third day; Wednesday, 10th August, at 8:29 p.m. it had been agreed in advance that a Ouija board would be utilised during the second fieldtrip and a portion of the budget was spent on a flatpack table and chair. Flatpack items were decided on for ease of transportation, both to the sight and between floors once there.

The intention was that four of the team would attend the Ouija board while the fifth witnessed and took notes. Originally John Pelton was designated to observe. He had little enthusiasm for a repeat of the previous Ouija board incident. He had repeatedly dismissed the first Ouija session as a waste of time, claiming the first movement of the planchette had been his doing, and the tilting of the table had been greatly exaggerated. Although he could provide no explanation for the later movements of the planchette nor the claims of the other witnesses that it was seen to levitate. Maintaining that the table in the dining room was unstable and the tilting could have been achieved by someone – by intention or chance - leaning on it, Pelton took charge of selecting the table for use with the Ouija board. He selected a square, four-legged item. The tabletop measured 95cm x 95cm, and the height was 72cm. The four straight-back chairs that Pelton purchased were in the same style as the table and clearly designed to be used with it. Pelton also had some input into the placement of the cameras.

Late in the evening of the second day, Mable Noakes tentatively raised the subject of Gerald Cardino's active participation at the Ouija board. Issues of his mental state at that point were not being considered, but there was some doubt about his ability to sit calmly long enough to take part in the session.

Carol Crossland always offers a smile before answering my questions. Sometimes her eyes appear a little over bright, but she isn't given to parading the emotional toll of talking about Fantoccini Street. When I ask her about the Ouija board session in the attic, the smile falters.

"At first I thought we were wasting our time. Once it had been decided John would be at the table, I lost my enthusiasm for the idea. I'd seen the video of the first sitting and it was terrifying. Amazing, but terrifying. Something had happened, some power had been released. Possibly a malevolent power. And that was in the dining room, May was adamant that Viola had contacted the Doll twins. May and Viola both agreed that the dining and attic rooms were active, psychically active. Hot spots if you like. Worryingly, they both agreed the presence in the dining room was the more benign. There had been a lot of speculation that, if the presence in the dining room was the twins, then the presence in the attic was probably Kenneth.

"Viola and May called him the father, but I can't think of him as anything other than the murderer. That's what made the prospect of working in the attic frightening. But, and I'm ashamed to say this, it was also exciting. Like going on an adventure. I know, that sounds horrible and childish. In my defence, I was younger than.

"Watching the tape of the first sitting, the thing that stuck with me was Viola asking if the presence was Patsy or Ann.

The way the planchette jumped to 'yes' and then 'no'. I talked with May about that. Her impression was of something trapped, the feeling that whoever, or whatever, they'd reached was trapped. May was convinced that was why the table tilted. It doesn't show up on the video very clearly, but she told me, the way the table moved was very sudden. Not so much tilting, more rearing up. It was like an animal, trying to bolt for the door. She felt very strongly that the twins were trapped in that house, maybe even in that room.

"That's why we moved the sitting to the attic room. If the presences in the house were specific to the rooms where they passed, May thought we had a chance to contact Kenneth Doll. May had always said that, for her, the strongest presence was the one in the attic. She also said the feeling she picked up was of something brutal. I had the same feeling. The kitchen and dining room triggered very little for me, almost nothing, but the attic room was … something else again.

"It's hard to explain the feeling because it doesn't come to me through my eyes and ears. Though, sometimes, I'll pick up a lingering smell that no one else gets. Strangely, it's always the same smell, a metallic tang, like when you leave a pan on the heat too long. The attic room stank of damp and mould and mice, but that hot metal smell was there too. But that was the least of it, the feeling of something … something else in that room was huge. Huge is the best way I can describe it. Huge and I guess … roiling. Walking into that room was walking into a storm of utter despair, violent despair, lashing out. The moment the door opened I felt it, and I knew, without a shadow of doubt that it was Kenneth Doll in there.

"May's a far better person than I'll ever be, because she felt it too and she talked about the pain the presence was in. She wanted to help it. For my part, I wanted to destroy it. We couldn't of course. I often wonder where that force is now, now the house is gone."

I ask if she thinks the house was containing the presence. Until then the impression I was under was that she and Gerald Cardino believed that the house, or possibly the doll's house,

172

were somehow generating the malevolence that occurred on the sight.

Crossland gives the question some thought before answering.

"I'm not entirely sure. Part of me hopes all that passed there was because of that bizarre building with all the odd numbers Jed discovered. but I can't be sure. Jed was convinced it was the convergence of the two structures. I found that hard to believe when he first mentioned it. He was talking almost constantly by the end of the trip and, if I'm honest, listening to him was exhausting. A lot of what he was saying went over my head, because I don't have the maths. But the convergence idea was something he'd talked about from the start, when he'd been calmer.

"He described it as 37 and 37a being parts of a puzzle, or a machine. One of the first things he did was measure the doll's house and compare it with the actual house. Once he saw how precisely the doll's house matched the real one, he was adamant about it. Strangely, it was remembering one of John's nasty comments that brought me round to the idea.

"I'd been warned that John was a cynic and to expect him to dismiss anything that didn't fit his petty, little world view. It wasn't something I was worried about; when you're tuned into something beyond most people's reach you learn to accept that many simply can't comprehend things outside their own realm. The way I describe it, the way most people experience the world, is like watching television on a radio. May and I were watching a kaleidoscope on a 62" flat screen TV. John was listening to someone on a radio describing the colours. I think, at some level, he knew that. I don't like the word jealous, but I'd struggle to find another one.

"He was always ready to make a disparaging remark, failing that he'd roll his eyes, whenever someone reported something. When May and I first arrived, we both walked the house. Tuning in you could call it. We agreed, there was a strong presence at the foot of the stairs, just as you entered the house. That was strange; there was no reason for there to be. None of the bodies had been found there[65]. Steve was with us, he had some hi-tech thermometer[66] and was taking readings with it. He reported there was a temperature difference of four and a half degrees between the ambient temperature at the foot of the stairs and at the back of the hallway. That's a significant change over such a small area. While he was showing us the reading on the thermometer, John made a point of closing the front door, hard. Then, because we'd jumped and were all looking at him, he paused and said, 'just keeping the drafts out'. Thing was, it was mid-August. It wasn't cold.

"We did the rest of the house, and there were more ups and downs in the temperature. Most of them happened deep in the house when we were miles from the front door. John wasn't there for any of those though, he was setting up his collection of toys. The only time we saw him again was as we went into the attic room, he was checking connections, or so he said. Maybe because he was there Steve was being very particular about getting the thermometer readings right. He waited almost a full minute letting the reading settle before he open the door to the attic."

"May and I both gasped. The force of the presence in that room bursting out … Steve didn't tell us what the temperature did at that point, but I felt like I'd just jumped in cold water. I spoke with May about it later and she agreed, the effect had been … well, chilling. That feeling of cold passed very quickly but the wash of emotions that pulsed from that doorway stayed. Neither May nor I spoke for a while. I became aware that Steve and John were both looking at us. Steve was staring

---

[65] At this point Carol Crossland was unaware that the body of Phoebe Reese, possibly the owner, or even builder, of the doll's house, was found in that spot by Guy Doll in 2001.

[66] This was the pyrometer belonging to Gerald Cardino.

174

in fact, he looked quite shaken. May said, 'It's gotten stronger'. Those were her exact words, I can still hear them today. Her voice sounded so small. I just nodded. Then John said, 'lucky the door was shut, it might have got out sooner.' I can hear his voice too. Totally flat, what's the phrase? Dead pan? I was so angry that he would say something like that, after what had just happened, that I couldn't speak.

"But the thing was, when I came to think about it later, he'd made some kind of sense; it wasn't a physical force we were talking about, like the ambient temp, it was a presence. The door being open or shut shouldn't have made any difference to how May and I felt it. But it did. A layer of wood was somehow holding it back, holding it in check.

"I didn't make that connection until later, until it was too late. I like to think I'd have spotted it if John's stupid comment hadn't got me so angry. But I didn't. It struck me when I was visiting Jed, this was the year after the house was earmarked for demolition and the council had shuttered it all away. He was having one of his up days. I'd been trying to keep the talk away from the house and the maths, but it would always creep in somehow. We got to talking about the doll's house. Jed had been reading up on doll's houses because he was going to try and remake 37a. He was puzzled about the doors in the toy house, all the books and articles he read about making doll's houses, said not to include internal doors, but whoever had made the one in the attic had put them in. What puzzled Jed was that they were all fixed in place. They didn't open and close, they were all fixed in an open position. If there was any kind of presence 'in' the doll's house, then it had been given free reign.

"I did mention the idea to Jed, and he didn't look even remotely surprised. I think he'd already worked it out. He just nodded and went to fetch one of his files (see appendix 2)[67].

---

[67] Again, the referenced appendix isn't available. According to Mr Croix's notes,

He'd measured the doors of course, on the model and the real house. I couldn't follow the math, but every dimension on them, even the thickness of them and the positioning of the knobs would circle back to 37."

The filming of the 2nd Ouija board session, by chance, provides one of the few clear views of the frontage piece of 37a. Having prepared the cameras and lighting, to film the use of the board, Steven Ward made a brief video showing the equipment before the four participants sat at the table. The film is five minutes in length and details the equipment and names the participants. Filmed using a handheld camera, the video is, in contrast with most material recorded by both him and John Pelton, indistinct and shaky. The opening of the film proper is of the table with the Ouija board resting on top of it. The lens swings around the empty chairs and around the room, describing a full circle. This circle takes approximately ten seconds to complete. It ends back where it starts, which happens to be on a hanging flap of lining paper that has come unstuck from the angled ceiling. Behind the flap can just be seen the bottom corner of the doll's house frontage. The picture wavers as Ward reaches forward and lifts the flap out of shot, revealing the frontage in full.

The frontage is made from two pieces of what appear to be plywood. It is a matter of record that the body of the doll's house was made of plywood, so it is safe to assume the frontage would have been too. The two pieces have been nailed to the sloping wall/ceiling of the attic room. The image is not clear enough to make out a great amount of detail, but the sections appear to have been papered with scale brick effect paper which is a normal technique amongst doll's house builders. In contrast to the frontage of the number 37, the miniature has five separate windows, two on ground and first

Jerald Cardino's files consisted mainly of comprehensive lists of measurements. (R.D)

176

floors and a single one for the attic space. Each of these windows is blank, this maybe to give the impression of drawn curtains, the quality of the image is not sufficient to be certain. Strangely, given the quality and detailing evident on the rest of the model there is no representation of a front door. Where the door should be, given the layout of the model's interior, there is a blank area of brick effect paper. The only acknowledgment that it should contain a door, is the number 37, crudely applied with white paint.

Just before the flap of paper is release, obscuring the frontage once again, a voice off camera, possibly John Pelton's, is heard to say,

"There's something else for Jed to measure."

What has come to be known as the 2nd Session Tape, is an edited conglomeration of the footage taken from all four cameras. The four separate films made of the second Ouija board session have all been retained in their original form. The two analogue recording have been copied in digital format for ease of editing. The editing was carried out by Steven Ward with the assistance of Carol Crossland.

The date and time signature of the recording(s) appears along the bottom edge of the picture. A recording time, denoting the duration of filming, appears at the top right-hand corner. These times remain consistent throughout the frequent point of view (POV) changes where the four original tapes have been spliced together. The only discrepancy is found when the recordings taken from camera B, situated in the north-west corner of the room, are used. The digits from this camera appear as pale blue, whereas, in the other three recordings they are white[68].

---

[68] Mr Croix seems unaware that the two analogue cameras would not generate an on-screen time signature. At least in the case of the analogue cameras, time and duration

The edited recording starts with the participants already seated at the table. Starting with Steven Ward they each identify themselves. After this Ward states the address of the house, and the location of the room they are seated in. After giving a date and time check, both of which correspond to the figures on the screen, he gestures towards Carol Crossland and says,

"If everyone's ready ... Miss Crossland, would you like to start?"

Until this point the recording has been obtained from camera C, it is situated at the east wall of the room and gives a view of all four people although the angle does not give a clear view of Crossland's face. Now, the editing of the tape gives the POV from camera B, this allows a clear three quarter's view of Crossland as she takes control of the session.

Crossland does not appear nervous, but she is conscious of the camera. She clears her throat,

"Before we start, I'd just like it to be noted that the Ouija board we're using today is the same one as used in the previous visit to this house. It belonged to Viola Mezco, but she threw it away shortly before she took a leave of absence. I took the liberty of retrieving it. The planchette is my own."

This is a revelation to the other members of the team. Mabel Noakes gives a yelp of surprise. At this point the camera changes, briefly, back to C. From this camera it is possible to see John Pelton roll his eyes. Clearly, the tension between him and the rest of the team is not resolved.

POV returns to Crossland, as the session begins. She glances around at everyone,

---

markers must have been produced during editing. (R.D)

"Let's begin. Everyone, place a hand on the planchette. Your non-dominant one please."

Although it is not seen in detail during the recording, the planchette was later photographed. Unlike the wooden item used by Mezco, made specifically for the task, Crossland's planchette is a Victorian drinking glass.

The four people at the table each place their left-hand on the glass, there follows a period of shuffling as they adjust their positions.

The POV changes again, this time to camera A. Camera A films from the northwest and is significantly closer to the table than the other cameras. It gives a clear view of the Ouija board. All four hands are resting on the bottom of the up-turned glass. Crossland asks that people place only their fingertips on the planchette. Ward is seen to adjust his hand.

POV changes again to Crossland who closes her eyes, her breathing slows and deepens. She asks,

"Is someone here?"

After thirty seconds she repeats the question. After a further 30 seconds the glass twitches. The duration reading, from the time the recording started is 10 minutes 37 seconds.

Without opening her eyes, Crossland says,

"Okay, can we concentrate please. Who's there?"

For the next five minutes nothing happens. A POV from camera C is maintained for most of this but on three occasions views are changed so the clearest view is of Pelton. On each of these changes he is looking around at the others. His expression is one of exasperation. On the last of these occasions when the POV switches back to camera C, the colour saturation of the image has changed. Crossland's face is still clear and focused, but the colour has largely drained from it. The background, by contrast, has darkened. The impression is off the wall behind her moving deeper into the background.

The scene remains fixed until the 17 minutes 14 seconds point when the POV changes to camera D. This is one of the only two occasions the footage from this camera in used in the edited tape. The view from camera D is the only one to include the doll's house, that is situated behind Ward[69]. At 17 minutes 51 seconds something in the attic room of the doll's house moves.

The doll's house has been thrown largely into shadow by the efforts to illuminate the table, board and participants. All that can be seen in the film is a small shape moving toward the open frontage of the doll's house. Pausing the recording and using the zoom function adds no more clarity and only produces a larger image of something that cannot be identified.

The visible movement lasts less than three seconds. At the culmination of this short sequence the POV changes to a view from camera B, this shot includes the faces of Pelton and Noakes. Pelton who has the doll's house on the periphery of his vision, gives no indication that he is aware of the movement. Noakes, who sits opposite Ward and has the clearest view of the doll's house, is obviously distressed. Wide eyed she stares at the attic room of the doll's house. The view returns to Crossland. She still has her eyes closed.

Throughout these scene changes the disruption to the colour quality on the recording from camera C continues. Crossland's image is still pale while the background darkens. She repeats,

"Is somebody there?"

---

[69] This detail of the seating arrangement conflicts with that shown in the sketch reportedly produced by Carol Crossland (See Fig,i). (R.D)

On the table the glass jerks onto the 'yes'. Crossland's eyes open and she regards the board. Her face is calm but the breath she takes is noticeably deeper.

"Who are you?"

The glass slowly moves down, away from the yes/no, onto the alphabet. It picks out the name 'Edward'.

By this point, the worsening colour saturation renders the area behind Crossland as a field of dense black. The high points of colour, formed by the faces around the table, are now white splashes of brightness. At 18 minutes and 19 seconds the image of the glass becomes a spark of intense white light. This lasts for four seconds after which the screen turns black. The pale-blue figures of the duration and timekeepers are unaffected and continue to count off the minutes and seconds of darkness.

At 18 minutes and 28 sec the POV switches to camera B. We see Ward and Noakes in this shot, although the clearest view is of the table and board. Ward is looking at the glass that is in motion again. His expression is calm but concentrated. Noakes is not looking at the board, her eyes remain fixed on the doll's house. The glass, after a series of jerking movements, comes to rest. It is resting over the letter H. The glass moves again. The POV changes to camera A, we see Crossland glance towards Noakes, then at the board. She says,

"E."

The POV changes back to camera B. Noakes is still fixated on the doll's house. Ward and Pelton are both looking at her. Only Crossland is watching the board, as the glass moves again. She says,

"L."

The glass jerks again.

181

"P."

She takes her hand away from the glass and sits back in her chair. She has her hand to her mouth but continues watching the board. The glass moves again.

At this point, 19 minutes 5 seconds, the image from camera B turns from colour to black and white. The now monochrome image holds steady for eight seconds then becomes increasingly pixilated. At 20 minutes 19 seconds, the screen turns black. The POV changes to camera A at 20 minutes 29 seconds.

Cameras B and C are not used again in the film. The faults in them remain consistent for the duration of filming. At the time the malfunctions were in progress a real time monitor was functioning in the room. On a single screen it showed the feed from all four cameras. At the time of the session no one was watching it.

The soundtrack of the session is maintained throughout. While the screen is blank, for the ten seconds between camera B failing and the POV switching to camera A, Crossland says,

"M – E."

Vision returns just as she announces,

"Help me."

Ward and Pelton both look up sharply at the words.

"At first I thought she was calling for help; help *me*. I hadn't been paying any attention to the glass, it took me a second to realise she was reading what had been spelled out. I think Steve thought much the same, we'd both been watching May. I was half wondering if she was having a stroke. It wasn't her usual awe-struck routine."

I ask John Pelton what he means by that.

"Look, I'm not slating her, alright? She was a lovely woman, caring, considerate all that and she was smart too, in her way. But the thing is, like all the true believers, she'd spent her life clinging onto this belief that somewhere, out there, just beyond the vail, is a whole other world of unimaginable wonders. And, like all the other true believers, she'd spent her life desperate to see it. They're all the same, they talk about these great cosmic powers, and all they can show you are a few creaking floorboards.

"It wasn't just May, they were all doing it, Steve, Crossland, Jed. They'd decided, before we went through the door, the place was haunted. Or possessed, or a doorway to another f__king dimension. Fifty times a day May would see signs or find marks that 'couldn't be explained'. If she didn't find anything she'd just tilt her head and proclaim 'I think there's a presence with us'. It not that they made stuff up, but it's like saying to someone, 'don't think about a pink elephant'. Once the idea's there, they can't *not* think about a pink f___ing elephant. May couldn't help seeing supernatural phenomena. But that night in the attic room was something different, she looked genuinely scared, not awe struck.

"No. I don't think she was pretending or faking it. She was totally sincere, always seeing things that she could fit into the idea of another realm. That night in the attic, it looked like something had come to find her.

"There was nothing there. I've seen the tape Steve and Crossland put together; something moves in the doll's house. That's it, something moves, maybe. It might be a trick of the light or a spider. This was on the third night. They spent three days convincing themselves the place was crawling with ghosts and restless spirits, then they break out a Ouija board. Kids telling ghost stories.

"The equipment failures? Equipment fails from time to time, and look, Steve is a top man with video, but – I'm just saying – none of my sound equipment played up. Even after it went flying."

At 20 minutes 56 seconds, the view from camera A shows the four participants sitting motionless at the table. Crossland still has her hand to her mouth. The glass is shaking. Ward nods encouragingly to Crossland, and says,

"You talk to him. Go on."

She reaches out hesitantly but doesn't touch the glass. Instead, she grips the edge of the table.

"Is that you Mr Bartlett?"

The glass slides up and to the right of the board: 'yes'.

"Why are you here?"

This is said by Noakes, who still has her gaze fixed on the doll's house. She waits for seven seconds before repeating the question. The glass begins to move. As before, Crossland takes it upon herself to read out the message.

"D – O – L – L. Doll." [70]

---

[70] On Mr Croix's transcription of the 2nd Session Tape there were several handwritten notes. Most were routine corrections of typos, but this line of dialogue was heavily unscored and had been crossed out and rewritten many times. It appeared to trouble Mr Croix that it was not clear if D-O-L-L was being used as a name or as a reference to a figurine. As far as I can tell, after spending some time trying to decipher his notations, he finally settled on the latter, choosing to encase the word

"*Doll? Is that right?*"

This is said by Noakes, who is now looking at the board. The glass moves. Crossland says,

"*Yes.*"

Noakes is now looking around the room. She asks,

"*What happened to you?*"

Again, the glass spells out the word 'doll'.

At the 22 minutes 28 seconds point, Noakes raises her hand and looks up. Ward begins to speak, possibly addressing her. She shakes her head.

"*Shhh. Listen, can you hear it?*"

The four people at the table sit in stillness. There is total silence for three seconds then a distinct scratching sound can be heard. Crossland draws a sharp breath. The noise stops, then resumes after seven seconds. It is faint at first but steadily grows in volume.

At 22 minutes and 45 seconds a loud metallic crack is heard. Crossland starts screaming and jumps from her chair, moving out of shot. Noakes, Ward and Pelton all stand. Noakes has her hands to her mouth. In the process of standing, Pelton knocks his chair over. As it falls it catches the tripod on which camera A is standing. The camera is jolted from its position. It continues recording but is now facing a section of blank wall.

---

doll to indicate a figurine. I may be
mistaken in this. (R.D)

Someone curses.

POV changes to camera D, the only working camera still focused on the table. The view, however, is obscured by Ward, who has now stood, stepping away from the table. Crossland is still screaming. At 22 minutes and 48 seconds there is a single loud bang followed by a burst of feedback. The sound recording is maintained but the quality of it is different.

Ward moves left of camera. Although mostly obscured there is a point, in the upper right corner of the screen, where Noakes can be seen attempting to calm Crossland. Both women are at the very edge of the frame. Crossland is pressed into the northeast corner of the room. We hear Noakes efforts to calm her.

"Shh, dear, shh. It's gone now, it's gone."

Ward moves around the table, allowing the camera a clear view. We see him and Noakes leading Crossland out of the room. All of them appear fearful. We hear footsteps and a door opening as, out of shot, the three people leave the room.

On the screen we see the abandoned table and Ouija board. Pelton is picking up the omnidirectional microphone that is now laying on top of the Ouija board. There is a muffled scraping sound, and the audio recording ends. Pelton leaves the shot, carrying the mic.

The 2nd session tape ends at 21 minutes 16 seconds.

Chapter Sixteen: Rat, Squirrel, Thing?

"Steve had his back to it, so he didn't see what happened. The first he knew of it was when the mic landed on the table. I think it actually hit him, but it was fairly light, the pole thing it was hanging from I mean. May wasn't in a good place to see it, she might have seen it out of the corner of her eye, that's probably why she thought it was just a rat.

"I was the only one who saw it properly. It was just like nothing on earth. And it was too big to be a rat, far too big. So, there's no way it could have got out of that room. The door was closed."

"I didn't see it. I mean I didn't see what happened. I had my back to the corner where the mic stand was set up and I was looking up, not behind me."

After watching the 2nd Session Tape, Steven Ward is quiet for a long time. In fact, I begin to worry that he's about to terminate the interview. Clearly the experience has affected him deeply. He shakes his head and carries on speaking has he closes the PC's video window.

"The scratching was coming from above our heads. It couldn't have been anyone at the table making that sound, and Jed was downstairs. I'd wanted him to stay in the room to monitor the live feed from the cameras, but May didn't think she and Carol would have been able to concentrate with him there. He couldn't keep quiet, you see. If he wasn't talking out loud, he'd be mumbling to himself as he worked through a set of figures. I suggested he do a thorough assessment of the dining room while we tried to make contact in the attic.

"After we got out of the room, we were all shaken. Carol especially. She couldn't stay in the building, so we went and sat in the caravan. May was shaken up as well. At first, she'd thought the materialisation was a rat. She'd had a phobia about rats since she was a child.

"We met Jed on the way up the stairs, as we were coming down. That was another strange thing about it; all that noise in the attic, things getting knocked over and thrown about, but he hadn't heard a sound. He asked what had happened. I was more concerned about getting Carol out of the building than holding a debriefing session. I just told him we'd made contact. When he heard that, he ran up the stairs. May called after him to be careful.

"Once we were in the caravan Carol calmed down a lot. We were all shaken up. She said, *What was that thing?* or *What was it?* I don't remember exactly. Than May told her it was just a rat, she was close to tears. For her, a rat was a big deal, she was holding it together for Carol's sake, I think. Carol was adamant though, whatever she'd seen, it wasn't a rat. I said, I'd go back and check the recordings. Of course, that was a waste of time, but I didn't know that then.

"When I got back to the attic, John was setting his equipment to rights and Jed was peering into the hole in the ceiling. John asked me if Carol was okay. I couldn't believe how matter of fact he was being. It was like nothing had happened. When I said so, he looked at me and rolled his eyes, then asked me what I was talking about. I couldn't believe he could ask me that. I lost it a bit and pointed at the hole in the ceiling and the overturned gear, I shouted, 'What do you f__king think?' He looked at me like I'd gone mad and said,

'It was a squirrel, you muppet.'

"Of course I jumped when the mic boom fell over. People jump if a car backfires, that doesn't mean they're ready to call an exorcist, and Crossland had started screaming. Primeval instinct, you'd have jumped too. The noise you hear on the tape, the scrabbling sound, it was squirrels. I'd hung an omnidirectional mic above the table to pick up sound from as many angles as possible. It was about the best mic I had, the pickup range was as close to a full 360 degrees as you can get from a single unit. I'd set it up on the boom so it was up high, out of the way. It was right under the ceiling. There were squirrels in the rafters, probably other things too, animals I mean, not monsters. The mic picked up the noise and, because it was so close, on playback it's clear as a bell. At the time we had to strain to hear it, really concentrate on it. Steve and Crossland forget that of course, to listen to them you'd think a brass band was playing up there.

"I heard a clunk from the corner where the mic stand was, a squirrel had fallen through the ceiling and landed on the boom. It run along it, realised it was running towards us and jumped off. That's probably what toppled the mic. Don't know where the little f__ker went but the lights where concentrated on the table so, looking out from the table meant we were squinting into them. They forget that too. Steve saw nothing, he admits that. May saw it and mistook it for a rat, at least that was her first idea. Crossland was worked up already. She saw something moving and filled the blanks in with panic.

"By the next morning, they'd all convinced themselves the hordes of Mordor had materialised in the room. Even when I took Steve back to the attic and showed him the hole in the ceiling, he wouldn't have it. I pulled a piece of the plaster board away and a load of nut shells fell out. Ask Jed. He counted them."

"John convinced himself nothing out of the ordinary had happened. For while he almost convinced me we were all jumping at shadows. I suggested we stopped talking about it and instead each recorded, independently, what we'd seen. John had a cassette recorder and a huge stack of tapes. We took turns sitting in the minibus, recording our versions of events.

"It didn't take that long. Start to finish, from sitting down, to bolting out the room, had only taken about twenty minutes. We were all hyped up that evening, even John, although he'd probably deny that now. After everyone had put down what they'd seen, I listened to them all, sitting in the minibus. That was the first time I heard about the movement in the doll's house. I knew the doll's house was in shot from camera D. I went back to the house, to the attic. The Cameras were turned off by then. I'd glanced at the pictures on the monitor earlier, so I knew there had been a problem with the gear, but I hadn't studied the recordings. I isolated the feed from camera D and played it back. It wasn't obvious, even with the monitor screen showing nothing else; the image of the doll's house was small. If I hadn't known to look for something, I'd have missed it.

"The first time I played back that recording, it was just me in the attic. I don't mind admitting this; I exited that room pretty quick."

"Whatever was in that house had agency and intelligence. It was playful. But then so are children who pull the legs off spiders."

Carol Crossland and I have moved outside to her garden. Its late in the day and far from warm but sitting in sunlight makes it easier to talk about the events in the attic.

"If you look at the tapes of the Ouija board sessions it was clearly playing with us. On the first tape the most significant event was the tilting. And it took place in such a way that the record made it hard to gather clear details. For the second tape Steve made huge efforts to make sure the footage of the table would be crystal clear. Then the most significant event takes place in the background, in the shadows. And of course, the films didn't capture the feelings.

"When Steven insisted we all record independent accounts of what we'd seen, it was already dark. Nobody was eager to go back into the house[71]. We took turns sitting in the minibus.

---

[71]In fact, John Pelton and Gerald Cardino hadn't left the house at this point. Steven Ward recalls going back into number 37 to

I took longer than anyone else, because I had to keep starting over. I just couldn't get it clear in my head, and when I did, I was so scared I began to stammer and couldn't get my words out. I remember putting the light on in the bus, then not being able to see what was happening outside and turning the light off again. On off, on off. The rest of them must have thought I was mad. In the end I made my tape with the light on, and my eyes shut."

She laughs at the memory. If someone was walking by at that point, they'd be forgiven for thinking she was recalling something she was embarrassed about. There's a contrast between her laughter and her haunted expression.

I've heard her account, along with everyone else's. Steven Ward spoke of them during our interview, but time constraints made it impossible for me to hear them at that time. I asked if copies were available. I was told there were copies, but the rights to them were owned by London North University and their distribution was tightly controlled.

John Pelton, when I mentioned the tapes and Ward's comments, laughed. He told me he'd send me copies, and whatever I did with them was between me and my conscience. Three days later a sixty-minute cassette tape arrived through my letter box. There was another delay while I scoured eBay for a second-hand cassette player.

Maybe because of the build-up involved in getting hold of the tape, its contents were slightly disappointing. The first voice on the tape is Ward's. His testimony is a clear, measured and largely worthless account of seeing nothing. Pelton's account is flat – maybe too flat. He states that Carol Crossland was badly shocked when a squirrel knocked the mic boom over. Mable Noakes's account is calm and professional, as might be expected from a psychic investigator with her years of experience. She recounts what she has seen methodically,

---

find Pelton, so he could record his account
of events in the attic.

scientifically even. She describes the mic boom being knocked over by 'something' she couldn't recognise.

Crossland's recording is a stark contrast. It has clearly been made by someone in a state of distress. Sitting in her tiny garden, hearing her talk about the recording she made, I picture a scared young woman, sitting in isolation, giving testimony of a resent trauma. The courage this must have taken is worthy of respect[72].

"I don't know what came through the ceiling. I do know it wasn't a squirrel. It was too big for a squirrel. The next day, when it was light - " she laughs again " – I went back to the attic room. John showed me the hole in the plaster board, he kept telling me about the nut shells he'd found and how squirrels get into roof spaces. I don't know who he was trying harder to convince, me or him. But I know what I saw wasn't a squirrel."

"What do you think it was?" I ask Steven Ward. I'm referring to the shadowed movement in the doll's house. We've just watched the 2nd Session Tape on the screen of his desktop computer. It is nearing the end of the academic day and the shared office is undergoing a brief flurry of activity. Ward

---

[72] Having interviewed Carol Crossland my view of the tape changed. Having been underwhelmed when I first listened to it, after sharing - in a small way - the experience of its making, it became deeply disturbing to me. My copy of the tape, still in the player and waiting for transcription, was neglected for some weeks as I found myself unable to press play. When I did finally muster the courage, the machine, that until then had worked perfectly, chewed the tape, damaging it irreparably.

192

glances around him. Someone is tidying their desktop, two more people, a student and a lecturer, are discussing something in the doorway. Ward doesn't want to talk in front of them.

The attitude of the university toward the fieldtrips is one of embarrassment. The press coverage that followed the final trip to Fantoccini Street wasn't favourable. The press either affected outraged at the waste of funds or, and this may have been more damaging, regarded the business as something fit only for ridicule. Ward was referred to by one paper as a mad professor. The article, and nickname, was picked up by a score of internet sites catering to self-styled sceptics. His standing in the university suffered greatly. It's a tribute to his level of expertise that he didn't lose his job.

While his colleagues prepare to leave for the day, Ward discreetly darkens the screen of his monitor. We talk in a stilted manner for a few minutes. I'm sure it's obvious to everyone present that we are waiting for them to leave. When they finally do, Ward watches the door. From outside someone laughs. It may or may not be connected to my presence in the office but Ward flinches, and I assume he's been the butt of barbed comments and bad jokes in the past. We're both embarrassed by the incident and sit in silence for a few moments.

Ward turns the screen back on and plays again the brief recording of something moving in the doll's house.

"I wish I had an answer, even an idea. But I don't."

I suggest it was an unlucky choice to sit where he did. Had he been in Mabel Noakes's position he'd have witnessed the movement first-hand.

"I've lain awake at nights, wondering what would have happened if I'd taken a different seat at the table. The conclusion I've come to is it wouldn't have made any difference."

He looks at me and something that isn't quite a smile pulls at the corner of his mouth. He can see I'm missing his point.

"You can see the irony, can't you? I was the vision man.

193

John did audio, May and Carol where the sensitives and Jed was on the structure of the house. Me, vision. My job, my area of expertise. And I was the only one in the room who didn't see anything. And, as I'm sure people are happy to tell you, my equipment failed. Let me tell you something Mr Croix, my equipment set ups don't fail. I check and check and check again. And in that f__king house I'd go back and check some more. So, for me, the clearest sign that something was at play in that house, is the fact I couldn't get a recording worth a damn. Whatever that is - " he waves a hand at the screen and the frozen image of the doll's house " – it was playing games with me. And it won."

The image frozen on the screen is the digitalised version of the analogue film taken by camera D. It's poorly defined and zooming in just pixelates the image, turning it into a collection of grey and black squares. Techniques exist whereby frames of analogue film are sampled and analysed by computer to form a composite average, enhancing the image. The tech for this has existed since the seventies, but its limited application, particularly in our digitally obsessed world, means it is hard to obtain, and correspondingly costly. London North University has refused to fund such an exercise. It has also forbidden both its academic and IT maintenance departments to get involved. Fearful of further bad press, the seat of learning has decided on a course of ignorance.

Seeking a fresh viewpoint and possibly a better line of enquiry, I contact Ella Caine and ask if she is aware of the 2nd Session Tape. She surprises me by telling me she's not only heard of it but seen it. Shortly after the team returned from the second fieldtrip, Steven Ward contacted her and sent her a VHS copy.

Initially sceptical of the claim[73] - neither John Pelton nor

---

[73] This would have been the first contact Steven Ward had made with Ella in over a year. Ward, during our interview, had told me he'd stopped corresponding with Ella

Ward had mentioned copies of the tape being made - I questioned her about the contents of the recording, and it soon became clear she was telling the truth. Either that or she had been extensively briefed on the tape's contents.

I ask the obvious question,

"What do you think was moving in the doll's house?"

She gives the equally obvious reply,

"A doll I suppose."

While the evidence seems to point to something strange, maybe even malevolent, I'm not ready to accept the idea of animated toys appearing at the behest of a Ouija board. As I'm debating the best way to put this to Ella, she laughs.

"I don't mean literally. Physically a doll is nothing more than a collection of parts assembled to resemble a human. No, I don't believe a little wooden man was causing mischief in the attic. But maybe the idea of one was. In some ways dolls are just that, a form of focusing."

It's possible to find your thinking roadblocked by Ella's passion for dolls. Taken in isolation it's little more than an obsessive hobby. Something on a par with anorak clad misfits, perched at the end of a platform, jotting down lists of train numbers, and building a well of knowledge as pointless as it is narrow. But step back and take in the breadth and width of her studies and the analogy doesn't stand up.

Not insignificantly, her fascination with dolls and their study, includes a degree of introspection. Though it would be churlish not to accredit some of this ability to her environment and the efforts of her case workers.

"Not long after I arrived here, I had an epiphany of sorts. At the time I thought it was a crisis, but I began wondering

---

when it became apparent her only interest in the Fantoccini Street case was the dolls. He refused to confirm, or deny, that he had sent Ella a copy of the 2nd Session Tape.

about the things I've done over the years. Questioned myself. My … I won't say beliefs, let's say my … ways. It wasn't a very nice time in my life, but I found my way through it.

"My fascination with dolls isn't unique. It can't be really, not when you sit and think about it. Almost every culture, every society has made dolls. Dolls, puppets, figurines, statues. The need to reproduce the human form in facsimile is part of the human condition, in the west we give children baby dolls to practice childcare on. The Russian dolls; one inside the other, humanity inside humanity inside humanity. People stab voodoo dolls to cause ill to their enemies and we put a miniature Jesus with a miniature Mary and Joseph inside cavernous churches, so we can get the nativity in focus. Focus, you see? Big events, concepts, rendered in miniature so we can try and understand them. If you can understand things you can hope to control them. Go anywhere in the world and you can find examples of people loading dolls with meaning, in Mexico they make puppets of skeletons for the Day of the Dead, in Guatemala they make Trouble Dolls, little figures that children can tell their worries to. Psychologists in the west use dolls to get abused kids to talk. In ancient China doctors used dolls to diagnose female patients, rather than risk offending a woman by asking her to undress.

"All over the world, all through human history, dolls have been there, taking on our problems, listening to our woes, our pain. Little mirrors on the human condition. The question should be, why the f__k isn't everyone fascinated by dolls?"

Ella stops and wipes a sheen of sweat from her forehead. She smiles across at the two orderlies, standing by the door, whose own conversation has halted. They exchange nods with her.

I change the subject, as far as that is possible when talking with Ella, and we spend the rest of my visit talking about her impending relocation to Pucklechurch and her sister's spare room.

Other than her brief return to the attic, when John Pelton attempted to explain away the toppling of the mic boom, Carol Crossland didn't return to the attic room again during the second trip. This decision was supported by Mabel Noakes who, although willing to return to the room herself, believed it would be dangerous to hold another contact session there. Crossland recalls it was Steven Ward who suggested they try again, but this time in the room below the attic. She says he seemed nervous about asking her and she wondered if the request had actually come from Noakes. This isn't something Ward spoke of during my interview with him.

"I was a newbie if you like," Crossland tells me. "While May was a battle-scarred veteran. When I watched the film Steve had made of us at the Ouija board, she looked terrified. Of course, that's because she thought she'd seen a rat. Once she'd got over the shock and digested the scene enough to realise what she'd really seen, she was relieved. Me, I'd give anything to believe what came through the ceiling was a rat."

For the remainder of the trip the attic became the focus of Gerald Cardino's survey. His attempts to measure every aspect of numbers 37 and 37a redoubled. The information he amassed on the attic room filled page after page of file paper. Over a hundred and fifty sheets of A4 were dedicated to the doll's house. More than forty of them to the miniature attic room alone.

John Pelton recalls that for the last two days of the trip, Cardino barely left the attic. He maintains there was an unspoken agreement between the other members of the team that Cardino should be left to his own devices. Having him at the top of the house kept him out of the way of the real work[74].

"We all knew he was a liability. He was so fixated on finding

---

[74] When I spoke to him, Pelton put the words 'real work' in finger quotes.

the number 37 he regarded everything else as a waste of time. Crossland and May wanted quiet so they could tune in, or connect, or whatever they called it. Steve was interested in ambient temperature changes, and I was trying to get baseline sound levels. In a way the business with the Ouija board was a God send. It turned the attic into a little world of its own; Jed could spin round in ever decreasing circles relating the room to the hole in the ceiling, the ceiling to the doll's house, the doll's house to the table ... " Pelton draws a circle in the air with his finger, round and round and round ...

"We should have got out of that place, got him out of it. Living in close quarters the way we were, everyone working themselves up about every knock and tap, all our nerves were frayed. I'm not excusing myself here, or anyone else, but we concentrated on getting Jed out of the way because he was driving us crazy. We should have tried harder to get him out of there."

Carol Crossland takes a different view.

"We all had a part to play. That was the idea, we were all specialists. Jed was there to survey the physical structure. May and I had identified a point of massive psychic energy, dangerously powerful, and since I wasn't ready to return to the spot, it just made sense to allow the physical investigator to take it on.

"The mistake we made, and the mistake everybody made, was thinking only sensitives, like myself and May, were in danger from it. But what you have to understand is this, number 37 was possibly one of the most powerful instances of psychic phenomena encountered in modern times. We were on a huge, huge learning curve. I think whatever was in that house was scared of Jed, or at least what he was doing. After that ... thing in the attic showed itself, almost nothing else happen, not on that trip. It was almost as if it had drawn the curtains and was pretending no one was home. But it couldn't hide from Jed. He kept finding those 37 measurements, the house couldn't hide its nature from his

198

incredible mind. That's why it drove him insane. It was on the defence."

"Because of the business with the squirrel and all the bulls__t about recording what we'd seen, we sort of forgot about Jed. None of us, me included, realised he hadn't come out of the attic again. I slept in the house that night, in the front room 'cos it had the least damp, and left the others to squabble over the beds in the caravan. I woke up in the small hours, two or three in the morning, when I heard Jed going out the front door. He'd been in the attic all night. I spoke to him about it later and he said he'd lost track of time.

"We all agreed that Jed should be given a set period to work to. Steve gave him some mooey about *health and safety* and *duty of care*, to get him to agree. I remember he spent an hour scribbling sums down until he came up with start and finish times he could work a 37 into, or couldn't work a 37 into. It was one or the other. I don't remember them exactly, but it was something like 7:33 and four seconds until 18:21 and 7 seconds. Then May said, you'll need to take a break for lunch. That's what I mean when I say May had a good heart on her. Though, at the time I could have strangled her because, of course, Jed then had to calculate a lunch hour that wouldn't include a 37 and f__k up the start and stop time. That took another f__king hour. However, he figured it out so we ended up stopping for lunch around 11 o'clock and he'd only take 58 minutes, not a full hour. If you f__k around with the numbers long enough you can divide 60 minutes by 37, apparently."

Cardin's precise time tabling put him in the attic between the hours of 07:38:09 and 19:10:57. With a meal break at 11:09:00 to 12:01:04. I obtained these times from Cardino's mother, through who all my correspondence with him were conducted. Her email exchanges with me were polite but cold. When I asked about the exact time of the agreed lunch breaks, she provided the figures and, as a side note, told me that since my visit, her son had reinstated the routine.

Chapter Seventeen: The Kitchen Session

There were two more attempts to communicate using the Ouija board after the attic session. One on Friday 12th August, in the front bedroom, and another on the 13th, in the kitchen. The first yielded no results.

It took place at 12:30, the timing was suggested by Steven Ward. During my interview with him he told me the decision to set the board up just after lunch was a practical one. For filming, he wanted as much light as possible. The front bedroom was ideal for this as it was east facing[75] with a large window that had not been boarded over. It was also empty. The only 'furniture' being the base sections of a box divan double bed. This reduced the number of shadows and hiding places.

For this session Ward used every video recording device available to him at the time. A total of seven cameras were deployed to cover every angle and plane of the room. Of the cameras, only two were Ward's favoured VHS type. The decision was made to use one of these to film the ceiling. The other was fitted with a wide-angle lens and positioned inside the door.

Because of the failures of equipment two days earlier, Ward left nothing to chance and his usual check, check and check again routine was expanded, reaching, in his own words 'the edges of obsession'.

The result, from a technical point of view, was successful.

---

[75] In this case author is referring to a compass direction rather than his own orientations (see footnote 56). (R.D)

All seven cameras performed flawlessly. The result was seven, one-hour long films, capturing nothing happening for forty-five minutes.

"I kept the tape from the camera I posted at the door. It shows we were there, and nothing happened. I kept it for the sake of having a complete record, sceptics always accuse us of cherry-picking results. I really didn't see any point in archiving the ceiling footage."

So, the second séance was a wash out? Ward isn't entirely sure.

"It's something I've wondered about. It was a washout in that nothing came forward, but it did show I could set up cameras that didn't fail. Believe me, I've watched every minute of all seven recordings. They're perfect, not a slip of the film, not a speck of dust on a lens. Perfection, surely that proves that two simultaneous equipment failures, with no traceable cause, simply isn't possible. And I covered every aspect of that room. A spider crawls across the ceiling at one point, then down the wall behind where John was sitting. I could actually trace its route along the ceiling, down the wall and along the skirting. Nothing could happen in that room, that those cameras wouldn't catch. And, amazingly, nothing happened. When there were shadows and blind spots … boom. It didn't like coming into the light."

Carol Crossland shares Steven Ward's opinion.

"Whatever was in that house, didn't want to be recorded. The more careful Steve was with his equipment, the less there was to record. I suppose I took a strange comfort in that. I was young then, don't forget, and scared. It began as a bit of an adventure but then it got real, very real. It was easy to get scared. May felt the same; that Steve's video gear was putting the presence off. It was the way we saw that that differed. I was grateful for it while May was resentful. She kept saying 'we', meaning she and I, were being pushed out. She grumbled that the attic had been given over to Jed and his measurements and numbers, and now the door to the other realm was being blocked by Steve and John with their boy-toys. It made the atmosphere a little tense. It didn't help that I started getting closer to Steve after the business in the attic."

By now the team was beginning to feel the tension, and the unity of the group was failing. After the failed contact session in the bedroom, the rest of the day was largely spent in argument.

While Gerald Cardino continued measuring the attic, the other four members of the team debated holding a third contact session[76]. The consensus was that it should go ahead. The first point of contention was the location. Ward thought the kitchen was the obvious place, his reasoning being that the dining room and attic had both been sites where bodies were found, as was the kitchen. Crossland, possibly still shaken by the 'successful' result in the attic, was more inclined to try a less charged location. As Ward had stated, on more than one occasion, that Naokes and Crossland were the specialists when it came to reading the psychic activity, it fell to Noakes to decide the matter – Pelton having effectively abstained from the discussion.

Pelton's recollection of the discussion – arguably the most reliable as he adopted the role of passive observer – was that

---

[76] Steven Ward and Carol Crossland both reported that while John Pelton was present during the discussion, he didn't express an opinion. Crossland said he had sat through the argument without taking part, his sole contribution being his agreement to the decision reached. She added that although he was silent, she could feel the negativity radiating from him. In effect the meeting only involved three of the five team members.

Noakes was trying not to upset Ward, while at the same time shielding Crossland.

"May was trying her best to please both of them. I think she genuinely believed it was best to try the kitchen. She kept using the same phrase, 'site of psychic trauma'. Her thinking was along the same lines as the Stone Tape Theory. Steve was on the same track. Maybe Crossland was too and wasn't that keen on getting caught up in the replay of a murder. I wasn't getting involved. I'd had enough of it by then. I'd have thought they'd have learned their lesson when Viola got spooked after the first show, but it seemed to have the opposite effect.

"I'd given up trying to talk sense to any of them by then, no one wanted to hear, not even Crossland. I guess they'd invested so much into jumping at shadows they couldn't afford not to be right. When I took them up to the attic and showed them where the squirrels had been nesting, they just refused to see it. Crossland had actually walked away while I was talking. I think I came the closest to doing anything supernatural: I became invisible."

"I finally agreed to try the Ouija board in the kitchen. May convinced me. She'd always had the feeling that the presence in the attic was malevolent, but she didn't pick up on that in the kitchen. We'd both gone from room to room when we first got to the house, of course for her it was the second time she'd been there. She said the overwhelming feeling she got from the kitchen was sadness. A mother died there don't forget. One thing I know, I'd stake my life on it, she wasn't the first to die. She died knowing her children had been murdered."

There is no visual record of the fourth contact session, or the Kitchen Session as it is usually called. The tension within the team increased when Mabel Noakes and Carole Crossland requested the session be conducted in private.

Steven Ward, not unsurprisingly as the head of the Visual Technologies Department, maintained that the whole purpose of the exercise was to obtain a record of paranormal activity. Without credible, and undeniable evidence, anything that took place inside the house was largely irrelevant. Unsupported eyewitness testimony was, in his opinion, worthless as it would invariably be dismissed as delusional or simply false.

Crossland recalls him saying repeatedly, 'This isn't a court of law, the burden of proof works against us'. It was to become something of a mantra for him over the remainder of the fieldtrip.

Noakes and Crossland's thoughts on the matter ran along a different line. Contrary to what John Pelton thought, neither of the two women were taken with the Stone Tape Theory. As sensitives, they dismissed the idea that what they'd experienced was something akin to a recording. They maintained that the presence, possibly the house itself, was aware of Ward and Pelton's equipment and their attempts to catch it on tape. Each recorded session, they argued, had produced less and less that met Ward's needs. The intimacy of a private session they reasoned would likely yield better results.

Results, that Ward argued, no one but the four of them would believe.

For a time the group was at an impasse. Eventually Ward agreed to the session going ahead without being recorded. He had little choice; Noakes and Crossland refused to use the Ouija board again if the cameras were in place.

Finally, at 3:30 p.m. on Saturday the 13th, the table and Ouija board were once again set up. This time in the kitchen. As with the attic session, Ward and Crossland's recollection of the seating arrangement differs. While at pains to record all aspects of the previous session, Ward, now, bereft of his equipment, seemed to regard the exercise as irrelevant.

That an audio recording exists of the Kitchen Session is, depending on your point of view, a mark of professionalism or betrayal. Steven Ward claimed, during our interview, that John Pelton acted alone and his recording of events in the kitchen was presented as a fait au complet. Pelton claims otherwise.

"Steve had the hump after the big conflab about whether or not he was going to film in the kitchen. May had flat out refused to use the board if she was filmed and Crossland backed her up. He knew he was beat. His parting shot was to ask if I could at least run off a cassette. He was just being snide about it really, but of course it started another round of nattering.

"I'd had it by then, so I told them to let me know what they'd decided and left them to it. I went out to the caravan and made a cup of tea. In the end they, May and Crossland I mean, decided it was too big a risk to run audio. Ward came out to the caravan and told me. Like I said, by that point I'd had a bellyful of the whole thing, I didn't think we'd achieved anything other than film a lot of people having hysterics. Not wasting tape on another hour of nonsense was fine by me. Ward didn't agree. He asked me if there was any more water in the pot and made himself a cuppa then sat down across from me, like we were best mates. I knew what was coming. He rattled off a few of his stock phrases about burdens of proof and evidential recordings. I don't even know if evidential is a word. I just waited him out and of course he finally got around to asking me how hard it would be to record the session 'discreetly'. I just nodded.

"The thing was he knew it would be easy. The whole house was wired for sound, I had a bank of cassette tape recorders hooked to mics that triggered if a mouse coughed. They'd only be turned on once we'd left the building for the night. There was no point putting the system on during the days, with the five of us in the house, the tapes would have been worthless. Well, they all were really. The point is, recording the kitchen wasn't any kind of problem at all. When everyone went into there that afternoon to set up the table and board, I told them I was going to turn off the tape deck, then I just went and turned it on.

"When I went back into the kitchen, they were setting the

chairs in place and Steve made a big display of looking at his watch and announcing, 'Okay, as of fifteen twenty-six, all recording halted'. I guess he was hammering the point home. That man's good with a camera but he's no acter, when it came out later that there was a tape, I don't think May or Crossland were surprised."

Of all the rooms in the house, the kitchen was in the worst state of repair. It is likely that after the death of Mrs Doll senior, when the property's sole tenet was Phoebe Reese, the building had fallen into disrepair. Nothing is known of the habits of Phoebe Reese, but the condition of number 37 when Kenneth Doll took ownership would indicate that she had rarely ventured from her attic flat.

At some point the long ignored lower floor kitchen had begun to quietly leak. Much of the flooring below the sink area had rotted away to little more than soft mould. The kitchen was duly stripped out, presumably to clear the way for a renovation that never happened. It seems likely that when the house was occupied by the Doll family the room would have been shut off and cooking would have been carried out in the attic space. John Pelton recalls gingerly picking his way between holes in the floor when he installed his recording equipment.

The area immediately under the location of the original taps and sink was mostly gone. Shuttered and ignored for many years, the house was gently rotting. Carol Crossland recalls the state of decay.

"The floor had rotted away in a huge halfmoon shape. It was horrible really. The patch of floor where they'd found that poor woman had mostly vanished. There weren't even broken floorboards to mark the spot, just a gap surrounded by this circle of rot. It was like a cancer. That's the word that kept popping into my head, cancer.

"Steve went ahead of us and stamped around on the remaining floor, making sure it was safe. I guess May and I looked nervous, but of course we weren't worried about the floor. It's funny, but for all his understanding and acceptance of the way a sensitive inhabits the world, Steve could be incredibly dense.

"That room was howling. Imagine walking into a concert hall, but instead of an orchestra and audience there's just people screaming in utter, utter despair. It was like that. I could almost taste the suffering. That poor woman. I remember thinking how lucky Steve and John were, being deaf and blind to it all. People talk about psychic gifts. Well, it didn't feel like a gift when I was in that kitchen.

"We set the table up as far away from the missing section of floor as we could. That suited me. I didn't want to be there at all, but that … that howling, that despair, it was boiling up out of that hole. I could feel it, when I spoke to May about it later, she said she'd felt exactly the same. It wasn't the way the attic felt, or the dining room, what came out of the kitchen was scary, yes, but it was heart breaking. If there was a chance, any chance, that I could help end just a fraction of that woman's pain, then I had to try. I don't think I'd have been able to live with myself if I hadn't.

"By the end of that day I was pretty mad at Steve. All he was interested in was making his films. When I mentioned the sensations … the psychic trauma, Steve came out with that nonsense about Stone Tapes."

The following is an edited transcript of the tape John Pelton made of the 13th August contact session. In its unedited form the tape is 47 minutes 26 seconds in duration. Approximately half of this is largely unidentified noise, another portion is Mabel Noakes announcing each letter indicated by the planchette, before stating the completed word or name. For ease of reading, I have omitted Noakes's announcement of individual letters and simply reported each word.

The transcript starts at 18 minutes 19 seconds. Carol Crossland, who again leads the session, has already attempted to make contact nine times.

Crossland: *Is someone there?*

<There is a sharp rapping sound that has a vaguely metallic quality. When the noise stops Crossland attempts contact again. Her previous attempts have been couched in generic terms. On this occasion she is more specific.>

Crossland: *Barbara, are you there?*

<There is further metallic rapping. Then the sound of the planchette moving. Although there is no video record, the duration of the sound and the time between Noakes's announcement of the individual letters makes it clear the planchette is moving far slower than during the two previous contact sessions.>

Noakes: *Not. Yet.*
Crossland: *Can you tell us what that means?*
Noakes: *Want. To. Finish.*
Crossland: *What do you want to Finish?*
Noakes: (sounding hesitant) *The. Ironing?*

<There is silence for five seconds. The metallic rapping noise starts again. This continues for 32 seconds.>

Ward: *Carol, ask who it is.*
Crossland: *Are you Barbara Doll?*
Noakes: *No.*
Crossland: *Then who are you?*
Noakes: *Liddy.*
Crossland: *Do you know where you are?*
Noakes: *The. Attic. Coming. Here.*
Crossland: *Why are you coming ... why are you coming here?*
Noakes: *Finish.*
Crossland: *Finish what?*
Noakes: *D ... I*

\<There is the sound of breaking glass, unidentifiable clattering
and violent retching.\>

Ward: *Oh, my god, are you okay?*
Crossland: *Of course she's not. We have to get her
               out of here.*

\<Confused sounds and footsteps. There is silence for
approximately a minute then the metallic rapping starts again.
It continues for the remainder of the tape.\>

As the planchette began inching its way around the letters
Mabel Noakes was violently sick. The three other members of
the team escorted her from the kitchen and, on Carol
Crossland's insistence, left the house to shelter in the caravan.

"She was in a bad way," Steven Ward tells me. "White as a
sheet, she was crying so hard I thought she was fitting. I was
about to call an ambulance, but Crossland kept a cooler head
than me. She calmed her down, talked her down. We helped
her, May, to clean up, and of course we made tea. We needed
to talk about what had happened but May said she was too
tired. But it was more than just tired, you could see her eye
lids drooping. We almost had to carry her over to one of the
bunks and she practically passed out.

"Crossland and I both stayed with her for about an hour,
we didn't know what to think. I was worried she'd be sick
again. She was so deeply asleep I don't think it would have
woken her, and I could picture her choking. We were clearly
dealing with something dangerous. Even if they weren't
directly malevolent, the forces in play were a risk to us. I was
at a loss. I didn't know what to do.

"Once I was happy May was just sleeping normally and not
about to choke, I went back into the house. Crossland stayed
with her, just in case."

While Ward and Crossland took care of Mabel Noakes, John
Pelton went back to the house. First to his tape deck and then

to the attic room.

"I had intended to pocket the tape I'd made and discreetly add it to the collection of material we'd been amassing. But when I went to the tape station[77] I saw it was still recording so I left it alone[78]. Then I went up to look in on Jed.

"I'd got in the habit of checking-in with him every now and again. I was more worried about him than about the nonsense with the Ouija board.

"He was okay ... well, physically. When I went into the attic, he was peeling a section of wallpaper away. He'd already exposed a big chunk of one wall. It looked like he'd been running his crazy calculations again because the bare patch of wall was covered in a scrawl of figures. I told him what had happened in the kitchen and said the others were in the caravan. He was very interested in the kitchen stuff, normally he was on the edge of manic, bouncing around like a puppy, but when I told him about May puking, he got very still and intense. Then he said he wanted to check something in the kitchen, and he was all energy again and almost jumped down the stairs. I didn't follow him, but when I pulled the kitchen tape later and listened to it, the second half was just him in the kitchen. You could hear him shuffling around, muttering

[77] The Tape Station was the bank of reel-to-reel recorders, cassette recorders and a pair of PCs, for storing digitally.

[78] The sound activated recording were triggered by any noise at or above the level of a normal footfall. Once triggered the recorder would run for as long as the sound level was maintained. When the sound ceased, recording would continue for two minutes before shutting down. This window of 'known' silence made it possible to identify the separate recording episodes as discreet events.

strings of figures. I find that part of the recording far more upsetting than the Ouija board stuff."

"May slept right through; she didn't stir until the next morning. She said she felt okay, but she couldn't remember what had happened. All she remembered was sitting down at the table, and the name Liddy. She looked puzzled as she tried to remember what had happened. Then she said something that sent a shiver down my spine. She said, 'it's almost as if I wasn't there'. Neither of us mentioned it again.

"Everyone was really down the next day. We were all worn out, physically and emotionally. I think everyone's nerves were stretched to breaking point. Even John was affected by it, but I expect if you ever speak to him, he'll tell you we'd all worked ourselves up over nothing and he was the only one of us not having hysterics. But that hadn't stopped him booking into a hotel for the night. Mind you, he invited me to join him, so I think he might have had an ulterior motive[79]."

On the last day of the fieldtrip Steven Ward collected the tape recordings made during the night. In total the auto trigger mics had collected over five hours of recordings. The packing

---

[79] When interviewing John Pelton I didn't make any mention of this comment, however the subject came up unprompted. His recollection of the incident is that he'd booked a room for himself at the local hotel to get a goodnight's sleep. He claims to have spoken to each member of the team asking if they wanted to do the same, they had all declined. In the case of Carol Crossland and Mabel Noakes, who he believed were most upset by the events in the kitchen, he claims to have offered to pay for their rooms.

away of equipment was a long procedure. John Pelton had runs of wiring that traversed much of the house. Ward had a smaller quantity of power cabling for lighting equipment and rather than help Pelton, who was particular about how his gear was handled, he decided to begin analysis of the nocturnal tapes.

"Myself, Carol and May set up in the caravan. Jed was inside measuring and, even if we'd had the appetite for running more investigations inside the house, John was decanting his equipment. May was still tired, even after sleeping for fourteen hours straight."

The analysis of the tapes revealed that the auto triggers had been activated a total of 67 times. On 51 of those occasions the triggering sound was unidentified and isolated. Meaning recording had stopped automatically following two minutes of silence. Of the remaining 16 trigger events, 12 took place in the kitchen. Three of these had a duration greater than two minutes and consisted of a series of knocking sounds. On the two earliest recordings, 21:07 to 21:12 and 02:35 to 02:53, the knocking is a series of short seemingly random bursts, none of which endures for longer than thirty seconds. The third, which starts at 06:31 is a louder, continuous bout of rapid knocking.

"We'd listened to the kitchen tapes first because of what had happened during the contact session there. It sounds stupid to say it now, but when Carol and May were working the Ouija board, we barely noticed the knocking. That may seem impossible but consider the world we'd entered. You adjust to what you consider normal or at least significant. Hearing the knocking again, out of context, all three of us drew breath. We listened to the whole of the kitchen tape three times, trying to hear if there was a pattern to it. May was ready to go for a fourth hearing but Carol, and if I'm honest, myself, found it too intense. I suggested we get John and Jed.

"Naturally, John wasn't interested. Jed needed some coaxing to pull him away from measuring, but he finally came out to the caravan. When we played it to him, he listened with his head on one side, as if he was concentrating on the sounds. At the end of the third section, the longest one, he laughed and said 'of course'. I saw then that he'd been staring at the timer on the tape player, counting the minutes. The final bout of knocking lasted exactly 37 minutes."

John Pelton refutes the claim about the duration of the knocking.

"Steve and the rest of them kept bandying the word 'exactly' about. 'Exactly' and 'precisely'. But it's impossible to say exactly how long the knocking went on for. My equipment was pretty good but there's always going to be a delay between the triggering of the recording and the actual recording, and the tape counters I was using were pretty basic digital timers. There's an error tolerance of around a tenth of a second per minute."

He didn't point this out at the time.

"I couldn't be bothered. I'd been there before, remember? They didn't want to hear anything that didn't fit in with the paranormal activity scenario. If they'd listened at all they'd have said, 37 minutes give or take is still exactly 37 minutes. It didn't matter how long the tape was anyway; Jed would have just sat with a sheet of paper and worked figures until a 37 appeared.

"If I'm totally honest, I barely listened to the tape. Steve came running into the house looking for me and Jed, wanting to play us the tape. Jed wanted to carry on measuring the bloody attic. I overheard a little of the conversation and he thought he was 'on to something', whatever that meant. When Steve finally got him to go, he turned to me. I think I may have said something about listening later on. I do remember he let it go straight away. I guess he didn't want the voice of a dissenter there. In the end I didn't hear the tape until mid-afternoon. I'd packed up all my gear up while Jed was still in the caravan with Steve and Carol. May had helped me put Jed's gear in the van. By the time I got to hear the tape Jed was in full swing about the 37 minute stuff. Carol and Steve

213

were sat staring at him like he was a vision of the Virgin at Lourdes. They'd listened to the tape four or five times by then, that's over two hours of listening to a banging noise.

"Jed was getting hyped up, I had an uncle years ago who had manic depression, bi-polar. Just before he'd fall into an absolute pit of despair, he'd have a day or so of insane excitement, it was easy to get caught up in it if you weren't careful. To me, it looked like Jed was about to pull the same trick and he was pulling the others along with him. When I put my head around the caravan door Carol jumped up and rewound the tape, she thought I was going to sit there with them, sharing the wonder. I listened to about a minute, said it sounded like water pipes rattling and let them get on with it. It must have been a bit of a buzzkill, because a couple of minutes later the three of them came out of the caravan and carried on the packing. That's when Jed started the bulls__t with the number plates.

"I was f__king glad I'd brought my own car and wouldn't have to sit in the bus. I wasn't going to win any popularity contests that day."

"That man was so cynical it drove me to distraction. All of us even, Jed, had listened to that tape end to end two, three times. I mean really listened, even Jed who couldn't normally stop talking, sat through it in total silence. We really listened hard, trying to catch anything about it that made any kind of sense, and there wasn't anything about it that did. There was no one in that kitchen, if there had been John's little toys would have picked up the door opening or footsteps. There is no reason, no possible way, that room should have been anything but silent, and yet there it was. And that clattering noise went on for a full 37 minutes. 37 minutes exactly.

"John waltzes in and barely listens to it. After about five seconds he announces, 'oh, that's just water in the pipes', and swans out again. Stupid man. If he'd listened properly, the way we did, he'd have heard the voice."

What Carol Crossland describes as a voice was, according to

Steven Ward, a collection of sounds that were recognisable as words.

"May was the first to hear the words. The three of us had listened to the tape once, we just played it straight through, then sat without saying anything. I rewound the tape and started it again, we listened again but after a couple of minutes May gasped and made me and Carol jump. She reached over and hit the rewind button. We couldn't hear it at first but once May told us what was there, it was clear as crystal.

'Liddy, Liddy, coming soon, so pretty.
Liddy, time to finish. Don't be scared.'

"We listened to the section again and again. It wasn't a mistake or our ears playing tricks. The words were perfectly discernible if you were willing to listen."

John Pelton, after packing up his gear and persuading Jed to get into the minibus, blankly refused to listen to the tape again.

"I just wanted to get home, have a hot bath, a decent meal and a couple of Scotches. Steve and Carol ran on a quiet level of hysteria that wore me out. May was calmer about everything, in her way, but she was still hard work to be around. And Jed was off the scale by then.

"I was exhausted, and the last thing I wanted to do right then was sit in the caravan listening to a tape of the plumbing and get told it was a chorus from beyond the f__king grave."

Chapter Seventeen: The Walls that Bled Numbers

<u>Fantoccini Street Photo Log (14/08/2011)</u>
<u>Attic room 3 of 16 (North facing wall)[80]</u>

The photograph is in colour. Taken from across the room, the expense of the north wall takes up approximately three quarters of the image. At the bottom right corner of the picture the removed wallpaper can be seen. It has been neatly folded and stacked. The upper right corner of the wall is discoloured with a mottled patch of dark mould. In this picture, the remainder of the wall appears to be covered with finely spaced horizontal lines.

<u>Fantoccini Street Photo Log (14/08/2011)</u>
<u>Attic room 4 of 16 (Detail of north facing wall)</u>

The close up of a section of the north wall takes up the whole frame. At this distance the horizontal lines can clearly be seen as digits and mathematical symbols. The figures are perfectly legible, neatly written and accurately ordered in evenly spaced lines. To the left of frame, the photographer (Steven Ward) has put his hand flat to the wall to give an indication of scale. It is possible to estimate the size of the written characters at less than a centimetre tall.

"Once we'd packed up the gear, I went around the house taking photos of each room, so we'd have a solid record to

---

[80] Again, this direction probably corresponds to a compass bearing rather than Mr Croix's method of orientation (see foot note 56). (R.D)

compare the way we left it to the way we found it, if we came back. At the time I wasn't sure that was on the cards. Yes, we'd found a huge amount of evidence and had a lot to look into and try to make sense of, but frankly I was debating with myself whether anyone's nerves could take any more. That feeling redoubled when I got to the attic.

"I hadn't been up there since the Ouija board session, none of us had really apart from Jed. John would go up to check on him a couple of times each day, but he didn't report anything back to us."

Alone in the attic, Jed had stripped away most of the wallpaper.

"The paper had been falling off the walls any way, but Jed had obviously put a lot of work into exposing as much of the plaster as he could. The only wall with any covering left was the one behind the door, I suppose being an internal wall it wasn't so riddled with damp. There was a lot of mould up there, the wall behind the doll's house was almost entirely black, but, in the places where you could see through it, the plaster underneath was covered with numbers. It looked as if the room had been repapered with pages from a book of logarithms. Equations, calculations, column and columns of digits, thousands and thousands of them. For a second I was angry, it was a form of vandalism, a destruction of a study in progress.

"But then of course, I came to my senses. There was no way Jed could have done so much in just two days. Clearly, he wasn't responsible for the figures. He'd just uncovered what was already inscribed there."

"I didn't hear the fuss about the writing on the walls until we came back to uni that September. I hadn't spoken to Crossland or Steve since we left the house. I was pretty much persona non grata.

"Someone I knew who lectured in maths told me Steve had been hassling him with these pages of calculations. He asked me if it was anything to do with the trick-or-treat malarkey - that was what a lot of the people in the uni were calling it. I didn't make the connection at first but when he told me the figures where meaningless I assumed some of Jed's jottings were being handed around.

"At the time this guy spoke to me, Jed was still in hospital. He'd been found in his bedroom by one of his flatmates, unconscious. They called an ambulance. He had a nasty respiratory infection, one of the ones that don't respond to antibiotics. He was in there for about three weeks.

"Jed was clearly having some sort of breakdown, and it wound me up that Steve was more worried about playing with those stupid calculations. I went to Steve's office and asked him if he knew Jed was laid up. He did, and to be fair, he had been to see him, which is more than I'd done.

"We were both sort of embarrassed. I'd been ready for a shouting match and then it hadn't happened. That's when Steve showed me the photos he'd taken of the attic. I'd asked if that was what he been showing the maths bod, but he told me what he was showing them was the reconstructed pieces Jed was working on. I didn't know what he was talking about. He pointed at the patches of mould in one of the pictures and told me Jed was trying to reconstruct the figures they were covering.

"I told him I'd seen Jed writing on the walls when I checked up on him. He just shook his head. He wasn't having it, as far as he was concerned, the figures were what he called a 'manifestation'. He said, 'did you sit with him and watch him do all of this?' Of course, I f__king hadn't. Steve shrugged and looked pleased with himself. 'All you know then is that Jed wrote something on the wall, that can't possibly account for all of it'. Stupid b-----d.

"I went to see Jed in the hospital. He looked awful. Far worse than he should have for a simple chest infection. I could tell there was more to it than that. I genuinely believe that house attacked him, physically, mentally, spiritually. Spiritually at least he fought back. That whirl wind mind of his wasn't letting go.

"The day I went to see him he was sitting up in bed,

propped up on half a dozen pillows with a stack of exercise books next to him. He was filling them in when I arrived. He tried to explain the maths behind it to me, but I've got no head for figures. He was adamant he was close to a breakthrough though. I didn't know it then, but John had been talking to Steve about the numbers in the attic. He was claiming they were fake, that Jed had just made them up. That was nonsense, complete rubbish. No way could a human being have filled those walls with that much writing. It would have taken weeks, probably months.

"Scared as I was, as we all were, I think John was more frightened. To have a mind that closed and be confronted with the things that happened in that house, that must be terrifying. At least the type of fear we had, me, Steve, May, at least that let us confront it. John condemned himself to a life of running.

"That said, there was no way I was going to go back to that house with a Ouija board."

"I'd be more inclined to buy the *walls that bled numbers* malarkey if I hadn't seen Jed working away with his pencil, and I know what you're about to say, the same c__p Steve came out with; *you didn't see him write all of it*. It's the same with those a__holes that follow Uri Geller around picking up his cast-off spoons. There's nothing that fella ever did that hadn't been done before by a thousand stage magicians, but the acolytes'll just say, 'yes, but the stage magicians use trickery, Uri does it by the power of his mind'. Geller's been caught cheating, on stage, on camera, time and time again, and the faithful just bleat out the same old refrain; 'he cheated once, but what about all the times he didn't cheat?'"

It begs the question, why would Jed claim the numbers on the walls of number 37 were already decorated with figures if, as Pelton believes, he'd applied them himself. What did he stand to gain?

"I'm not suggesting he was trying to fake something or pull a fast one. I don't think he knew he was writing on the walls. He was clearly on the edge of a breakdown or in the midst of a manic episode. To me the only mystery about that house is why the f__k did the uni let Jed go back there again."

Doctor James Slidesmith - the nearest I have to an inside source on the University's attitude toward the fieldtrips – thinks he knows why Gerald Cardino was allowed back to Fantoccini Street.

"I was in a funny position there, being one of the few alumni they had chasing a PhD. Not exactly staff and not really a student, I probably heard more of the management's side of things then most of the campus.

"They wanted to distance themselves from the stories in the press about running courses in ghost hunting, and they were doing flips and turns to avoid taking responsibility for Viola and Jed.

"Viola had dropped out and as far as I know didn't come back, Jed was getting close to being 'put off' the course[81]. That's uni speak for 'kicked out'. Another rock and a hard place situation. If they endorsed the idea that Fantoccini Street was dangerous, not only would they look like quacks, they'd have to explain why they sent students there. If they said the house was harmless and the fieldtrips were just an academic exercise, what was the rationale for stomping on a third trip? By then there was a lot of student interest in Fantoccini Street.

"As for letting Jed back on the team; the gossip, and I happen to believe it, was that there was a lot of pressure to get Jed through his course, to show how good the pastoral care was. Well, the only thing that would persuade him to attend classes was the promise of going back to the house. Politics."

---

[81] After leaving hospital and returning to his studies Gerald Cardino's attendance became erratic. By the beginning of the New Year, he was close to arbitrary dismissal due to the number of classes he'd missed.

Chapter Eighteen: A Brief Musical Interlude

"For about ten minutes, just before we went on stage that last time, we thought we were rockstars. It turned out to be the end of the band really. That last night was a packed house."

I'm talking to Victor Donoghue. Now a successful landscape gardener, from 2010 to 1012 he was the guitarist for Doll's House Autopsy. We've met in the extensive grounds of one of his clients. I ask if the demise of the band was the end of his musical ambitions. He laughs.

"I never had any musical ambitions. The band was just a bit of a laugh. There were four or five student bands on campus already and they were all squabbling over who'd get the Friday night slot, playing the big stage. They were all into playing this sombre, melancholy stuff and taking it all very seriously. They all sounded the same. Me and my flat mate, Peter Craine, he played keyboards, decided to form a ska band, and do something a bit more upbeat. We put up a notice looking for a singer. We said in the ad, *singer wanted, talent optional.* That says it all really.

There must have been something in the water at Uni. We had a dozen applicants; one half were trying to be Kurt Corbain and other half were Robert Smith look-a-likes. Then this skinny, chain smoker turns up, says his name's Kiren Patel and he does Elvis Impressions. Pete told him we were a ska group, and he says *fine, do you know House of Fun?* Pete played house of fun and Kiren sang it as Elvis. It was bloody awful, but it wasn't Kurt Corbain, so he was in.

The big stage at the uni was in the media department, 'cos they ran a TV production course. The set up was pretty good in all fairness, and the Student Union were allowed to stage gigs there with a pop-up bar most Fridays or Saturdays. Only the serious bands got those slots. The likes of us only ever got the midweek slot in the Student Union bar, where the stage was about six inches off the floor and not a lot wider. Wednesdays were always stone-dead for some reason, so that's where we ended up.

We never tried to sell tickets or anything, we were just in it for a laugh. People generally had a good time. We were so bad we were good, if you know what I mean. We kept changing our name. Someone who fancied themselves as a music critic wrote about us in the student rag. They made some snide comment along the lines of, *the only way anyone would go to see this band twice was if they changed their name.* So that's what we did.

Originally, we called ourselves Zombie Elvis, on account of Kiren looking half dead most of the time. It became our thing to have a relaunch every time we got a Wednesday night. The funny thing is we gained a sort of following, for a little while we had 20 to 30 people coming to see us. Not exactly big time but considering how bad we were it was quite impressive. There was another piece about us in the uni rag, written by a mate of Kiren's. He said if you went to more than two of our gigs you might be suffering from Stockholm Syndrome. That's where the idea for the flyers came from."

The flyers the band put together for what was to be their last public outing, showed the frontage of 37 Fantoccini Street. Slanted across the page in neon pink:

DOLL'S HOUSE AUTOPSY
The Stockholm Syndrome Tour

The example I'm holding has a dayglo orange sticker in one corner. It's an update to the original time and location.

The photograph of the house is overexposed, making it hard to recognise, though not impossible. To clear up any ambiguity, the number 37 has been added to the door, also in pink.

I ask how the band got hold of the photograph.

"I just drove over and took it myself. The address was meant to be confidential, but the whole campus knew where it was. Steve Ward and Carol never stopped talking about the place. Even so, if you asked them outright about it, they'd go all coy and tell you they couldn't divulge its location. Once the stories about the séances started doing the rounds, quite a few people started making runs over to Fantoccini Street. London North had its share of Goths and emos, they loved the place.

The gig at the big stage was very strange. There'd been a lot of interest in it, so we were moved from Wednesdays at the bar into that week's top spot. On the night there must have been a couple of hundred people there. I was p__sing myself. This was the first time we'd really had an audience. Until then we'd just been playing for friends really, we knew everyone who'd show up. Most nights we'd get people on stage with us and they'd end up doing more songs than we would. They weren't so much gigs as mini parties.

Kiren was loving it. He'd got hold of a blow-up doll that he took on stage with him. The atmosphere was odd right from the off. I don't know what people were expecting. I don't think most of the crowd realised we were a joke band. A lot of the Goth and metal crowd had showed up, along with the usual Friday crew, who all wanted Coldplay or Snow Patrol covers. What they got was Elvis and a sex-doll.

We'd lost about half the audience by the third number. Some people got into the mood, our mood, but a lot took offense. We were getting cheered and booed in equal measure. There were a few scuffles, not fights really, just people pushing and shoving too much. The real trouble only broke out when Kiren threw his doll into the audience.

Did I say Kiren chain smoked? Even on Stage? Well, we were doing *It Must be Love*. Kiren was singing it to his doll and … well you can probably imagine. Trouble was he had the doll in one hand and the mic in the other and a fag on the go. He was singing out of one side of his mouth and playing kissy kissy with the doll. Of course, he ended up burning a hole in the things head and it started deflating. Once he saw what was happening, he gave up on the doll and slung it into the crowd. Any other night it would have got a huge laugh but that night a tug of war started, and it got nasty. When bottles started flying our way, we called it a night.

We came close to getting expelled over it. The next student rag run a piece about the gig. Whoever wrote it was ranting away about misogyny and the cheap shock tactics of death metal music. Us, death metal? We'd generally opened our sets with the theme from the Magic Roundabout.

It was the doll that got people riled up. By the end of the night, it had been torn to bits. Someone had taken a photo of it laying on the floor with a dirty great boot print on its face. They used the photo with the article about us, and the author had a lot to say about our stage act glorifying sexual violence. It was only a doll, for f___sake.

The atmosphere at uni the previous term had been horrible. People were so ghoulish about what had happened. We did what we could to be discreet but word of what was happening leaked out somehow. People would keep coming to us wanting details and gossip. I wouldn't tell them, of course.

"What was worse than the ghouls though was the lack of respect. I don't mean people poking fun at us, although there was plenty of that, but the way people talked about the house as if it was a tourist attraction. Three women were murdered in that house, and people thought it was something to joke about.

"There was a concert by some heavy metal band. I didn't go, thank God, but I heard about it the next day, and a lot of people complained. The front man simulated sex with a blow-up woman then ground a cigarette out on her face and threw her to the audience to be torn apart."

224

Part Four

Wouldn't Mind Dying (If Dying Was All)

The 2012 Fieldtrip

Tuesday 31ˢᵗ July to Monday 6ᵗʰ August

Members of Investigative Team

Carol Crossland	*Sensitive*
~~*John Pelton*~~	~~*Audio Capture Technician*~~
Gerald Cardino	*Surveyor*
Mabel Noakes	*Sensitive*
Steven Ward	*Audio Visual Capture technician*
~~*Viola Mezco*~~	~~*Sensitive*~~
~~*Edward Bartlett*~~	~~*Archivist/Investigator*~~

Chapter Nineteen: Ironing

"Once we had the go ahead for a third fieldtrip, we had endless discussions about the house and how we should handle it. We came very close to abandoning the project, purely because we couldn't reach a consensus.

I know I'm repeating myself, but the more I think about it, the more I'm convinced that house was playing with me. Maybe still is. That first trip, with the table tilting in just the right way to be barely visible to the camera. Then the second trip, things walking around inside the doll's house, things coming through the ceiling, but just out of shot. Everything just slightly away from the table. The table I'd spent the whole morning preparing to shoot.

I initially thought the safest way forward was to redouble on the recordings. I was willing to switch to digital, just to make it possible. With digital equipment I could have recorded throughout the house 24/7. With film, the main expense is the physical copy. With analogue recording the quantity of film stock limits your recording time. Even using video tape, where you don't have the processing costs, the shear meterage of tape required to produce a constant record would have cost a fortune. Going digital meant it could all be stored on a couple of cheap hard drives.

The counter argument was the possibility that the presence of so much equipment would just mean that whatever was in the house wouldn't show. I took a lot of persuading. At that time, I was only beginning to understand that we were dealing with an intelligence, not just a random collection of phenomena.

Steve was incredibly stubborn about his filming. May and I thought his plan to load the house with cameras would be counterproductive. The presence had made it known it didn't want to be filmed, or was playing with us, making sure the cameras would only grab snippets of what was going on. It was almost as if it was trying to make us look stupid.

I think Steve saw the project in a whole different light to me and May. He wanted recorded proof of paranormal activity, whereas we were hoping to bring some peace to the poor souls trapped in the house. Steve didn't understand that. Having no sensitivity to the other side, he simply didn't feel the pain in the building. Even Jed, who'd convinced himself that he had no sensitivity, was tuned into it at some level and was trying to work it out.

May said something to me, after we'd had a very unproductive meeting with Steve. She said it was something she'd noticed over the years, men and women had a different way of interacting with the paranormal; men, even ones with strongly developed sensitivity to other's pain, acted like big game hunters. They wanted something they could mount on a wall, or they wanted to eliminate it entirely, under the guise of 'freeing' someone they'd labelled a victim. None of them ever considered that what they were dealing with might be the thing that needed help. May was one of the sweetest people I've ever met, but, when she said that, she sounded deeply bitter.

When May and I told him we thought filling the house with cameras would only put the house on its guard, he started well … well, sulking is the only word I can use. He told us if we were going on the trip without a view to getting a visual record then he was largely redundant and might as well not go.

This might be disingenuous of me, but I suspect he thought the trip couldn't go ahead without him. At the start of the project that may well have been the case, but by 2012 there was so much interest in number 37 that the project was bigger than any one of us."

The date for the third fieldtrip was specified by Cardino. After his collapse and admission to hospital he had spent almost a week in a state of intense confusion, the chest infection combined with severe dehydration caused a degree of delirium. During this period, he filled pages with line after line of tightly packed figures. When he recovered his senses, he had no memory of writing them and no idea of their significance.

That the pages of, what appeared to be, random numbers survived was the result of Mabel Noakes's intervention. She had visited Cardino in hospital daily. Later, talking to Crossland she would report that Cardino was almost unconscious for the first 24 hours. When he came around his speech was largely incomprehensible.

By chance Noakes was present when a member of staff was attempting to take Cardino's lunch time meal request. Seemingly oblivious to his mental capacity, they had given him the menu to read and a pen to circle his choices. Instead of circling items on the menu, he frantically wrote numbers in every available space. Noakes asked that he be given blank sheets of paper, and that they be saved when he had filled them.

Over the course of three days, Cardino filled 16 sides of A4 paper. The sheets were all retained by the hospital staff and Noakes collected them daily. When he was lucid again, following a course of antibiotics and IV fluids, Noakes presented the collection to him, asking if they were significant.

Noakes, again reporting to Crossland, said Cardino stared at the sheets blankly for a time before nodding. Although he had no memory of writing the numbers, he could see a pattern. He started work on deciphering the sheets while still in his hospital bed, filling several A5 notebooks with calculations.

Noakes returned the original A4 sheets to Cardino, but not before making copies that she passed on to Steven Ward. In the course of decoding what he calls his 'mind free writings' Cardino would make more copies, dozens of them. He shows me the copies, as well as the originals.

The photocopied reproductions have all been subjected to varying degrees of modification. Many sets have been mostly obscured by notations and calculations, some are overlaid with carefully drawn grids, another has been connected to a collection of graphs and Ven diagrams.

"This was the breakthrough though," he tells me and carefully unfolds a huge map-like sheet, formed from narrow strips of paper, Sellotaped together. The strips are lines of figures that have been painstakingly cut from the A4 sheets.

I had to try several combinations. I thought it was going to drive me crazy sometimes, but I worked it out in the end. I separated the individual lines and laid them out in their original order. Then I took the first line and moved it down three spaces, the second line I moved seven spaces, the third line three spaces, seven spaces, three spaces, seven spaces, three spaces ... and so on. It wasn't right, but I could feel something was beginning to gel. I spent four of five days on that trying to see where I'd gone wrong, then it struck me, it was obvious really. Three, seven, three, seven, until I got to the 37th line. The 37s were set in place, static, I didn't need to move them. After that it all made sense and it was just a matter of condensing the figures to a single point; the date. The house was telling us when we should go back. When I told the others they all agreed, the house was telling us to go back."

Unusually for Steven Ward, the quality of the footage is poor. Colour saturation and focus constantly shift and the images are uniformly grainy. A date stamp in the corner of the screen reads 31/07/2012. The clip, little more than five minutes in duration, has audio, although it is purely ambient. At the start of the clip, Mabel Noakes – out of shot – can just be heard,

"Can you feel it, Carol? Can you feel it too? It's ... oh. The pain."

The next voice, much clearer, is Ward's,

"Oh my God. This is unbelievable. This is insane."

Faintly and for a short time, Carol Crossland, can be heard

weeping.

The first 97 seconds of the footage, having no context, is largely meaningless. The camera, later it is confirmed the filming is being carried out on a mobile phone, moves along a slightly mottled green surface. As the film progresses it becomes clear that what's on the screen is a section of the wall of the staircase of 37 Fantoccini Street. It is not possible to exactly locate the section of wall as no indication is given of which staircase is being filmed.

During my interview with him Ward maintained the footage was taken on the second staircase, leading from first floor to attic. Crossland however, interviewed at a later date, was adamant that Ward had started filming almost as soon as they entered number 37 and the film was taken on the first staircase, leading from the entrance hall to the first-floor landing.

The poor image quality and uniform colour scheme of the hallways and landings make it hard to definitively settle the matter, even when the footage is compared with the 127 photos Ward would later take.

"There were 370 of them," Steven Ward tells me, *them* being the series of regular, peak like shapes that had appeared on the internal walls of number 37. He is showing me some of the huge collection of images, captured on the first morning of trip three.

Jed counted them, of course. He was hugely excited about that, the number 370. Although, and I did note this in my report at the time, four of the markings he included in the count I thought were questionable".

He shows me photos, taken in isolation, of four individual markings. All the markings, except for these four, are remarkably regular. Three of the four rogues are roughly the shape and size of the others but end in vague blurs rather than a clearly defined apex. The fourth is little more than a dark smudge.

When we went into the house that morning my first

thought was that the damp had really taken hold, because it looked like the walls were covered in patches of mould. There was no electricity on, and the ground floor windows and doors were boarded up against vandals, so it was pretty dark in there. It was a really bright morning as well, so coming out of the glare into the dim hallway meant our eyes needed to adjust. When I saw how regular the marks were, I realised they couldn't be just mould, or anything else natural. They led up the stairs, so we followed them."

The chill of the late afternoon has driven us from Carol Crossland's garden. She leads us to the seats at the end of her dining table, which sits directly in front of sliding glass doors, overlooking her lawn.

She is glad to be nearing the end of her story.

"Steve said something about branding, the way you brand cattle, you know? At the time he said it I hadn't been too close to the marks, so I didn't appreciate they'd been burned into the walls, which must have been what he was thinking about. To me, they looked like teeth. I thought the house was baring its teeth at us, warning us away. I was very unsettled by it. Of course, Steve wanted to film it. He pulled out his phone and started taking a video as soon as he was through the door.

The atmosphere between the group was off, even before we left the uni. The effect that house was having on us didn't end at the borders of the property. People talk about hauntings and possessions and contacts as if they're something that can be contained in box. It's one of those ideas that's almost universal. It's ludicrous, if people sat and thought about it for even a second, they'd see that. Forces, spirits, ghosts - whatever label you like to apply - exist outside the physical realm, but somehow people think if you close the door on the way out, they'll be contained.

That mode of thinking was part of the reason we'd become discordant. To be blunt, I've always had a problem with the masculine approach to para investigations. May felt the same, but she was always very discreet about voicing it. That might have been a generational thing. The work of Eddie Bartlett and Steve and even the big-name players like Geller and Playfair, is doubtless sincere but, and I don't mean to devalue it by saying this, the obsession with recording risks fetishizing it. The compulsion to document and observe – repeatedly - things we don't understand is almost pornographic. I don't mean that in a sexual way, but if you look at the way the adult film industry works nothing is considered to happen unless it's graphically shown, not portrayed: shown.

Once we'd realised the marks had been burned into the walls, we decided to take some scrapings. I was still thinking in terms of branding, it was May who saw the marks were the size and shape of a flat iron. I was taking a sample of one of the darker markings, it was one at the top of the stairs leading to the first floor. May said, 'It looks like Liddy[82] has started on the ironing'. I didn't have access to the Jed's thermometer on that last trip, but I'm willing to swear the temperature dropped when she said that. We all felt it. It was more than just the old cliche about your blood running cold; you could actually feel the ambient temperature fall. I clearly remember glancing across to Carol and being able to see her breath hanging on the air.

We were nonplussed for most of that first day. We were also very scared. Me, Steve and May stayed as a group most of the time. We spent the whole of the morning with the markings, following them and mapping and photographing them. We didn't want to be alone in any of the rooms, and we only looked into the bedrooms and living room after lunch. Nothing was said, but none of us wanted to go into the Kitchen. Even Jed, who'd taken himself off to count and

---

[82] 'Liddy' was how group referred to the presence that had made contact during the kitchen/14th August session. The message spelled out by 'Liddy' had stated she were coming to, 'do the ironing'.

measure the markings, didn't go in there. If John hadn't appeared I don't think we'd have gone into the kitchen at all, at least not that day.

He didn't get there until after lunch. God, that sounds crazy, doesn't it? With everything that was going on, we stopped for lunch. May insisted. She was worried about Jed, worried he'd just keep slogging away at the house and forget to feed himself unless we reminded him to."

"That last trip? I wasn't invited. I was so out in the cold by then I wasn't even told they didn't want me to go. They just didn't bother speaking to me. Then I get a phone call, Stevie boy himself, nearly in f__king tears because, by his telling, big things were happening and none of it would be recorded. I thought at the time he was trying to drum up my enthusiasm. He did come out with some s__t about how stuff was happening that would convince even me, but I wasn't in the mood to be charmed. He wanted me to drop everything and run for another poxy ghost story. I told him what my hourly rate was for private work and asked how much he wanted to spend.

We agreed I'd give the house three hours. I don't know who footed the bill, but I've always suspected he paid me out of his own pocket[83]. That's why I wrapped it up ASAP."

"We discussed whether we should ask John to come back to the house. It wasn't a matter of whether or not to use him but whether or not to record at all. Steve was desperate to get records of what we were doing. We kept kicking the same argument around, May and I were scared of losing contact, we could see the house didn't want to be filmed. It's a recognised phenomenon that paranormal activity is reduced in the presence of sceptics, those with closed minds. We were

---

[83] If this was the case, Ward chose not to mention it when interviewed.

convinced the intelligence in number 37 viewed the attempts to collect proof as an extension of that effect.

Steve kept saying that the audio equipment hadn't seemed to be a problem. May's view, mine also, was the house might be increasingly communicative if we simply tried to make contact, rather than 'catch it in the act', those were her words. I felt the same, but … well I was scared too. The contact was important, of course it was, but the feeling in the house had changed, even in the short time I'd spent there. At first there were different vibrations coming off the different parts of it, the living room had an aura of fear laying over it, the attic had something bad, malevolent and the kitchen had that despairing feel to it. By the third trip, all you could feel was the pain. Not a physical pain, nothing like a stubbed toe or a broken bone, say. This was a spiritual pain, like the essence of the building had been boiled down to a cup of psychic suffering. For me that was the frightening thing.

Whatever had happened in that house on the morning of 9/11, it hadn't ended at murder, that was just the start of those poor souls' pain. I was scared by that. There's an old song I heard, long after we'd ran out of that hellish place. I remember hearing it and just bursting into tears. I've not a clue who wrote it or sang it, but it went, *'wouldn't mind dying, if dying was all.*[84]' That was the essence of that place, you couldn't escape it, not even in death. Look at us, none of us ever really left it behind us. Not even John. Whatever happened in that kitchen - and he'll deny anything did, I'm certain of that - he never really got over it. Ask him why he lives the life he does, if you really think he got away clean."

"I got there about one. They'd got the caravan again and they were all having lunch. Apart from Jed, who was gibbering

---

[84] *Bye and Bye I'm Going to See the King*, gospel blues song, recorded by various artist over the years. (R.D)

away as usual, they all looked pretty shaken up. When I knocked, someone yelped in surprise. When they opened the door the smell of the food was overpowering, whatever they were eating was badly overcooked. I had the impression they'd locked themselves in to eat.

For a long time, no one moved. May had opened the door and she just stood there, at an angle, staring at me. I waited for someone to speak, and no one did. Finally, I said, 'Well offer me a cup of tea, at least'. They didn't. Instead Crossland sort of giggled and said, 'Show him'. Then Steve stands up and says, 'You need to see this'.

I nearly laughed. It was so over the top, they didn't seem to know how dramatic they were being. I think they'd worked themselves into such a state they didn't know what to do next. They were acting like characters from a Hammer Horror film. They didn't know what to do, so they copied the script."

"It was amazing in a way. I didn't see it at the time, perhaps I was too scared to think straight, but in its way it was amazing. There's a condition called hysterical blindness. Some PTSD sufferers get it. Reality's just too hard to deal with so the mind turns the eyes off, so it won't have to see what's happening. It was like that. Only it was like John's eyes had turned his mind off. He was looking at all those marks and seeing something else. He was spouting rubbish about April Fool's jokes. Delusional, complete denial. He was scared through, and damn close to losing it."

"Steve led me to the house, then paused at the front door and turned. I thought he was looking through me, but he was looking over my shoulder. May and Crossland were trailing behind us like a parade.

We get inside, and he just points at the prints on the wall. No one said anything. I swear, it was like they were observing a minutes silence. I must have been pretty well keyed up myself, because when I realised what they were so excited about I remember I let out a huge breath, that I hadn't known

I was holding. Then I laughed.

"I think it could have got nasty there, but Jed chose that point to come bursting through the door and start jabbering about the hidden 37s again."

"John insisted the marks were just someone playing a prank. I think he even convinced himself in the end. I wish he could have convinced me. It would be so much easier to think that someone had just come in with an iron and vandalised the building. I guess everyone copes with stress in their own way, has their own defence mechanisms. At the time I envied his ability to just pretend the reality of what he was seeing away.

"Like all armchair sceptics he insisted he was being logical while ignoring all the evidence. When we showed him the markings, he just pulled silly faces and said it was kids messing about. At first, he said something really stupid about stencils and tagging. Obviously, we had already discounted that. If you looked at those marks properly, you'd know that wasn't what was happening.

"He wouldn't let it go though. When we pointed out the marks had been burned into the walls, he came up with this ridiculous idea about someone sneaking in with a steam iron. Has soon as he'd said it, he realised it was a stupid thing to say, because he tried to backtrack on it. I pointed out there was no power in the house, so even if someone had randomly chosen an abandoned house to vandalise, what did they do, bring a generator? He made a snide remark about how people had been ironing clothes long before electricity.

"It was classic denial. The facts were there in front of us; the house had been locked up since we left it, almost a year before, and there was no graffiti or tagging on it, none – that alone was strange, given the area. And this wasn't a few vague blemishes here and there, this was a huge number of clearly defined markings. It would have taken days to produce them, even with a modern iron and a working electric supply. And rather than admit that something beyond his understanding was going on, John constructed this elaborate fantasy about

236

kids with flat irons, branding the walls.

"Even if it was vandals that doesn't explain away the huge coincidences. Why that house, why 37? It wasn't the only abandon house in the area, and even if this magical vandal knew the history of the Doll family and the house, why an iron? There was no mention of irons when the murders happened. The only time anything about irons came up was during the third contact session. Only the team knew about that. Steve wrote it up in his reports, so did I, and there were the tapes, but all that was confidential information. We never spoke about it on campus. We just ... we ...

"I'm sorry. Give me a moment. It just upsets me, still upsets me. All the evidence, all the proof, anyone could ever want, and people explain it away with fairy stories because they're too proud or too scared to accept it.

"I'm still angry at John, but I'm sorry for him too. At least the rest of us had the strength to admit we were frightened. Still are. And I suppose for sensitives, like me and May, ignoring the truth will never be an option. John, Steve, even Jed - though I'm sure he's a sensitive of a type - rely on sight and sound, they have the option of putting their hands over their ears and shutting their eyes. But the signals I was picking up ... Despair comes to you through the heart not the eyes.

Sorry, I've got to stop now. But if you ever see John, ask him what happened in the kitchen."

"Oh, for f__k's sake. Look, write this down, tattoo it on your f__king forehead so you can see it in the mirror: *nothing happened in the kitchen*. And before you bring up the subject of the recording I'm supposed to have wiped, it didn't exist[85]."

---

[85] This outburst was the only reference ever made to accusations of a recording being wiped. John Pelton refused to be drawn into further discussion on the subject and no

Chapter Twenty: The Space Below

The witness accounts of events in number 37 are, for the most part, in accord. How the team members interpreted what they lived through often differs, as does the reasoning behind their opinions but, with a few exceptions, references to observable facts are consistent. However, the accounts given of John Pelton's exit from the house, on 31st July 2012, vary significantly from one another.

Other than a few seconds of audio tape, which cannot be accurately accounted for in terms of location or chronology, there are no physical records of Pelton's departure from the house and no records of what he encountered in the kitchen.

"Carol was getting upset. I don't know if John was trying to wind her up deliberately, he could be pretty obnoxious when the mood took him, but she was still very shaken by what had happened and John, just refusing to see it, was annoying her. May and myself were used to it. We'd both dealt with him before and, being that bit older, we'd developed thicker skins in general.

"The armchair sceptics are always desperate not to be convinced, after a while you learn not to waste time listening to them. It's the only way to get anywhere.

"It was the usual thing, I'd seen it before, and since. Carol was pointing out the obvious truth and John had his fingers in his ears shouting, 'la la la'. She was nearly in tears. By the end John was just blanking her, and May, who was backing

one else I interviewed recalled hearing of such an event.

238

her up. He turned to me and said; 'If you want me to, I'll stay here all day talking fairy studies, but I'm charging by the hour.' *Fairy studies* was what he'd taken to calling the study of the paranormal. It was his way of getting out of the discussion without admitting defeat. I told him what I wanted setup and he went to collect his gear.

"We'd agreed to reinstate sound triggered, recording devices in the attic, living room and kitchen. Basically, the places where the bodies had been found. In truth I'd have liked more comprehensive data collection, but it was a degree of compromise. And the budget was tighter for the last trip. We had no power supply, so all John's sound gear would have to be battery powered. Not ideal.

"He worked really fast. He was doing his usual thing of trying to look completely unfazed by the house, but ... well you could tell he wanted to get out of that place. It was obvious he was wary of going into the kitchen. With hindsight I feel bad that I didn't go in with him. In my defence, he was being bloody obnoxious at the time, and I wasn't at my best that day.

"It's hard to describe, but I was scared without really knowing it. Finding those marks was a huge event; clear, unambiguous evidence of paranormal activity. I was intensely excited about that, but then there was the other side of it, the nature of the marks. They were clearly hostile. We weren't welcome in that house. A good part of my excitement was fear, and at the time I didn't recognise it. Of course, that made me edgy and less patient with John. In Short, I wasn't about to offer to go into the kitchen with him unless he actually asked me to. And, of course, he didn't.

"I wondered since if the house didn't act on us in a way. Bring out something in us, maybe the worst of us. John got more stubborn and narrow with every visit. Jed's obsessiveness, my own impatience. Only Carol and May seemed able to keep sight of themselves, even then, the toll it was taking on them was plain to see.

"When he couldn't put it off any longer, John went to the

239

kitchen. He'd only been in there a few minutes when the door slammed shut. I'm sure he'd explain it away by blaming the wind or a draft, but it would just be the voice of his denial. There wasn't the vaguest hint of a breeze that day. We'd all remarked on it. There wasn't a breath of air. It was what people used to call close. Regardless, that door didn't just swing shut, it slammed. Jed was with me in the hall, pointing out some detail about the height of the first marking, and I remember we both jumped when the door banged shut. Then John screamed."

"I didn't scream. Christ, where does he get this s__t from? I might have yelped or cried out, I'd just landed on me arse. Mostly I swore, especially once I'd gashed my leg open. That was the end of the story.

"The door slamming? That was me. I was setting up the mics for the kitchen and all I could hear was Steve and Jed in the hall. Jed was jabbering a load of s__t about the marks and Steve was acting like he was hearing the 10,000 names of God. It was getting on my nerves. I backheeled the door shut, lost my balance and stumbled onto a section of the rotted-out floor. The bit by the sink. My right foot when straight through one of the boards and down I went. That's when I cut my leg.

"I've read Steve's account of it all and it's complete b_____ks. All that s__t about the house biting me is pure fantasy. I went to A and E after I'd finished up and got a tetanus jab. It was a rusty nail, not a bite."

"I hesitated. I'm ashamed to say that, I really am, but for a moment I contemplated running away. That's how scared I was. Then Jed barged past me and wrenched the kitchen door open[86] and I followed him. I still wonder what would have

---

[86] The phrase 'Wrenched open' suggests the kitchen door opened outward, into the hallway. If this is the case, it contradicts John Pelton's statement that he

240

happened if Jed hadn't been there at that point. I want to think well enough of myself to say that I'd have unfrozen and gone into the kitchen anyway … but I'm not sure."

"I was with May, in the living room when John started screaming. She was already shaken up. I'm not sure if it was because of the vibrations in the house or because of the scene with John. At the time I was very angry at him and I assumed May felt the same, but it may have been purely the house effecting her.

"I remember we were having a funny kind of conversation, very stilted, and for us that was unusual. We'd had a real rapport from the outset. But, after listening to John's stupid comments and snide remarks, I felt as if I was walking on eggshells for some reason. I've heard Steve's theory that the house worked on us in some way, played around with our psyches. When he first suggested that I didn't really put much store by it, because I thought, as the group's sensitives, May and I would have been hyper susceptible to such an influence, and, at the time, I didn't think we'd been affected. Now I'm not so sure. The way it was between us two that morning wasn't normal.

"When we heard the screams, neither of us really reacted. I know Steve said he froze up and couldn't go to John straight away because he was scared. I'll take him at his word on that, but for my part, I wasn't scared when I heard John screaming,

---

'backheeled' the door shut while inside the kitchen. At the time of interviewing Steven Ward, I did not realise the significance of his wording, and would not do so until after he had closed communications with me. No floor plans of the 37 Fantoccini Street are available and none to the photographs in my possession show the door in enough detail to settle the question definitively.

241

I was triumphant, happy almost. The thought flashed across my mind: *'try explaining that away'*.

"That sudden blast of spite, it was me, I have to own it, but it's as if it was being magnified. Though maybe that's not the right word. Amplified would be better. It was only there a moment, then it was gone, and we were both running to the kitchen.

"When I think about that day, and I think about it more than I'd like to, I can't help but wonder at what May must have been going through. Very few people could really appreciate what a talented, what a powerful, psychic she was. Whatever I might have gone through in that place, she must have gone through tenfold."

"He was in the floor, it looked like the house was trying to swallow him. He wasn't making any sense, just bawling really. He was terrified, flailing around. Jed got to him first and when he put his hand out to help him up John grabbed him like – I'm sorry if this sounds melodramatic – like his life depended on it. As soon as we got him out, he started trying to tough it out, cussing and swearing, trying to look angry rather than scared. He might have pulled it off if May hadn't cried out when she saw the state his leg was in. There was blood pouring down his shin. He was wearing trainers and the blood was pooling in the laces.

"There was a first-aid kit in the caravan, so I took him out to dress the wound. I had to stop myself locking the door once we were in the caravan. I don't know if John was just really tough or just desperate not to believe his eyes, but once we were out of the house, he acted as if he'd done nothing worse than bark his shin. It was a moderately bad wound, it wasn't life threatening, but it needed attending to. The thing about it though; it wasn't a scratch, the skin breaks weren't longitudinal, they were puncture wounds. Bites.

"I know how that sounds. Frankly, I don't care if you believe me or not. I know what I saw."

"I didn't see John's leg, not really. Steve described it to me and May just after he'd bandaged it. I did see John's jeans were ripped and bloodied. Steve had tried to photograph the wounds, but John wouldn't let him. Apparently, he got quite aggressive about it when Steve tried to insist. So, I can't say if the marks were bites, like Steve says. But bear in mind, Steve is a trained observer.

"What I can say with certainty, will swear to on my life, is that whatever drew blood that day, it wasn't a simple hole in the floor. I saw the hole in the kitchen floor and there was nothing that could have done that, the wood was soft as butter, it was so rotten. It had been rotting away for years.

"Jed, wanted to measure the hole[87], he was edging forward, feeling for sections of flooring that might give way. We all stayed while he started measuring, it was a safety thing. By that point we didn't want to be isolated. I kept thinking about those silly horror films where the teenagers go into a haunted house or a shack in the woods, and one of them wanders away on their own. You know how that story goes.

"It felt like Jed was taking forever but really he can't have been at it for that long, because Steve and John weren't in the caravan that long, and they came back to the house just as Jed realised there was a cellar under the kitchen."

"John didn't say as much, but he wanted to get his gear together and get the *hell out of Dodge*. The second he got his jeans back on he stomped back to the house. As soon as we stepped through the door, we heard Jed shouting. I bolted for the kitchen, I thought he was being attacked too, but he

---

[87] The hole was irregular and yielded dimensions dependant on which points were chosen as datums. However, Gerald Cardino did find a high number of points measuring 37 inches and a lower number measuring 37cm.

bowled out the door and nearly knocked me flat. He was shouting about needing a torch."

Cardino points to the base of the miniature house he has constructed. Like the genuine doll's house, it sits on a 15cm high plinth.

"Until I was edging around the kitchen, measuring the hole in the floor that had opened up, it hadn't occurred to me that number 37 had a cellar. It wasn't that common for a house of that age and style, and there was no entrance to it. We never did find one. We all paced around the footprint of the place looking for a coal chute or something, at least signs that one had been closed off or bricked over. There was nothing. There was no way down under the stairs either, that would be the obvious place to situate an entrance.

The only logical explanation might be that the house was originally designed to have a cellar, but the specs were changed after it was excavated, and it was then built over. I suppose it's possible, but it doesn't sound very likely. Even if that is the case, it doesn't explain what the staircase was about, or how the dolls got in there.

"I told Steve and John about the cellar. They came into the kitchen about a second after Jed ran out, looking for a torch. I hadn't seen it at that point. Neither had May, but she was frowning, and her eyes were glazed over. She wasn't speaking, and I'm sure she was picking something up from the space below.

"John refused to take an interest. He started collecting his toys and just acted like we weren't there. Steve went to see it for himself, peering into the hole. The maw, really, that's what it looked like, a diseased mouth. In some ways I suppose it was. Steve was squinting into the darkness and had just said there was something down there, when Jed burst back into the room again with one of those big MAG lights. He got down on the floor and shone it into the space. Steve gasped out loud and a second later May, who still hadn't moved, let out a moan. Jed swore, and that was unusual for him. He beckoned me over. I remember moving very slowly. I was scared. That hole ... I swear to you, I could feel it throbbing, as if it was vomiting, heaving out bile and hate.

"I looked into the cellar and ran straight for the door.

The cellar was full of dolls. The torch light caught their eyes, making it look like they were gazing up at the light.

No. No. I won't pretend; they *were* gazing up at the light."

"I heard John mutter something under his breath when Carol ran out the room. I said to him, 'you really need to see this.' He just said, 'No, Steve, I really don't', and walked out.

"I don't blame him. Not after what he went through. Even if he does pretend nothing happened.

"I took some pictures with my phone. They're rubbish. That cellar just swallowed the flash. But as soon as I took my phone out, Jed's MAG light failed. By that point I wasn't even surprised."

Chapter Twenty-One: Beautifully Hideous

The photograph has been taken on Steven Ward's phone. The image quality is low. The phone's flash facility has provided a narrow point of illumination, leaving large parts of the image in near complete blackness.

In the upper section of the frame, it is possible to see a flight of stairs, lying on its side. The structure is in deep shadow, and it is not possible to make out any details beyond its shape and location. In this copy of the photograph the upper most edges of the stairs have been highlighted with a fine white line. The appearance is of a tilted zigzag running across the image.

The lower portion of the photograph has a number of bright points. These are caused by the camera/phone flash reflecting off the glass eyes of approximately twenty dolls.

Not all the doll's faces are visible, the ones toward the outer area of the frame are lost in darkness. All the dolls visible in the picture, lay face up.

Although it is not possible to see in the photograph, witness reports agree that the floor of the cellar was flooded. The depth of water is unknown, but it was sufficient to allow the dolls to float.

Ella, despite her connection to the Fantoccini Street fieldtrips, has never seen the photograph of the cellar dolls. The low-quality image, from Ward's phone, is lower still in the photostat copy I show her. Despite the lighting issues and poor print quality, Ella is able to identify around half the dolls

246

by brand and date. In her opinion, given what she can make out, the dolls appear to be a moderately expensive collection of seventies Victoriana. She describes them as,

"Nice enough, nothing spectacular."

The photo doesn't hold her interest, although she does ask me about the bizarrely situated staircase, laying in the brackish water on the cellar floor, seeming to provide a senseless route between the angle of two walls. I tell her there is no explanation for it that makes any sense. In the same way there's no explanation as to why a cellar was built with no entrance and, least of all, an explanation of how the inaccessible space came to house a collection of dolls.

The mysteries too, fail to hold her interest, but that is not really surprising. In less than four weeks' time, Ella is due to leave her 'home' of the last thirty years and move in with her sister and her family. By any measure it is a big step.

I put away my badly reproduced photo and talk about the new life that will soon open up for her.

It's been a little over two years since I first made contact with Ella. It's a relationship that's hard to define. Most of the activities that form or constitute friendships are denied to us by Ella's circumstance. The extensive correspondence we have shared and the far less numerous meetings, have revolved almost exclusively around the subject of number 37, even then, Ella's interest was almost completely on the dolls.

I know little of Ella beyond her reputation, both within doll collecting circles and beyond. While she doesn't give the impression of being unwilling to share her personal history, I am left with the feeling that she regards most of her life as secondary to her collection.

In many ways she is the perfect foil, or even reflector, of the overarching story of number 37. Facts present themselves but offer no revelations and produce questions, not answers.

I know enough of Ella's background to know the upcoming residency at her sister's household represents a massive

247

change for both of them. Sadly, given the nature of my own relationship with Ella, I feel unable to discuss it with her in all but the vaguest, shallowest terms. I want to know what her feelings about her brother-in-law are, but instead I ask where she'll be sleeping. The answer's as banal as the question. The boxroom, front of the house. I'm still thinking of her brother-in-law and any concerns he may have about the new contours of his shared home, when I ask if she'll continue expanding her collection.

I'm surprised when Ella shakes her head. Doubly so because she gives a huge and genuinely happy smile.

"I've nearly finished the collection, I'm making the last doll now. It'll be the final piece".

To imagine Ella without the attendance of dolls is almost unsettling. The conversation becomes ever more stilted, and it is evident without the common ground of dolls, there is little reason for us to stay in touch.

I wish Ella luck and happiness with her new beginning and leave, expecting this to be our last contact.

Less than a week later I receive a package from her. It's a gift, one I find strangely moving, despite the letter that comes with it explaining I wasn't originally intended as the recipient.

It's the last doll, the final piece of the collection. The letter explains that Ella had intended to present the doll to her sister and her husband as a sign of her gratitude for being welcomed into their home. After discussion with her counsellor, she agreed the gift might not be appropriate.

The doll is beautifully hideous. To understand this you need to be familiar with the dichotomy of Ella's craftmanship. Ella's methods, which if not secret are largely private, vary depending on the type of doll she is working with. For plastic varieties, such as the one she gives me, she uses a decommissioned steam iron, heating the tip manually using a chef's blowtorch. This delicacy of touch produces the precision disfigurements that her creepy dolls are renown for. Ella tells me the finishes she achieves are further enhanced by

248

first layering the iron with aluminium foil. With patience and years of practice, she perfected the art of combining coloured foils and semi melted plastic to produce differing hues of burn marks. In her own words she, *'renders the plastic flesh with just the right amount of gloss, so the flecks of foil shimmer like jewels of scar tissue.'*

The doll Ella gifts me is a fairly scares 'Lydia doll'. It was released and sold in America toward the end of the nineties, part of a range of biblically themed figures that the manufacturers predicted would be the must-have-present that Christmas. Lydia and her companion dolls where destined to become obscurities, sought out only for specific collections, or by someone with a sister named Lydia.

Despite the artistry of the doll and the care that has gone into its creation, I can see why Ella's therapists warned against giving it as a sign of affection. The doll's remaining hair has been styled to lay over the scars, although the strands accentuate their presence rather than hide it.

I send Ella a sincere letter of thanks and this time as expected, never hear from her again.

Chapter Twenty-Two: The Last Recordings

"May never went back inside that house again. I know Steve and Jed – at least to a point – were disappointed in her, but they couldn't begin to understand what she, what both of us, were going through. It took all my strength just to stay on site. I stayed in the caravan, making mugs of tea of course, how banal is that? But I wouldn't have gone back into that place if I hadn't had to.

"It wasn't just about being scared, we were of course. We all were, even John, especially John, but thinking beyond the fear; it was dangerous. Dangerous and pointless. Running into a burning house to save a life, that's brave, running into a burning house to check if it's hot, that's just stupid.

"I remember May and I kept opening and closing the curtains and changing seats; trying not to look at the house and too scared not to.

"In the end we only stayed the one night anyway. A big part of that decision was Steve's. At the time he told me he was concerned that Jed would get injured. Later I heard him telling Jed that they should leave for the sake of *the girls*. I was so relieved to be leaving, that we were all leaving, it wasn't until later that I got angry about it, patronizing b_____d. And worse than that, he was blaming everyone but himself for leaving. At least John had had the decency to just run away.

"Steve was all for staying, until we listened to the tapes from the night's recordings. That was typical; *the girls* had been telling him there was something malevolent in the house from the moment we landed, but he had to hear it from a machine if he was going to believe it. Maybe he'd have taken our word for it if we'd had a wifi connection to the other side. Or if we'd been men."

"Jed and myself went back into the house at six a.m., or there abouts. I've got a record of it somewhere, but it doesn't really matter. I wasn't in any hurry, but with four of us in the 'van it was hard to sleep anyway. And of course, Jed barely slept at all. I was really beginning to worry about him. Especially given the state the house was in; the rot had taken hold since our last visit, I don't remember what the weather was like that winter, perhaps it was a bad one and it accelerated the decay, but I don't know. There was a feeling about that place, you didn't need to be a sensitive to pick it up. There was a tension there. I don't know if the place was trying to draw us in, or drive us out, but it was like the fabric of the house was reacting to what was happening.

"You had to watch your step. That's not a figure of speech, I mean it literally, the kitchen floor was falling through, it was only luck that we didn't all end up in the cellar. If that thing was a cellar. The top of the house was in a bad way too, particularly the attic and the top half of the last staircase. You had to be careful.

"Me and John had been creeping up and down the stairs like cat burglars, but Jed couldn't slow it down. I had visions of him putting his foot through one of the treads and going down the rest headfirst. He was too excited; I was worried he was edging into mania.

"May and Carol wouldn't go into the house after we found the dolls in the cellar, and with just the two of us in there I couldn't do much more than keep an eye on Jed. I wanted to check the recording devices to see if they'd picked anything up and Jed wanted to find a way into the cellar. We did a tour of the outside walls looking for a door, he practically ran around the back garden. He was getting more and more hyped up when we didn't see a door. He was all for climbing down the hole in the kitchen floor. I was worried that he'd throw himself down there the minute he was out of my sight.

"I persuaded him to stay with me while we collected the tapes, then he agreed to listen to them with us. At the end of it we were all pretty shaken up. Well, even more shaken up.

251

Carol especially. Even Jed, manic as he was, could see that.

"After all that had happened and all we had seen in that house, those tapes were terrifying. That silence. Hours and hours of ... of void. Somebody, and even though there were only four of us I can't remember who, said it was like the house was holding its breath. For me it didn't' feel so benign. It was more like the house was a snake, waiting while it decided whether to strike.

"Carol was upset, and I could tell she didn't want to be there anymore. I could understand that. People at the uni had been talking about the trips like they were big jolly ups, but they'd never been like that, and now they were downright unpleasant. It was May I was really worried for. I knew she was a talented psychic, but it wasn't until that last trip I had any idea how talented. I could see her being beaten down by whatever was in that place. I can't imagine what it must have been like for her, I imagine it would be like you or me sitting in a roomful of people screaming in our faces. She kept drifting off from us. You could see her eyes losing focus sometimes, then she'd look around her, as if she'd just woken up and couldn't quite place where she was.

"I wanted to get both of them away from that place, and Jed too of course. After we played those tapes[88] Carole was close to tears. May was trying to comfort her, even though she was distressed herself. For the time being I was unwilling to leave them alone. While I waited with them, Jed went back to

---

[88] During the interview Steven Ward didn't make it clear if he and the team had listened to the tapes in their entirety. It seems unlikely that four of them sat together in the caravan for the full duration of three tapes, each four-hours long. I can only assume that Ward means they listened to enough of the tapes to ascertain their nature.

the house."

"The tapes were very odd. Because that house was never quiet. I agreed with Carol's comment, about it sounding as if the house was holding its breath and waiting for us. After we'd listened, Steve muttered something like, 'Sweet Jesus', and then Carol burst into tears. Steve and May were both looking after her. I thought she looked uncomfortable about the fuss being made, so I slipped outside and went back to the house.

"For some reason the recording made in the attics gave me an idea. It was obvious really, I don't know why I didn't see it from the start. The doll's house was clearly a model, albeit a distorted one, of number 37. It followed that if 37 had an entrance to the cellar then it would be represented in 37a. I went straight upstairs."

"I hadn't slept much and, as I've said, I was scared myself. That morning my head was spinning like a top. I knew May and Carol were both in a bad way, but I was acutely aware that Jed had gone back to the house. At that point I think he was a danger to himself. Combine that with that house …

"I told Carol we needed to get Jed out of that place. I remember telling her because May wasn't with us at that point, she was staring directly at me but I'd swear she had no idea who I was.

"I Dropped the keys a dozen times getting the front door unlocked. As soon as I got through the door, I saw there was a doll on the bottom stair. I almost turned and ran."

Chapter Twenty-Three: The Last Photograph

Fantoccini Street Photo Log (01/08/2012)
Base of ground floor staircase. 1 of 1

The picture is out of focus and poorly defined. It has been taken on Steven Ward's mobile phone. The camera/phone flash has produced a red and orange 'bloom', slightly to the right of frame, further obscuring the contents of the photograph. The few discernible details have been enhanced with white outlining. Had this not been done it is doubtful if the subject matter would be recognisable.

A series of horizontal lines highlight the leading edges of the stair treads. Staggered vertical lines, to the left of shot, indicate the uprights of the bannisters. On the bottom step, partly hidden by the red and orange 'bloom', is an irregular shape. The shape, too, has been outlined revealing it as humanoid in form. Using the known dimensions of the step, recorded in Gerald Cardino's existing survey, it is possible to estimate the height of the humanoid figure at five to six inches. If the figure is intended to represent an adult, this would mean it is 1/12th scale. This is consistent with the doll's previously discovered in 37 Fantoccini Street.

This is the last photograph taken inside house.

"I shouted out to Jed and didn't get an answer. The obvious place to look was the kitchen. I don't know how long I stood there, too scared to move. When I finally got up my nerve and pushed the kitchen door open, Jed wasn't there. My first thought was that he'd gone through the floor. I called out to him again, a lot louder than I intended to, if I'm completely honest I probably screamed his name.

"For a long time, I told myself I didn't want to risk going into the kitchen and the floor collapsing under me. I can admit it to myself now; I was terrified of what I might see if I looked into the underside of that house.

"When Jed shouted down to me from the attic, I really did scream. I was so convinced he was laying in the cellar, when his voice came down the stairs, my first thought was it was the doll."

"When the screaming and shouting started May mumbled something. She was scared senseless. People say that as a figure of speech but when you see somebody in that state, it's awful. Awful. She was staring around her and just mumbling. I wasn't thinking clearly at the time but obviously the psychic energy, even outside, sitting in the caravan, was immense. My hair was standing on end, and I was covered in goose bumps. Looking at May now it's easy to forget what a powerful sensitive she was - it could be she still is, we can't know - I can't begin to imagine what that house was doing to her just then.

"I don't know how I managed to get out of that caravan and go to the house. Fight of flight reaction I suppose, the adrenaline kicked in. I ran up to the front door and saw Steve bolting up the stairs. I ran after him. Jed was in the attic, we could hear him shouting.

"The doll on the bottom step? No, I didn't see it, it had gone. At the time I didn't know about it. Steve didn't mention it until we were all back at the uni. I thought he might have been imagining it or seeing what the house wanted him to see. Then he showed me the picture he'd taken. But when I followed him up the stairs, it just wasn't there.

"I caught up with him at the foot of the staircase leading to the attic. I was still pumped with the adrenaline and made to charge up them, but he blocked the way and told me to stay where I was."

"That last staircase was rotten. I wanted Carol to stay there so

255

there'd be someone to get help if me or Jed went through it. It wasn't going to be safe to have all three of us coming down it together anyway. So, I went up alone. That probably sounds braver than it was. Now I was closer to the attic I could hear Jed wasn't distressed, he was excited. He was shouting that he'd found it, 'come and look, I'm got it, I've found it'.

"I assumed he'd come across another of his 37 finds. It's a sign of how twisted that house was, that those recurring 37's were close enough to normal to be calming. Then I got into the attic room and the first thing I saw was the blood. I'd got there just in time. To this day I don't think Jed realises the danger he was in.

"He was over at the far end of the room. He'd torn the doll's house to pieces and there was blood, his blood, smeared over the walls."

"I frightened the life out of Steve."

Cardino laughs, then looks abashed.

"It's not funny really, it wasn't at the time, but now I can see the funny side. I don't know if Steve does. I'd guess not.

"I'd been looking at 37a again, trying to find where the entrance to the cellar was. Of course I couldn't see the back elevation of the house without moving the model. So, I pulled it away from the wall. It was on a three-legged half table affair and, when I inched it out from the wall, one of the legs just folded underneath it. I grabbed the model to try and save it. I caught it by the roof, and it came away in my hands. It was badly swollen with damp by then of course, falling to pieces. I made another grab at it, and it sort of folded in my hands, collapsed. I managed to slow its fall a little but that was about all. It hit the floor and fell apart.

"I couldn't believe what I'd done. I'd just destroyed an important paranormal artifact. I just stood there for a second staring at the wreckage. I even ran my fingers through my hair, the way they do in TV dramas. It was only then I realised I'd cut my hand because I smeared blood across my forehead. It's possible I staggered or tripped because I remember putting my hand out to support myself, I guess that's when I put the handprints on the wall.

"In a funny way it was lucky, cutting my hand, banging into the wall, it distracted me from what I'd done, so I was able to actually see what I was looking at. The doll's house, what was left of it, had separated from the plinth and I'd been right. The plinth wasn't just a platform to display the model on, it was a miniature cellar, with a miniature staircase in it.

"It had broken free when I dropped the model, but it was possible to see where it had been. It didn't make sense, not in terms of normal architecture, but I had a pretty good understanding of the way 37a represented a twisted version of our dimension. I knew all I had to do was take the measurements and I'd be able to locate the way into 37's cellar.

"I made a judgement call and decided finding the cellar was more important than preserving the doll's house. So, I set about pulling the plinth-cellar out of the wreckage, so I could measure and calculate from it. About then I heard Steve calling. I shouted back that I'd found the way in.

"A few seconds later he burst through the door, screeching that we had to get out of there.

"Such a waste. If only we'd stayed, the things we might have discovered. I tried explaining about the miniature cellar. He just stared at the wreckage and told me to bring it with me. I grabbed the plinth, it was still in one piece, and went. I figured it was the most vital part of the puzzle. Of course, even that was lost in the end. This is all that's left."

He's holding the miniature staircase that had come adrift from the doll's house cellar. Unlike the rest of 37a, it is a crude piece of work. A basic representation of a flight of stairs, made with a series of cuts in a block of wood. Cardino holds it tenderly and smiles at it. It's not a happy smile.

"If only I had the original model to work with, I'm sure it had a lot to reveal. Guess how many steps."

He holds the miniature staircase up for my scrutiny, and I count.

257

"ten."
He nods,
"Exactly. Ten, three plus seven."

"I had to coax Jed away from the attic. I've no idea what had happened up there. He wasn't making a lot of sense. There was blood on his face and hands, he was on his knees tearing away at what was left of the doll's house.

"I expected him to object when I told him we had to leave. After seeing the state he was in I thought it might be a case of calling the police. But Carol appeared in the doorway and gasped or yelped. It was probably the blood. I saw something cross Jed's face, so I told him we had to leave for the sake of Carol and May. And I told him we'd come back later. He agreed, I could see the effort it was for him.

"He said he had to bring part of the doll's house with him. I didn't realise at first it was the base the thing had been resting on, I didn't see it was the doll's house version of the cellar. Jed didn't explain what it really was to me until it was too late. If I'd known, I'd have tried to save it."

"We sent Jed ahead of us. It sounds sort of callous, because we were worried about the stairs, but Steve didn't want him suddenly announcing he'd need to do one more thing and diving back into the attic. The last trip, we'd had a real struggled to get him to leave. None of us spoke on the way downstairs, we didn't want to break the spell I suppose. I didn't even ask about the blood.

"When we got out the house May was already in the minibus waiting to go. It felt like a scene from a heist movie. Steve got in the driver's seat, and I jumped into the front. That was a mistake because Jed made to get in the back. He was smeared with blood; his hand was still bleeding. May had no idea what had happened in the attic, not that we were much better off really. When Jed tried to push the remains of the doll's house, into the bus, May finally lost it and started screaming. He didn't seem aware that she was having

258

hysterics.

"It was more than just the blood on his face. May was pressing herself into the corner of the bus, trying to get away from the bits of wood he was holding. She never said as much but, with hindsight it's obvious, even smashed to pieces that doll's house was charged somehow. I began to feel it myself. it happens like that sometimes, you can feel your own sensitivity increase in the presence of another psychic, it's like running batteries alongside each other. I could feel the malice pouring out of that thing.

"In the end Steve and I wrestled it off him. We could only persuade him to get in the car by locking the plinth in the caravan and telling him we'd come back to it later. I don't know if Steve meant that. I know I didn't.

"May was still sobbing as we drove away. I can still hear her. The noises were bestial."

"The police put it down to random vandalism. How likely does that sound, really? The place was riddled with damp, there was probably a foot of water in that cellar, yet that house was razed to the ground. The investigator's opinion was that the caravan wasn't even targeted, it just got caught in the wave of heat and combusted. This 'random vandal' must have been carrying a hell of a lot of petrol with them when they randomly selected a building to torch.

"It was clearly a deliberate, premeditated case of arson. Who? I'm not saying anything. I've got no proof and I don't want to be sued. But I think we all know the most likely candidate.

"I drove Carol and May to Carol's flat. May had calmed down once we were out of Fantoccini Street, further from the influence of the house. She was still badly shaken though. Carol told me we shouldn't leave her alone and suggested I take them both to her place. Once we'd dropped them off, Jed was all for turning around and going back, so we could collect the plinth and maybe continue the fieldtrip alone.

"I told him we needed sleep. It wasn't even noon, but the

adrenaline had left my system and I was ready to collapse. I didn't have the strength to go back to the house at all, certainly not with someone I'd have to keep safe from themselves. I drove him back to his flat, we argued most of the way but in the end, I was driving, and he wasn't, so that was that.

"Then I made the biggest mistake of my career. I should have gone home and slept. Instead, I went to see John and played him the tapes."

"Oh, those f__king tapes. Steve came to me with them the next day. It was bizarre, he came to my house, not this one, I've moved since then, and he barged in the moment I answered the door. Kept spouting, 'You have to listen to this, you have to listen to this'.

"Trouble was there was nothing to listen to, the tapes were blank. They're a few scratching noises that could be anything, a loose windowpane rattling, maybe another squirrel, then nothing. Silence until the recording stops. The triggers in the attic activated the recorders three times in the night, four if you count the first time when Steve turns the system on and closes the door behind him, that happened in the living room and kitchen too of course. Other than that, the downstairs rooms didn't trigger at all.

"Steve says the machines recorded hours of silence, but that's just wrong, they were blank, they weren't recorded on. There was nothing happening.

"The whole thing was such a f__king farce. If we got a noise on the tape, it was a spook talking to us, if we got silence it was a spook cleaning the tape."

"May stayed at my place that night. I flat shared with two other students but luckily, they were away. Neither of us were up to handling questions that night. We didn't really speak about anything that had happened, just sat drinking cups of tea, or leaving them to go cold. I don't think I even asked if she wanted to stay. I just made up a bed for her on the sofa.

"I went to bed but didn't sleep for hours, I know the last

time I looked at my phone it was half three in the morning. Part of me was scared of having nightmares, but when I did finally sleep, I was completely out of it. If I did dream, I didn't remember when I woke up. It was quite disconcerting; I woke up the next afternoon and began to panic. Once I'd got myself under control I went to see if May was okay. She'd left though. She stacked all the bedding neatly on the sofa and left a note.

"I don't know what I did for the rest of the day. It was late evening when Steve called to tell me about the fire. I knew it was him before I picked up the phone. I remember listening to him, him in tears he so angry, and me not reacting because it was like I'd already heard it.

"He told me he thought it was [89]_____, and I just said 'yeh, it was'. It was just the natural route. People as scared as ____ lash out. I imagine listening to those tapes was very hard for him. Do I blame him? I don't know to be honest. Part of me is disappointed, angry that we've been denied that line of communication and the chance to help that poor woman and her children. But, and I'm being completely frank here, part of me is relieved. I'll never be able to go back there. It's been taken from my hands. It never goes away, not completely, but knowing that house isn't there or that doll's house ... well, there's a degree of comfort in that."

"I have no idea what happened to the house after they bolted. I know Steve's convinced I torched the place. Him and half the f__king campus, but why in God's name would I?

---

[89] Before the interview closed Carol Crossland requested that I didn't reveal the name of the person she and Steve Ward believe to be responsible for the razing of number 37. Although in her mind there was no doubt, she feared becoming embroiled in libel proceedings if her opinions were put on record.

"Look, Fantoccini Street was a s__thole. It was a rundown pit of a road in a pit of an area. By Stevie boy's telling they'd all got themselves hyped up to the point where they thought their lives were at risk. From what he told me, and from the stories that began to filter through the departments at Uni, they ran out of the house, piled into the van and left doing a ton plus. I'd bet good money they left the door open, and the caravan unlocked. Do that in any part of London and you're asking for trouble, do it in NW12 ...

"Anyway, I don't give a s__t if they do think I torched the place. If they want to come up with some tangible reason, or even, God forbid, some sort of f__king evidence then they can take it to the police.

"Anyway, that was the end to it. House gone, all gone. Were done here."

After the stifling heat of John Pelton's basement flat the chill of the outside world feels harsh, almost brutal. For a few seconds my head swims and I lean against the door that has just closed behind me. When I open my eyes there's a man in a uniform staring at me. He's holding a plastic tray of groceries and a look of suspicion.

The door of the flat is in a miniscule sunken yard at the bottom of a concrete stairway. For me to get past the delivery driver will require us to engage in a careful series of complimentary moves. He makes no such move and, in effect, blocks my way.

Still holding the tray of shopping he reaches past my head and raps on the door. It's opened almost immediately and I suspect Pelton has been watching me through the peephole, waiting for me to be clear of his property. The delivery man asks if everything it alright. He addresses him as Mr Pelton, his gaze on me.

The reply is brief, almost terse. *Yes, everything is alright.* Brief as it is, the reply satisfies the driver who finally angles himself, and his tray of goods, so I can get past.

On street level, I wait by the door of the delivery van. The driver raises a hand to me in apology as he approaches.

"Sorry about that. Mr Pelton's one of my regulars. You get to know the ones you need to keep an eye on."

I ask the question I wanted to ask during the interview, but didn't feel able to: does John Pelton ever leave his flat?

"Not much, I don't think. You can usually tell by the shopping lists. Toiletries, underwear, stationary. You know personal stuff you get for yourself or pick up while you're out and about. Normally the sort of stuff I bring here comes with three crates of cat food and a sack of kitty litter."

Part Five

Ashes

Epilogue

Guy Lyon Playfair acknowledged in his account of the Enfield Haunting that real life doesn't provide a compelling narrative. In fiction, mysteries are solved, questions answered, villains are brought to justice and heroes get the girl.

Reality might spare us the clichés but seldom provides resolution. I would like to be able to say differently for the story of 37 Fantoccini Street and those touched by it. Sadly, I can't. All I can do is bring my own involvement in it up to date and leave the reader to draw their own conclusions about what they've read.

At the time of writing, Mabel Noakes still lives in a residential care home. I visited her on three more occasions after my initial interview and was saddened to note the continued decline in her cognitive abilities. The staff assure me she is well cared for and comfortable.

After returning from a break in her studies, Viola Mezco completed one more term of her Occupational Therapy degree before dropping out completely. She is now a self-employed Complementary Therapist and lives with her husband and two stepsons.

Steven Ward continued to lecture at London North University until its closure in 2017. After the fieldtrips to Fantoccini Street, he gave up paranormal investigation and let his membership of the ASSAP lapse. He ceased responding to my emails in 2016.

Carol Crossland completed her Psychology degree in 2014 after taking a year's leave of absence. Although she maintains an interest in the paranormal, she no longer takes part in Ouija sessions. She requested details of her personal life and circumstances be kept private.

Gerald Cardino was put off his Civil Engineering course in 2013 due to poor attendance. In the same year he was sectioned under the mental health act and admitted to an Acute Mental Health Unit at St. Bailing hospital, NW10. He was released to the care of his parents two months later. He continues to live at his family home.

John Pelton left London North University shortly after the conclusion of the 2012 fieldtrip. He now works on a freelance basis, offering advice on audio surveillance in the private sector.

Guy Doll's email account closed in 2015, shortly after I interviewed him. Since that time I have been unable to locate him.

Ella Caine left the confines of Bucklechurch Psychiatric Hospital in 2016 and moved into her sister's home.

In 2016 Fantoccini Street and much of the surrounding area was demolished to make space for a road extension project.

Those responsible for the premature razing of number 37 were never found and no motive was ever discovered.

Postscript

I had thought that my involvement with Ella Caine and her interest in Fantoccini Street, or more accurately, her interest with the dolls associated with it, had ended when she presented me with the skilfully disfigured Lydia doll.

In a break from the usual rule, reality had seemed to provide a pleasing symmetry. My association with Ella first came about because I'd been hunting for a doll to gift to my niece, and my association with Ella came to a close with her gifting a doll to me.

In late 2017, purely by chance, I found a few water damaged and disembodied sheets of the Metro newspaper, dated 24th September 2016[90]. They were in too poor a condition to save but the page five story of a bizarre murder case was still legible. The name Caine, immediately jumped out at me.

In the small hours of 22nd September 2016 the fire brigade was called to attend a roof fire in a small suburb of Havering. Unable to rouse the residents the fireman forced an entry and found the body of a woman laying at the bottom of the stairs. On removing the woman, later identified as Ella Caine, they

---

[90] I managed to obtain a copy of The Metro, dated 14.09.16 and there is no report of the incidence Mr Croix refers to. The reference appeared on a handwritten page of the manuscript. It had been heavily notated and was linked to many columns of figures that filled the margins of the page. The section was not easy to read, and it is as likely that I misread the date as it is that Mr Croix got it wrong.

found she had wounds consistent with a severe beating.

The blaze was quickly brought under control and the firemen, now accompanied by police officers, searched the house. In the front bedroom they found the body of Lydia Lalka, née Caine, lying in bed. She too had head injuries consistent with a brutal attack. In the attic room space, they found the body of Robert Lalka. Cause of death unconfirmed but possibly smoke inhalation. The article went on to explain that the attic had housed a renowned collection of 'bizarre' dolls.

Two photographs illustrated the piece, a small picture of the fire damaged house, surrounded by emergency vehicles and police caution tape, and a larger image showing the ruined interior of the attic.

Remembering my own visit to the attic to see Ella's collection, I could recall the tiered display stand forming the centre piece of the room. The stand now lay on its side, looking at first glance like a staircase turned through 90 degrees. A number of the dolls, soot streaked and soaked through, lay in puddles of filthy water, appearing to gaze up at the camera lens.

I can only hope, that with that image, the circle of events of number 37 is finally closed

<u>List of Illustrations (scan QR Code for Hi-res)</u>

<u>Fig, i:</u>

Carol Crossland's sketch (not drawn to scale) of the attic room where the Ouija board was set up on 10/08/2021. Seating of the participants, reading clockwise from top: Carol Crossland, Steven Ward, Mabel Noakes, John Pelton. This seating arrangement is contradicted by Mr Croix's recounting of the video recording of the event. The figures surrounding Ms Crossland's sketch were added at a later date by Mr Croix. Many of the papers and photographs that made up the manuscript were heavily notated.

<u>Fig, ii:</u>

Plan of 37 Fantoccini Street's ground floor (not drawn to scale). Mr Croix made several drawings of each floor of the house, all of them covered with notes, symbols and calculations.

Fig. iii:

Two examples of the post-it-notes peppered throughout Mr Croix's manuscript. Eyes, set at 90 degrees to each other, were a recurring theme, as were doors opening onto flights of stairs.

Fig. iv:

One of Mr Croix's larger sketches. As with his post-it-notes, strangely angled doors and stairways were a frequent subject matter. The significance, if any, of these sketches is unknown. The list of words at the bottom of this sketch are the words spoken in error by Francine Corn (see chapter 11). This list appears frequently in Mr Croix's sketches and diagrams.

Fig. v:

Flyer for the student band Doll's House Autopsy. Their Stockholm Syndrome Tour was to be their last engagement and almost ended with their expulsion from London North University. The flyer features the only non-copyrighted photograph of 37 Fantoccini Street Mr Croix had access to. Image reproduced with the kind permission of David Frasier.

Fig,i

CC CAROL CROSSLAND
SW STEVE WARD
MW MAY NOAKES
JP JOHN PELTON

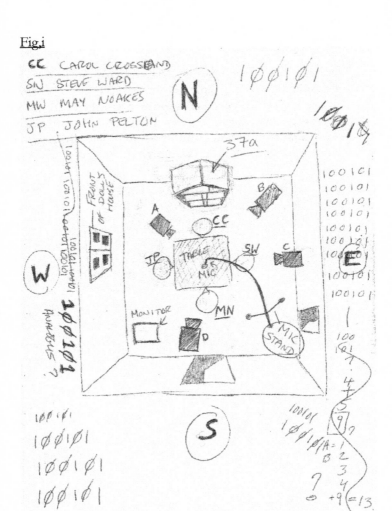

100101

1001010

100101
100101
100101
100101
100101
100101
100101
100101
100101

100
101
?
4
5
9 ?

100101
100101/A=1
B 2
3
4
0 +9 =13.
?

37a

FRONT OF DOLLS HOUSE

100101 101010101011010101
100101 100101
Apparatus ?

A
B
C
D
CC
SW
TABLE & MIC
JP
MONITOR
MN
MIC STAND

N
W
E
S

100101
100101
100101
100101

Fig.ii

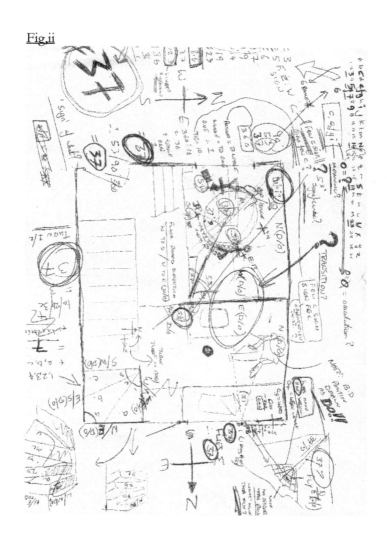

Fig.iii

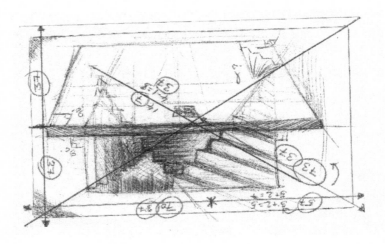

Fig.iv

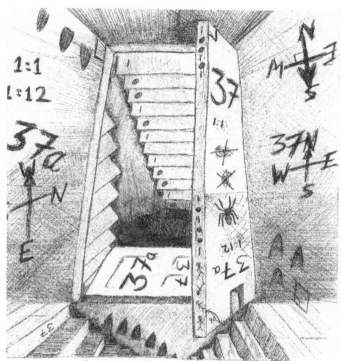

KITCHEN FLOOR BENEATH TABLE TOP THOUGHTLESS
MINDLESS MAISON ALTAR IMAGINARY NUMBERS
VINETY SQUARE ~~TWISTS~~ (TWISTS (IRONS EQUAL PRETTY) STILL
SISTER (IRONED FACE) → FRONT / BEHIND / BACK FORWARD
STAIRWAY WRITES (RITES?) RECORDINGS. PAINLESS
BURNING WOODEN BOARD BLACK WHITE GLASS

Fig.v

Bibliography

Clark, J. and Hitchings, S. (2013)
The Poltergeist Prince of London: The Remarkable True Story of the Battersea Poltergeist. Shroud: The History Press

Playfair, G.L. (2011) 'This House is Haunted: The true Story of the Enfield Poltergeist. 3rd edn. London: White Crow Books

Playfair, G.L. (2011) Twin Telepathy. 3rd edn. London: White Crow Books

Puthoff, H.E. Targ, R (1974)
"Information transmission under conditions of sensory shielding". Nature 251(5476): 602–60

Storr, W (2007) The Supernatural: One man's search for the truth about ghosts. Wiltshire: Ebury

Study365. (2000) How to Experiment with Zenner Cards. Available at: https://www.study365.co.uk/wp-content/uploads/2018/08/How-to-Experiment-with-Zener-Cards.pdf

About the author

Although Anthony Croix (1982 – 2019) had a degree in journalism, he chose not to pursue a career in mainstream media. He believed the constraints of deadlines, column inches and, above all, financial requirements were distractions from the simple goal of uncovering the truth. It is believed he was an enthusiastic contributor to a number of underground journals and magazines.

His final project, a deep investigation into the events following the Fantoccini Street murders, is the only surviving example of his work. Sadly, Mr Croix did not live to see it in published form.

About the editor

Russell Day grew up in Harlesden, NW10 – a geographic region searching for an alibi. From an early age it was clear the only things he cared about were motorcycles, tattoos and writing. At a later stage he added family life to his list of interests and now lives with his wife and two children.

In his first novel, *Needle Song*, an amateur detective employs logic, psychology and a loaded pack of tarot cards to investigate a death.

Russ often tells people he seldom smiles due to nerve damage, sustained when his jaw was broken. In fact, this is a total fabrication and his family will tell you he's always been a miserable bastard.

He has written 3 novels

- *Needle Song*
- *Ink To Ashes*
- *King Of The Crows*

All available from Fahrenheit Press